WINDS OF TIME

SACRED TIME TRILOGY

WINDS OF TIME

A. MARIE

Winds of Time

Copyright © 2023 A. Marie

ISBN: 979-8-9888696-0-3

Contact Info: author.ac.marie@gmail.com

A. MARIE
WRITING & DESIGN

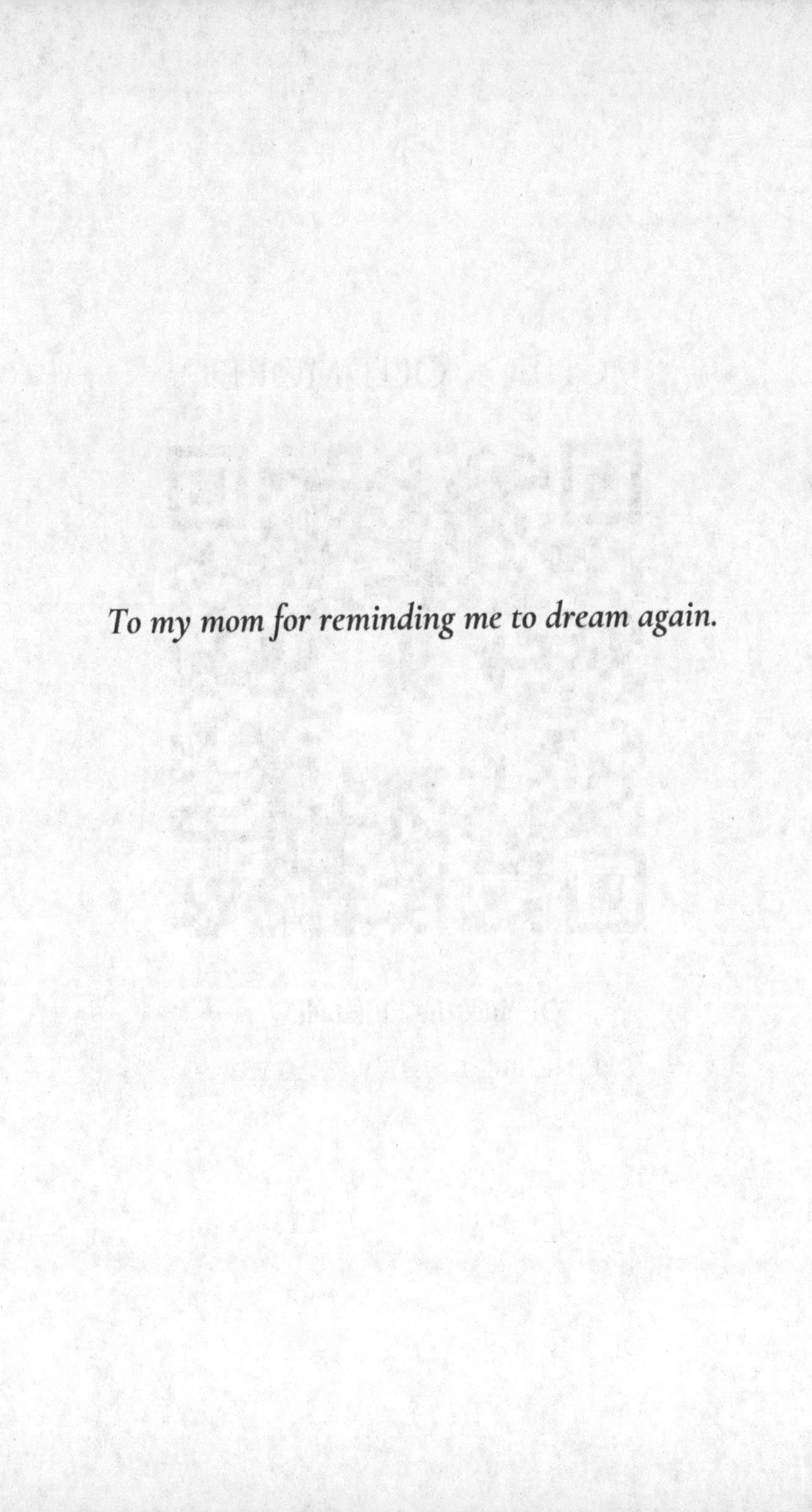

To my mom for reminding me to dream again.

CHECK OUT MORE!

Or click the Link below

https://linktr.ee/author_a_marie

CHAPTER ONE

❖

People always say home is where the heart is. Was that why Morra's chest ached as Chicago's skyline became a distant memory? Had pieces of her heart been carved out with each home she had to leave? It would explain the hollowness that sat heavy in her chest.

Morra gazed out of the dirty white hatchback as more hope escaped with each exhausted sigh that passed her lips.

Her stormy grey eyes watched another field pass by.

Open land felt different to after her living in the city. Rolling fields blanketed by different shades of gold and brown stretched endlessly before her eyes. But as much as she admired the view, she longed for her home. Towers and concrete, a jungle made of glass, metal, and strangers, was once where she lived before her mom decided they would move... again.

Slumping, she curled in on herself. Her bones ached from another loss, and this time she couldn't even be mad.

Pain shot through her chest and unconsciously she reached up to rub the spot. The chilling ache resembled the icy winds during winter. No amount of sun beating through the car windshield could soothe it.

Of all the places they had lived, she had loved Chicago the most. There was a freedom in not knowing the people who passed her. Each day was new, new people, new things. It was her favorite part of the city. But in the tiny valley town of West Virginia, people would recognize her. Morra would walk through town, greeted by strangers, but soon she would know every face. She would recognize each person before the first leaf of fall.

A shiver crawled up her spine and goosebumps bloomed on her tawny skin. The sharp tang of blood coated her tongue as her teeth sunk deeper into her lip. Morra could already feel her chest tightening at the thought of the small town. Her hope began to dwindle as the car trudged along, pushing them farther from Chicago. Morra's faith in her mother dwindled as well.

The cracked leather squeaked as her mom shifted in the driver's seat. The tension in the car grew with the silence. Morra realized her mom wasn't trying to uproot her each time she built a life in a foreign place, but it had become a pattern. A familiar one. In Chicago, she had a friend, which was a rare occurrence for Morra. Natasha and her were going to be the only sophomores to make varsity team in softball. One that went to national almost every year. That meant college scholarships; small towns didn't have those opportunities.

Bitterness burned the back of her throat.

It's not her fault, she thought.

Morra wasn't sure if she believed it, but she was trying to. After packing her things, she put them in the old car and said goodbye for the fourth time in five years. Each time, her mom had promised it would be the last.

It never was.

As her bitterness grew, so did her guilt; she knew her mom tried to keep her promises. Morra's eyes fell shut as another sigh escaped her lips. Whenever the fury of her displacement swelled within her, Morra remembered her mother's warm smile as she proudly presented the little shop in downtown Norwich. It didn't help calm her anger, but it caused her stomach to twist enough that she kept quiet.

Morra's mother, Adelaine, had always dreamed of opening a bakery. Morra knew her mother put aside her aspirations the day of Morra's birth. After sixteen years and purchasing the deed to the small brick building, she could finally live that dream.

With the last of the money her father left them, Adelaine found a small town where she could put a shop on main street and a small two-story house close to it.

Morra's shoulders sank as she thought about the father she never knew. A wave of bittersweet grief swarmed her. She saw his face in her dreams, or a amalgamation of the parts on her face that didn't match her mom's. With no pictures all she could do was imagine.

The dark curly hair bunched in a high pony sure didn't come from her mom's long line of Irish lineage; both her parents were red heads. Morra's nose and high cheeks matched her mom's, but her dark tan skin and silver eyes had to be her father's.

Her mother had always been silent about him, but Morra could tell that they had loved each other deeply. The navy blue button-up was a testimony to that love, her mother wore it every night, it had been threadbare for years, but it was the first thing her mom packed when they moved to their new home.

Morra's hands fumbled in the bag under the old leather seat, foraging for an old teddy bear. She ran her fingers over its threadbare fur, checking to make sure it was there. Its once dark emerald green eyes faded over time and its ear hung by a single stitch of thread. Her mother sewed them back on twice and still they were loose and ready to fall off again. No matter how many times they moved from city to city, she kept it close. It was the only thing Morra had from the man who had once been there, like a distant memory lingering in the back of her mind.

Stupid bear.

It made her feel closer to him, as if she could look up and see a shadow or a flash of someone recognizable. Or a childlike smile in a large crowd. One that felt familiar because it saw the same crooked grin in the mirror.

"Honey?" Her mother's voice pulled her out of her internal turmoil.

The sun started to fade on the fields of West Virginia. The pink and orange dappled sky cast shadows across the rolling field of crops, Morra traced them with her eyes as the town crested into view.

Her new town.

The robotic voice coming from her mom's phone guided them, the monotone static drowning out the radio playing in the background.

Stretching her arms in the air, a yawn escaped, heaviness clawing at her. The two-day drive caught up to her. The previous night was spent restless in a sketchy motel. Morra craved a comfortable bed, especially one without bugs. Shivers wracked her as the memory skittered across her mind.

"What's up?" Morra looked over, turning in her seat, unable to meet her mother's eyes. The gold light shined against Adelaine's strawberry blond hair and fair skin. With a wise look she glanced Morra's way, a soft smile played on her lips.

"Life is too short, and we must live, sweet girl." Adelaine peeked over for a quick second before reaching for her daughter's hand. "I know you wanted to stay, but this will be great for us. It's the life I always wanted for us... before your father died," she said, voice cracking, "he said he wanted to show me the world and then we would settle down in a little town just like this away from all the noise of... life. Create a haven just for us. It is not how he would have wanted, but I have tried to keep his dream alive."

Morra couldn't look at her mother, shame filling her. Shaking her head, Morra wished she could explain her feelings, but the words just caught in her throat each time she tried. Silence hung heavy in the car. Adelaine sighed gently when enough silence had passed, putting her hands back on the peeling leather of the steering wheel as she drove them to their new home. Morra refused to look up until they arrived.

When the rumbling of the engine stopped, she focused her gaze on her hands. Morra noticed the pain once she saw the blood coated nails. Picking at the skin around her nails till she bled was a bad habit she couldn't break. She looked up from her mangled fingers and she saw the home for the first time.

Light blue siding covered the two-story townhouse. White trim surrounded it and rose bushes lined the front windows as a stone pathway led up to the door. Lush green foliage filled the yard despite the blistering August sun.

The car door shut behind her with a loud thud as she gazed down the street. House after house lined the road, fresh paint and mowed grass. It looked like a good place. Grabbing some boxes from the back, she walked in. Between the two of them, it didn't take long to get all the boxes inside.

Morra began unpacking and lifted the cardboard top to the box labeled 'Kitchen', quickly putting away the white ceramic plates in the cupboard next to the stove. Her mom came in leaning against the counter watching her only child.

"I want you to have something." Reaching into one of the moving boxes labeled 'Keepsake', Adelaine pulled out an old worn book. Its brown leather cover creased from its use as the binding lifted, handmade stitches slowly unraveling with time. "Here, it's always been my favorite, and I want you to have it. Maybe gain some insight into life since you are growing up so fast." A kind smile graced her face, one Morra knew well.

She gently took the book out of her mom's hands. Reading the title, she almost rolled her eyes.

Le Morte D'Arthur by Sir Thomas Malory.

First edition.

Glancing up from the gift, she could see the corner of her mom's soft green eyes crinkle at the book in fondness. Morra never understood why the stories in this book mattered to her mom, but it became a tradition between them.

Her first bedtime stories were of chivalry and honor, snuggled under the covers she would read the lives of Guinevere and Sir Lancelot and the brave King Arthur.

Every time Morra's school did a unit on the stories of Camelot, she aced it. The knowledge was engraved into every fiber of her being.

"Thanks, Mom." Morra gazed softly at the book; this was an important peace offering. An olive branch, she thought. It didn't fix the problem because in a year or two Morra would have to repack and leave. It was inevitable but for now she would not turn it down.

After a moment Morra shifted her focus from the book, her gaze landed on the empty living room. "Hey, is it okay if I go wander around the town, see what there is to do?" Sleepiness tugged at her eyelids, but she knew sleep would be futile. The echoing of the empty house set her on edge. The pungent stale odor, the incessant ticking of the cheap clock that hung above the doorway, and the barking of the neighbor's dog grated her like sandpaper on delicate skin. She needed to feel the wind on her skin to clear her mind.

After getting permission and rifling through a box of clothes, searching for a jacket, Morra left the house gently closing the door behind her. The late august evenings were turning cold, slinging the jacket on she decided to leave in the direction they came.

Morra trudged down the dusty, broken sidewalk, her eyes darting around taking in the sights of her home for the foreseeable future. The brick buildings, dimly lit from the evening's sunlight, were clustered together like a tiny village. One in particular caught her eye. Black Bird Books, she felt a flutter of excitement at the thought of getting her hands on a new book. A place where she could let herself escape.

The evening air had already started to cool, causing goosebumps to dance across her skin, it helped ease the panic that had been consuming her.

It didn't take long to reach the shops. Morra paused and stared down the hill at the small town, the reality of her situation suddenly hitting her like a ton of bricks.

Her face twisted into a frown. It looked like something out of a Lifetime movie.

The lights in the bookshop were on and Morra sighed in relief but before her foot stepped off the curb, a glimpse of blue caught her attention.

The sun fell even deeper past the horizon, shining dark orange and red. The evening sky glowed, illuminating the banner with the words 'Opening Soon'. Emotions tumbled through her as she realized it was her mother's bakery. Cocking her head to the side, she decided to take a peek. Smushing her face against the outside glass, she cupped her hands around her eyes, trying to see inside.

The brown wood floor complemented the navy blue walls and the leather couches. The marbled counter tops had a painting of the shop's name, 'The Sweet Shop', in charming bubbly cursive.

An image of her sitting at the table doing homework as her mom whistled while frosting cakes flashed through Morra's head. As she gazed through the storefront, the anger that she held in a death grip eased, she knew it was time to let go. Her mother could finally fulfill her dreams after struggling with being a single mom, still she wished she could hold the rage and let it burn. She wished she could just act like a child for once. Shame caused her cheeks to burn at the thought as she stared at the acclamation of her mother's goals. Morra needed to give her support without protest.

Letting out a sigh, she stepped away when somebody suddenly turned up by her side. Her heart leapt to her throat before calming to its usual rhythm. Being met with strange people wasn't new to her, after all, she spent three years living in Chicago.

She had to get used to the occasional oddball.

The man stood enraptured, completely oblivious to her presence. Morra watched as deep set eyes brightened at the cobalt banner. A broad smile painted his face causing his crow's feet to deepen with the stretch of it. Pride splashed across his face and Morra found it odd. She looked the man up and down, trying to place the stranger. He looked... familiar. A Deja Vu kind of familiar that tickled the back of her brain.

Her curiosity got the better of her. As she started to ask, the man turned towards her and grinned, pride still heavy in his eyes, before turning around and walking away. Morra waited until he turned the corner. The night had fallen, and darkness pressed heavily around her.

Deciding to mind her own business she ignored the stranger, and she snuggled into her jacket as the wind kicked up her hair and lapped at her face.

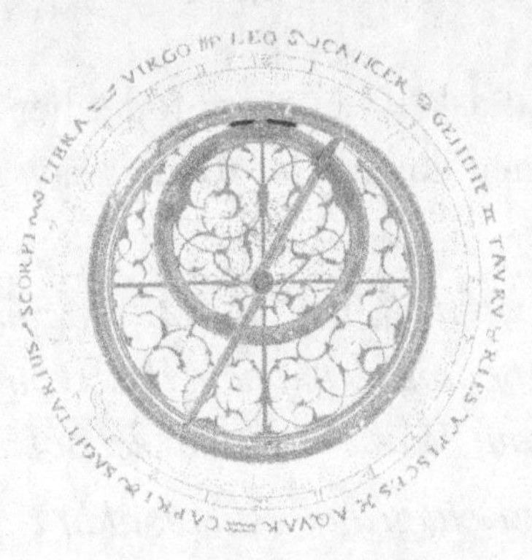

CHAPTER TWO

❖

Summer green turned to the first visage of fall as Morra and her mother settled into Norwich. Sitting cross-legged on a cream plush armchair, she watched while Adelaine danced around the shop blaring the radio. Morra's lips tugged into a small smile watching her mother's carefree attitude. She wouldn't consider Adelaine a high-strung person, but she spent more time worrying than not. Watching her cheerful and free caused the anger that still gripped her heart to loosen. If her mom could be happy, it would all be okay.

Sweat beaded on Morra's forehead as she stared at the pile of boxes. They had so much to do, but it didn't matter. Morra chuckled as she watched her mother dance in the background to some Queen song. It didn't seem to matter that they had only a day before the grand opening, or that they were up most of the night, or that tomorrow was her first day of school. It seemed her mom was enjoying every minute she could. Days before, Morra had asked her mom to let her help, but she had been quickly turned down. Her mother saw right through the ruse.

Adelaine peered at her, eyebrows raising in disbelief. "Nice try, kid, not going to happen. Plus, you can't miss out on the first day of your West Virginian school career!"

Morra smiled chagrined; she couldn't get anything past her. She never could.

"How about I make your favorite carrot cake and after your first day of school, we can celebrate together? Just us."

Morra looked around as the memory faded. Pastries were on display and the chalkboard had the menu written in neat bubbly cursive letters matching the logo that decorated the room. The chairs and tables were neatly arranged. All that was left to do upfront was to fill the shelves. She decided it was a task for later.

As she watched her mom prepare icing, her eyes wandered around the store. She could unpack more boxes, or she could go get coffee. With a small nod she decided the caffeine would be more productive. The two had discovered a small coffee shop down the street. The man who owned it greeted them cheerfully. Her mom and him created a pact of free coffee for them and free pastries for him; and she planned to cash in on that promise. Morra tried to carry her voice to the back of the shop for her mom to hear as she asked if she wanted anything.

"Yes! Bring me an iced latte!" Strawberry hair whipped around the corner, obscuring her mother's face. Morra snickered at the streaks of blue marring her mom's pale arms

Galahad interrupted their conversation by sitting down next to Morra. Engines rumbled as the plane taxied down the strip. Morra's nails dug half moons into the leather armrest.

Kahadin snorted around his muffin he was still picking at, and she cast a hard glare at him through pinched eyes.

"What are you laughing at?" she snapped.

"Nothing, I just never seen anyone as afraid of flying as you are," he replied with a smirk.

She spluttered for a response, face growing hot. Galahad smiled genially at the both of them as he patted Morra's hand warmly. "We will be there before you know it."

He wasn't wrong. After an hour in the sky, they landed in an open field with an airstrip. Morra surveyed the area with narrowed eyes, she had never flown before, but she knew this wasn't an airport. Getting off the plane and sending a silent thank you for being back on solid ground, all she could see was an rolling grass with a fenced area on the left.

Noises came from the direction, but she couldn't make out the sounds.

She followed Galahad and Kahadin as they walked on the cobblestone path. They wound up the path until they crested the hill, and the house came into view. Morra's breath hitched as her mouth dropped open.

It was huge. The house was an orange brown brick Manor. It reminded her of the color of earth, an old-fashioned kind of beauty that had become rare to see.

Tall white stone fences surrounded the Manor, beyond laid wide stretches of fields. It completely dwarfed the rest of the surrounding trees being over four stories tall, with large spacious windows peppered elegantly around. "This is what you call a house?" she asked, side eyeing the two people who have been casually describing their home as a modest house.

The cobblestone path they walked on bordered close to a road enclosed with trees, leading to the front of the Manor. A fountain sat in front of the home while the sides had a beautiful garden. Morra inhaled, smelling the lilacs from this far away as a gentle breeze passed by them.

Morra jumped as Galahad spoke, forgetting she had asked a question. "Yes, it has eighteen bedrooms and twelve bathrooms. It also has a large kitchen, library, billiard room, game room, several sitting rooms, study, formal dining room, sunroom, and conservatory. Oh, and the astronomy tower there on the right."

Kahadin smirked. "Obviously, the architects didn't want to go overboard." Sarcasm dripped from his every words.

Morra forced her eyes from her new home to look around.

She startled at the large sign:

Camelot Holdings Farm

Shaking her head with a dumbfounded smile, she peered at Galahad. "What is with this family and its obsession with Arthurian Legend? And why alpacas?" Seeing the smaller text under the larger words proclaiming the largest alpaca farm in America.

Kahadin chuckled, "You haven't seen anything yet."

"The Arthurian stuff or the Alpaca stuff?" Morra asked and was promptly ignored in favor of a mischievous smirk.

Kahadin stepped through the open door as Galahad opened it. Morra peeked inside and gazed around in awe.

The walls were made of stone, the ceilings high with long chandeliers reminding her of castles in Europe she had seen in books. The antique furniture made of mahogany wood and brass accents littered the space. Rugs covered the floors and art lined the walls, but nothing was overly fancy or modern.

It was warm.

It felt like a home.

They pass a set of stairs and enter an office with a sitting area where Galahad pulled out a chair for her. When she walked into the office, she was struck by the smell of leather and old books.

It was beautiful, full of antique, almost medieval-looking furniture. Bookcases lined the room, tomes and scrolls filled them. Galahad walked over to the large mahogany desk. Behind it was a massive window and French doors opening to a patio that overlooked the grounds.

Paintings of the family's crest adorned the walls. A wispy 'S' mounted on a shield of rippling gold with the words in a language she couldn't read were engraved in the bottom.

In the hearth, a roaring fire crackled as wood popped. Kahadin moved to stoke it before sitting down in the oversized velvet green chairs. Everything screamed old money and comfort.

Morra loved it.

She decided not to sit, instead exploring the room. Running her finger across the worn leather as she roamed the edges of the room. Not a single speck of dust coated the books.

The meticulous cleaning was done with a reverence that only comes from love.

Kahadin and Galahad's voices created background noise for her exploring as they chatted about family dinner, she decided to ignore them and continue her search. The books she touched must have been hundreds of years old.

Morra felt the blazing heat of the fire against her skin, embracing her in a moment of comfort as she neared the hearth. But in an instant, she felt the fire's strength intensify as a loud crack echoed, smoke flooding out and consuming her. Drums sounded through her ears as the room spun. It took a moment for her to realize the sound was her heart. Images and thoughts of her mother dying in flames ripped through her. She wasn't there to see her die, but she could imagine it. Hear the screams as flesh melted from bone. The heat of the flames reminded her of all she had lost. Morra found herself paralyzed as her chest moved frantically. She couldn't breathe.

Galahad was there in an instant, his powerful arms pulling her away from the flames, providing protection from the cruel inferno. She could feel her rapid breaths coming in short bursts as she clung to him, desperate for safety.

"Morra, what is wrong?" he asked.

His voice was so close, but drowned out by the torrent inside her. Pulling her close to his chest, he tried to soothe her panic. She sucked in breaths as though she were suffocating. Morra bowed her head, resting it on Galahad's shoulder, desperately trying to calm down.

"It's okay," he whispered in her ear, guiding her from the fireplace to the seating area. Barking a command that fell on her deaf ears, he placed her hand on his chest, coaching her breathing. The pain of her mother's death was still a fresh wound, seeping and pouring blood with each thought.

Morra desperately wanted nothing more than to forget.

Once the fire was out, the smoke dissipated and the harsh pops of firewood quieted, the panic Morra felt slowly drained out of her. Her cheeks reddened, but as the last vestiges of tension eased, exhaustion quickly took its place until she slumped her weight against the broad cardigan covered chest.

Galahad examined his granddaughter with concern laced eyes and saw the exhaustion. Standing, he offered his hand, which she unthinkingly took. He slowly guided her out of the office. "I was going to talk to you about the family and answer any questions you have, but I think that should wait until after dinner." He looked at the grandfather clock in passing as he led them down the hall and up another flight of stairs.

"There are about three hours until dinner is served in the main dining room. I will have Kahadin come get you, but for now, I think it's best for you to rest."

Ending in front of a door in a hallway of many doors,

Galahad opened it, showing off the bedroom. "This is your room. I had the luxury of setting it up for you. In the closet, there are some fresh clothes. If you need anything, there is a phone to call the maids, or they can find me."

With glazed eyes, Morra looked at the man gratefully, making her way into the room. With a last goodbye, he left her to what was now hers. She stumbled to the bed, barely able to kick off her sneakers before flopping down. Everything had become a blur. The meeting of a new family, the drive, the plane ride, and the long journey into the Manor and to her room all bled together into one memory.

Everything felt jumbled.

As her eyes grew heavy, her chaotic mind slowed as she pulled the blankets around her. Slumber wrapped its warm arms around her, blanketing her in comfort and she thought back and wondered why no one explained the alpacas.

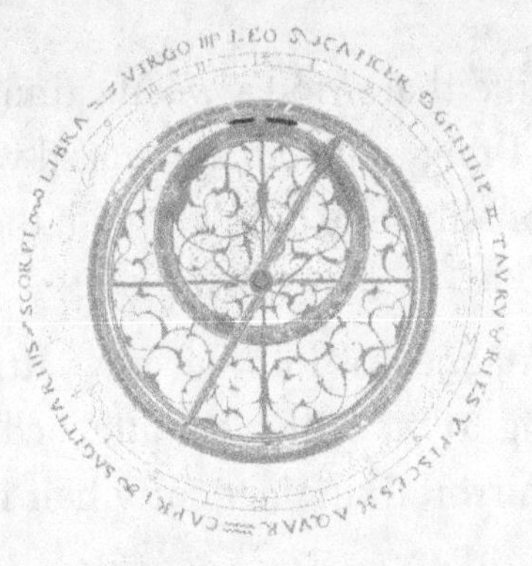

CHAPTER SIX

A light knock woke her. It was the only warning her cousin gave before bursting into the room like he owned it. Sweeping over to the oak wardrobe, he threw open the doors, rifling through clothes until he had a bunch in his hand.

"Dinner is being served in twenty minutes." He gave her a wolfish grin, setting the clothes on the foot of the bed. "Time to make yourself presentable. You're about to meet the whole family."

With a slight bow, Kahadin left the room. His head popped back into view. "Oh and fix your hair. If you thought I am judgmental..." he trailed off as he left.

She spent a few minutes trying to wake up. When she finally did, she registered the clothes left on the bed. Soft dark blue shirt and pressed tan trousers, wool socks, and matching oxford shoes. She shook her head, smiling. Of course, he would pick something like that. Morra was beginning to realize the pompous perfect thing that Kahadin oozed wasn't and act but his genuine personality. She didn't mind it though; his honesty was refreshing.

With a yawn, she got into her new attire, which fit her perfectly. Walking to the bathroom attached to her room, she peered into the mirror, fixing her curly hair into a pony.

"You can do this. You are one of them. There is no need to be nervous." She looked at herself in the mirror and tried desperately to convince herself of her words. The rousing speech failed, and she realized that these were the people her mother kept her from. There had to be a reason.

Kahadin came back to escort her back to the dining room, and it took Morra's breath away. White walls and a deep purple ceiling were lit by delicate chandeliers, causing light to bounce off the gold crown molding picking up other ornate details. Fine china and silverware were delicately placed on the large mahogany table. The windows were decorated with amber glass and the ceilings were coffered. Morra's eyes bounced around, unable to choose a spot to land.

When silence encased the room, Morra's gaze finally fell on her family. With a tilt of her head, she stood straighter and tried to walk with more grace than she thought she was capable of. Everyone's eyes were on her. Galahad motioned over to him, pulling out a chair, he waited for her to sit down.

Kahadin strutted to an open chair by an older man.

"It is my pleasure to introduce our newest family member, Morra," Galahad announces.

With a smile that didn't reach her eyes, she greeted her family. "It's lovely to meet you all."

Morra resoundingly thought it was not lovely to meet them. Part of her felt like she was replacing her mother with these people if she let herself be happy. She couldn't replace her mother, and she knew they couldn't replace the hole in her heart that broke open the moment she died, so what was the point?

She didn't want to be disingenuous, but she wanted to make a good impression. Galahad and Kahadin seemed like good people, but these people could control her fate until she turned eighteen. A lot could happen in fifteen months.

Giving over that type of control to strangers seemed impossible. Thinking about it caused her chest to tighten. No one other than her mother had been in charge of her and even then, there had been a certain level of partnership.

Sitting down, she sat straight, trying to exude confidence. Scanning over, the large group of people locking eyes with Kahadin. His slight nod reassured her. At least she had a friend.

The room erupted into polite conversation, and Morra tried her best to follow along without appearing completely lost. Busying herself, she started in on the rolls that were passing around. The wait staff brought out large silver platters that carried delicious smelling food, causing the room to quiet as people dished out food. The clanking of silverware became the only sound as everyone ate.

"How's the food?" the man next to her asked, causing her to jump.

"Really good," she muttered, swallowing her mouth full of roasted chicken. It had been years since she had this good of a meal. Her mother was an okay cook, emphasis on the okay part, as in she didn't burn most of their meals. It had been some time since she tasted something this rich. The orphanage certainly didn't provide this type of elegance.

"Is there anything you would like to know?" he inquired quietly.

Morra peered at the many faces peppering the large table. Her gaze sought out Kahadin's for reassurance. She found he was intently listening to their conversation.

"Names first, hmm?" With a nod from Morra he continues, "I am Balin. Next to me are my wife Lydia and my children." He pointed to the young child on Lydia's lap, introducing him as Edaris. "Next we have my lovely daughter Ladianna and I gather you have met my son," he said, nodding towards Kahadin.

Balin went on and introduced her to the rest of the family members gathered at the large round table. His sister Isolde and her husband William and their two children Madoine and Rion, Galahad's younger brother Ocursus and his children and his children's children.

Her brain swam through the plethora of names thrown at her. It would be impossible to remember them all.

Overwhelmed by odd names and aristocratic faces, Morra couldn't hide her discomfort and Galahad noticed. He leaned over whispering quietly, "It can be difficult. I am sure you will get used to it." He patted her hand gently before turning back to his wife.

She gazed around, trying to memorize each person's name.

Most were having conversations with those around them, occasionally asking her questions. She tried being polite while listening to the various voices.

A chill slithered up her spine. She glanced up to see one of the adults at the table, Isolde, if her memory served her correctly, glaring at her coldly. She was beautiful in a haughty kind of way, blond curly hair and glacier eyes watched her. Pure disgust oozed from her gaze, as if the young girl was something vile that had crawled out from under a rock. Something she wanted to crush with her perfect red bottomed heels.

Before she could read into it, Balin pulled her into conversation. "So, what do you think of our family?" he asked.

With a flicker of her eyes to Isolde, who continued to throw poison laced glares, she replied, "It's...it's so big." Everyone conversed with each other quietly as the waiters laid desert on their plates.

Balin looked at her with a tiny tilt to his lips, causing his eyes to crinkle slightly. "It was just you and your mother. Am I right?" The adults must have been informed about what happened and why she now lived with them. It was the confirmation she needed. Morra wondered if everyone knew.

"Yes, just me and her," she replied, swallowing the lump in the back of her throat. In her younger years, Morra craved a large family and an unchanging home; she longed for it on the days when she and her mother ate cold pizza in another newly unpacked house.

Now, Morra wished with all her heart for her mother to sit beside her and listen to the stories she had to tell and the jokes she wanted to share. Guilt gripped her in its unforgiving hold. She had wished for so long that her life would be different. Now she had a big family and no mom, as if she willed it into existence.

Bile rose in her throat as she pushed away the delicate pudding dish. Unable to face those around her, she fixed a polite expression on her trembling face and refused to look up until dinner ended.

Galahad stood. "My dear, would you accompany me to my study?" He offered his weathered hand and Morra accepted the help. With a gentle, weathered hand on her back, he guided Morra to the office. Sitting on the plush settee, Morra picked at her nail bed as warmth flooded her cheeks when she noticed a fire no longer roared in the hearth.

A lady followed behind, Galahad's wife, Morra couldn't recall her name. The older woman leaned over the coffee table from the sofa she sat on to gently grasp her hands. The trembling hadn't stopped, Morra wondered who else noticed.

"It is so lovely to have you here, Morra. I know so much has been going on and I wanted to introduce myself. I am Sophia, Galahad's wife."

Perking up slightly, she asked, "You're my dad's mom?"

Sophia was a beautiful older woman, probably a few years younger than Galahad. Etched lines curved around her mouth to her nose, lines that told of big smiles and happiness. Shaking her head sadly, she said, "No, I never got the pleasure of meeting Arthur's mother, but I loved Arthur like my own since Galahad and I married. He was only eight."

"I wish I could have known her though," she told Morra, watching her fight back the tears welling in her eyes. "I know, sweetheart, I know. This all must be so hard. I am sure you have so many questions. Hopefully, Galahad and I can answer some of them."

Without warning, the office doors open to a servant dressed in a suit. He walked to Galahad, leaning to whisper in his ear. Watching closely, Morra saw the note of surprise in his eyes and the quick glance he gave to Sophia.

The servant promptly got up and walked away, Galahad on his heels.

Stopping at the door he looked back at them. "My dear, please excuse me. I must take care of something. It may take my attention for the rest of the night. Sophia, would you give Morra a tour of the Manor, please?"

Morra sat jittery. She had so many questions, a dam burst within her and every barely held question came racing to the forefront of her mind. With a heavy sigh, she resigned herself to waiting, again. She had waited this long; a few hours longer couldn't hurt.

"Of course," Sophia said as he walked over, placing a soft kiss on her forehead.

Morra stood to stretch. It had been a long day, and she honestly didn't know how to feel about her new family. It didn't matter Morra pushed those thoughts into a box. She had to make the best of a bad situation.

Morra stepped out of the office and followed Sophia down the hall, taking in the grandeur of the home that resembled a palace. Artwork and furniture, not to mention the high ceilings and ornate windows, amazed her. The walls themselves were decorated with tapestries depicting battles between knights and dragons, or picturesque scenes of courtly life.

Sophia continued to show her the house. It had every room you could think of, from an astronomy tower, which they didn't visit much to her disappointment, to a room of maps and weird spiraling things that hung from the ceiling. When they got to the basement floor, they explored stock rooms, storage places holding old mementos and unused holiday decor.

They moved further down the hallway, eventually coming upon another door that hinted at something almost ancient, as if it had been here before the rest of the house. Sophia paused, her hand hovering against the old wood. "This is the one place you are not free to explore. It is locked at all times and its contents are never to be touched, understood?"

With a slow nod, she gazed at the forbidden door. It mimicked the others, oak with black iron fixture and hinges, but was older than the rest. Scarred with age. Intrigue filled her as something in her hummed, pulling. Sophia smiled genially, moving them along as Morra followed; she couldn't help wondering why they would have an entire room off limits. With a bunch of kids around, it was a truly terrible idea.

Eventually, Sophia led them to the first modern area she had seen in the entire house. Stepping foot into the Manor was like stepping into the past. The people and the things inside the home broadcasted another time, but as the door opened to the media room, her jaw dropped. Decked out in technology, there was a large screen playing a movie she wanted to see, beside it was enormous speakers.

Scattered around the soft sectional held the people who were now supposed to be her family. She recognized a few of them, but most she couldn't remember.

Kahadin sat in the middle of everyone, but when he saw her, he nodded. She would have thought it was a dismissal if he hadn't quietly shooed those on the side of him to make room for Morra.

Smiling gratefully, she moved to sit next to him, yet the whispers in her head were telling her she didn't belong didn't ease. Someone confirmed her fears as soon as she sat down. The petite brown-haired teen sitting on her other side glared, turning up her nose before storming out of the room.

Kahadin leaned over. "Do not worry about her, she has a propensity of being a bi-." He cut himself off as one of the oldest in the room raised an eyebrow a jet black eyebrow. "A propensity to be disagreeable."

Morra's shoulders slumped. Even now, after getting a family, some of them hate her. What did she do? She turned to ask Kahadin but stopped short as he grinned at the movie screen. It could be a problem for another day.

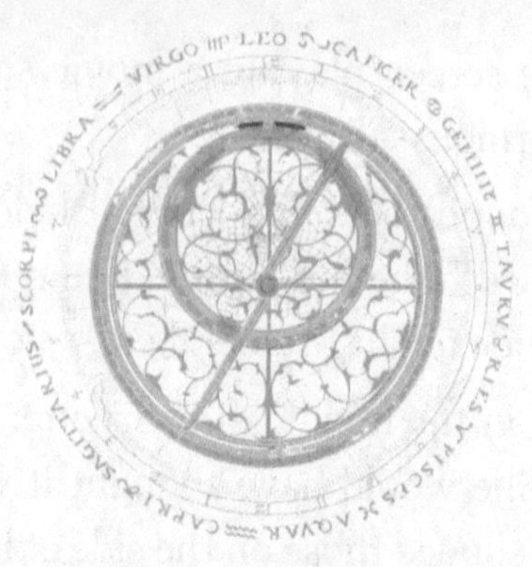

CHAPTER SEVEN

Galahad wasn't back in the morning.

During breakfast, Sophia let everyone know that both Galahad and Ocursus would be gone for an unknown time. It seemed to be a common enough thing, as no one seemed concerned. It helped settle her nerves. Days had passed and on a bright sunny Monday, Morra began to feel ill. When she woke, it started with just a chill and a slight ache that worked into a full body pain. By noon she was cocooned into her thick comforter, sweat beading on her forehead.

She hadn't felt this sick since the time her mother and her got those tacos from a sketchy food truck in Englewood. Her heavy eyes drooped shut before opening them again to a knock. The sun was no longer casting strips of light through the room, and she couldn't even begin to guess what time it was with her head pounding and her leaden limbs. Sitting up, she rubbed her bleary eyes, groaning at the pain throbbing in her head. Another knock sounded at her door, and she called out, voice weak, "Who is it?"

"It's me, Sophia," came the muffled voice from the other side of the wall.

Morra felt a wave of relief wash over her. She dragged herself out of bed, wincing at the sharp ache in her muscles, and shuffled to the door.

"Oh honey, you look a fright." Sophia's voice was laced with concern as she took in Morra's disheveled appearance. Morra could see the worry etched on her face, and it made her feel a little better to know that someone cared.

"I feel worse than I look," Morra croaked, her voice barely above a whisper. Sophia stepped closer and placed a hand on Morra's forehead. The coolness spread rapidly, causing shivers to shake her spine.

"A fever," Sophia said, her voice soft. "Let me help you back to bed."

Morra nodded gratefully as she leaned on Sophia, shuffling her way to the four-post bed. Pulling back the covers, her grandmother tucked her in pulling the thick red comforter high under Morra's chin. As Morra settled back into her cocoon of blankets, the sweet older woman bustled about the room, gathering supplies. She returned with a basin of warm water, and a washcloth.

"Here, drink this," Sophia said as she pressed a cold glass to Morra's chapped lips. "It has some honey and lemon in it. It should help with your throat."

Morra sipped the drink, feeling the honey coat her throat. Sophia placed a hand on her forehead again, and the lines on her face deepened. "I'm going to go get Balin. He's a doctor, he'll give you something to bring that down." Morra wanted to comment on it, but her throat hurt too much to speak.

As Sophia left the room, Morra drifted in and out of sleep. She was vaguely aware of her uncle, Balin, entering the room, but she was too out of it to pay much attention. She heard him murmuring to Sophia, his voice low, but she didn't have the energy to open her eyes and see what was going on.

The next thing she knew, she was being propped up by pillows, and Balin was holding a glass of water to her lips. She gulped the cool liquid, soothing her dry throat. Then Balin placed a hand on her forehead, and she winced at the heat emanating. "You're still burning up. Let's see if I can whip something up to make you feel better," Balin said gently as he guided Morra back to a laying position. After tucking her in, he disappeared and returned with a steaming cup of tea and some herbs that smelled like spicy lemonade.

"Drink this. It will help," he said as she handed Morra the tea.

Morra took a sip and felt warmth spread through her body. She smiled weakly at Balin and Sophia, who hovered behind, eyes shining with worry.

The next few days were much of the same. Morra drifted in and out of consciousness, taking sips of tea and water and nibbling on bland crackers. Balin and Sophia took turns sitting with her, checking her temperature, and wiping her forehead with a cool cloth. Kahadin slept on the couch in her room, but she rarely saw him. He was a quiet sleeper and hardly noticeable but, Morra was grateful for his presence.

On the third day of her illness, Morra awoke to a different kind of ache. Her body, still weak and sore, and her mouth felt stuffed with cotton, but she no longer felt a foot in the grave. Kahadin sat on the bed next to her, deeply absorbed, as he clacked on the laptop sitting precariously on his raised knee. It surprised Morra to see him there, blinking blearily up at him. "Hey." Her throat ached from disuse, but it felt good to speak.

Kahadin looked up from his computer, relief flooding his face when he saw that Morra was awake. "Hey, how are you feeling?" he asked, putting his computer aside and moving closer to her.

"I feel better, thanks," Morra replied, her voice still hoarse. "What happened? How long have I been out?"

"You had a pretty terrible fever," Kahadin explained. "You've been out for almost three days now."

"Three days?" Morra repeated, eyes widening. "Wow, I had no idea."

Kahadin nodded, his expression serious. "Yeah, it was alarming there for a bit. The adults were starting to get worried."

A small smile tugged at her dry lips. "Yeah? Even Isolde?" Morra started to feel more accepted in the family before she fell ill. However, there were others whose hate only seemed to grow by the day. Sharp, steely looks and snide remarks raked her nerves. Their behavior had worn down Morra's temper, and the flu had taken away the last of her patience.

He gave her a look before rolling his eyes. "No, I think she was upset by the attention you were receiving."

"What is up with her and her daughter?" The water on the side table caught her eye. Hoping it was fresh, she pulled the glass to her lip. The pain undercut the relief of the cool liquid trickling down her throat. Each swallow felt like that time she was seven and tried to eat sand.

"To be frank, I cannot make heads or tails of it. They may not be the most agreeable individuals, but their attitude has become worse since you have arrived. If it becomes to bothersome, just let Balin know he will handle it."

"It's just us here, you can just call her a bitch, but enough about them. How is everyone? What did I miss?" Her muscles twinged as she rolled over in bed, ready to be regaled with the current drama.

As the days went by, Morra shook off the last bits of illness and became more and more comfortable in the Manor. She often spent her time with Kahadin and his sister, Ladianna. Morra found that she quite liked Ladianna; her kind disposition and her good sense of humor had endeared Morra to her within their first meeting. The girl was still posh like Kahadin, but more subtle about it. She oozed it in a classically pretty way that only an aristocratic girl could pull off. Ladianna looked like she walked out of an old painting with her long wavy blond hair and her piercing grey eyes. Her words weren't as sharp as Kahadin's, but they were still eloquent and full of hidden meanings.

Morra was wandering the grounds, trying to find said girl. She had started to become restless waiting for Galahad's return. Instead, she found Lucan, one of the many grandchildren of Ocursus and his wife Beatrix, instead.

"Have you seen Ladianna?" she asked. Lucan, four years Morra's senior, towered over her with broad shoulders and a physique that spoke of strength. His long, windswept dark hair framed a handsome face with sharp features, while his deep blue-grey eyes glinted with mischief.

"Follow me," he mock whispered with a wink. Following him out the large double doors in the main family sitting room to the back of the house, Morra walked down the steps, taking in her surroundings.

Ladianna stood on a black mat in a fighting stance, her lithe body framed by her black ensemble of a tank and leggings. Her hands were bound in black fabric as she raised them in defense, a fire burning in her eyes.

Balin stood opposite of her, fists raised. "Again!" he commanded.

As soon as he spoke, she threw herself at him with a blur of movement. Each of them moved in fast flashes of arm and legs, striking, each angling at knees and hips. Balin took a step back, causing dust to rise from the mat as he tried to evade her quick attacks.

The fight raged on with incredible speed. Morra could barely track who had the upper hand, but as Balin turned fast on his left leg, she saw him gain the win. He held back, protecting his daughter from his full force. Balin barely swung at her, dodging her attacks. Soon they stopped, both panting, sweat beading on their brows.

"Good job, Ladi!" Lucan's older brother, Pallas, yelled from across the yard. He, too, was tall and lean with jet black hair that he kept short. His sun-kissed skin glowed and made him appear older than he was. Morra had only met him in passing a few times, but she liked him.

He always had an inviting smile pasted on his firm jaw, his gaze was both inquisitive and mischievous, much like Lucan's. He moved with grace, a natural athleticism, as if he could take on any challenge that he might face.

"What is he doing with them?" Morra asked. Pallas had moved on to a little cage off to the side of the main training ground. Inside little Rian and Edaris were in boxing glove swinging wildly at each other.

"The older ones can train with weapons, but the younger ones still want to be a part of the action," Lucan explained to her as he walked her around the yard.

Lucan gestured with his onyx painted fingernails towards the spot where Pallas had placed a series of faux-swords for Edaris and Rion to spar with. Then to Kahadin who pulled a bow taught before releasing with a delicate breath, hitting the target dead on.

"Do you think I could learn?" Morra eagerly asked Lucan as Pallas walked over to them. A hesitant look passed between the brothers.

"Please!" she asked, trying to give them puppy dog eyes.

Lucan laughed at her attempts, shoving her lightly before wrapping an arm around her shoulders. "That stopped working on us years ago, but nice try pipsqueak."

Melancholy spread across her face. She nodded morosely. "Okay, I just..." with another heavy sigh she glanced up at the boys, "I have never done any of this." She gestured to the family. "I never got to play with cousins or siblings growing up."

"Fine, but-"

The facade dropped from her face as a grin spread across her face. The brothers rolled their eyes at her trickery, almost impressed by her ability to fool them.

"But," Pallas said, "we can only spare some. If you want t o do more, you have to ask Galahad's permission."

"Okay," she said, slightly disappointed but still excited to finally feel part of her new family. Morra had been living with them for a couple of weeks and it was the first time they would include her in a family activity. These people *were* becoming her family, despite her reluctance to let them in. Briefly, Morra wondered when Galahad would be home.

"Let Lucan teach you a few tricks before I start training with you," Pallas told her before turning sharply. "Hey Rion, no." With surprisingly fast legs the little boy took off with a wooden sword forcing Pallas to chase after him.

After a few hours of training, she could see the blossom of bruises on her arms and thighs. "Okay, this is all I can teach you today. If you want to train more, you can do it with me tomorrow," Lucan said, ruffling her hair again.

"Thank you, Lucan. For everything!" Morra told him earnestly, as he wrapped her in a hug before sending her off to Kahadin and Ladianna, who were beckoning her.

Morra's days were entertaining, but her nights were restless. Nightmares haunted her sleep. Each time her eyes fell shut, shadows of fires and explosions plagued her. Images of her mother burned on a silver table in a cold morgue tormented her.

To keep the dreams at bay, Morra wandered the Manor when night fell. The bright moon's shadows cast through the enormous windows gave her a sense of peace as she strolled through the quiet halls. Cold stone against bare feet grounded Morra as she explored the place. In the quiet of twilight, the home felt foreign, almost like a castle from another time.

She loved it.

Wandering through the halls, and down to the lower level, she eventually came to the threshold she had been cautioned against. Morra had passed it multiple times on her late night explorations but had never got the courage to go inside. In the daylight, the forbidden room resembled the rest, only older, darker. But in the dim light, brightened only by candlelight down in the deepest parts of the Manor, it shapeshifted into something older. Darker.

The heavy and thick oak wood appeared dark as night, with black iron fixtures and hinges. It seemed forbidden, holding secrets yet to be revealed. Unable to curb her curiosity, she turned the knob and pushed on the door, which creaked loudly, the old wood protesting the movement. She paused, wincing, hoping nobody had a bedroom down here. When she didn't hear footsteps, she pushed into the room fully.

Dusty books covered the few shelves, the walls were made of exposed grey brick, and the floors were black laced marble. The entire room emitted the scent of burning candles, producing a light honey and cinnamon fragrance. It resembled a shrine of sorts, but Morra just didn't know who for. A beautifully carved and painted statue of a woman was in the middle, with others lining the circular room.

Captivated, she padded towards the statue. Her skin was a deep umber, and her hair resembled a raven feather, appearing like starless night with a bright full moon. The statue's eyes shimmered like stars themselves. If this was just an homage to the woman, Morra couldn't begin to imagine what she would have looked like when she was alive.

Morra pulled her eyes from the stone visage to the bottom of the statue, feeling the rough stone as she dragged her fingers over the engraved words she didn't understand. The same language on the crest, she noted.

Deciding to explore the rest of the room, she saw each statue was unique and ancient. Towards the back, a display case appeared to have never been opened, with a layer of dust centimeters thick. Inside was a sword with foreign words etched into the steel that looked similar to the ones on the statues. Looking around, she tried to find a way to open it. She wanted to hold it and feel the weight in her hand, sensing a longing inside her she didn't think upon.

A hand landed on her shoulder and with a jolt, a scream ripped from Morra echoing through the room as she spun around to face the stranger. Shadows ensconced most of him. The single light she toted into the room flashed against wire frames, revealing distressed eyes.

"You shouldn't be in here," he urged, surveying the room frantically before turning to her. "You need to leave before someone finds out you were in here."

Her heart thumped loudly as she stared dumbly at the stranger. "Who are you?" she eventually managed to whisper.

Without answering, the stranger seized her arm and pulled her out of the room. "Let go of me," she demanded, trying to break free from his grasp. He suddenly turned, slamming the door shut and locking it tightly, sliding the key into his pocket.

Who was this?

Morra wasn't angry about being forcefully removed from the room, but the stranger's iron grip made her uneasy. "Who are you?" she asked again, but before he could answer, the sound of heavy footsteps echoed down the long hallway, sending shivers down her spine.

The stranger once again pulled her by the hand. Forcing them behind one of the draperies, he pushed her against the wall. They stood in silence, holding their breath as the footsteps drew nearer, and he held a finger over his mouth. The boy, and he was a boy only a bit older than her, was illuminated as light streaked past the heavy tapestries. Green eyes shone, and the light reflected glints of shiny skin on his face. Though she couldn't fully see his face, her heart still raced at the glimpse.

His hold on her wrist loosened, but his skin still burned hot on her own. Puffs of warm air hit her face as he spoke. "There's something bigger at play than your curiosity. You need to be careful," he warned, eyes shining.

With that, he turned and left. She decided to finally go to sleep. It seemed that she caused enough mischief for the night.

As Morra crawled into bed, she couldn't help but think about the mysterious room in the basement.

And the mysterious boy.

CHAPTER EIGHT

❖

"**I** would like to know more about my father," Morra said, broaching the subject quietly. It took three weeks before Galahad returned. He immediately sought Morra out, apologizing for the long delay. Galahad explained that it didn't happen often, but long travel for work was sometimes expected of the family. Morra nodded politely, still not sure what they did for business. Alpaca farming didn't seem like a lucrative jet setting type of career, but what did she know? She had more important questions. Those had to wait until after dinner; Galahad told her he wanted to talk then.

Dinner came and went as they had previously. Morra endured the glares while laughing and joking with everyone else. After the food had finished, she followed her grandfather and Sophia to the office.

Morra had struggled while Galahad had been gone. Living where her father grew up, getting to know his family, his siblings, but she knew very little about him. She had asked in the beginning, but it continued to be a strained subject.

Everyone seemed to avoid talking about Arthur. Or at least talking about him with her. Eventually, she stopped asking, words dying on her tongue at the pinched looks or sweeping grief.

"Arthur was a good man," Galahad avowed, watching her with a melancholy tilt to his lips. "Kind and thoughtful, always trying to better himself. He attended an academy on a full scholarship. He had been such a bright boy. Arthur would light up a room, always seeking ways to expand his knowledge and always trying to get away for some new adventure."

Sophia gave a watery chuckle as she chimed in, "That boy was always getting himself into mischief. It calmed down when he met Adelaine, though. Arthur loved your mother so much; they were so happy together." Their gaze held the wake of devastation that grief left behind. Morra could see they were fighting the same battle she was.

The battle to hold the memories of their lives instead of the broken bodies that were left behind.

"My mother never really talked about him much. It was too hard for her, I think," Morra confided, wiping tears away with the back of her hand, "I don't even know what he looked like. I don't understand why she wouldn't tell me about all of you. I get talking about him being too painful, but why keep me in the dark?"

Galahad stood with a heavy sigh, showing his age. He came across as a young spirit. Morra forgot he must be in his seventies. Walking to the fireplace, he grabbed a photo book, handing it over to Morra. He sat next to her as she flipped through the photos. The first pages were of a younger Galahad and a beautiful woman with a baby in their arms.

Pudgy arms and legs and a toothy smile made Morra coo. Her dad had been an adorable baby. Grey eyes pierced through the photos, the same ones that she had.

Knowing she carried a piece of him with her meant so much more than any teddy bear ever could.

Reverently, Morra went through the childhood pictures, greedily devouring them. Her heart tugged seeing him so carefree and wild. Galahad turned the pages to the back.

The color drained from Morra's face as her heart sank like a leaden weight, stomach rolling with dread. She stared transfixed at the beautiful picture of Arthur and her mother, their two heads pressed together lovingly, his hands cradling her mother's pregnant belly.

"This was before he left on his final assignment," he explained, his voice barely audible over the thundering in her head. "That is the last picture of him alive."

Morra forced herself to listen as Galahad and Sophia spoke, but it felt as if her brain had frozen in fear.

"Where was he assigned to?" Sophia asked.

"Nyneve Thelusius's estates, his body was never recovered."

"He's not dead," she croaked quietly, her eyes on the photo. On him.

Galahad gave her a puzzled look before shaking his head.

"No, dear, I searched for Arthur for ten years. I know this is..."

The table clattered as her knee banged loudly into it as she stood, cutting him off. "No! I saw him. I have seen him before."

Galahad watched her carefully, studying her face for any signs of deception. His eyes shifted quickly from a sweetlooking grandfather to a sharp, perceptive patriarch of the family. It startled her for a moment as he stared her down.

Morra beseeched him. "I know what I saw. It was my dad." She tried to keep the tremble from her voice. The air forcefully pushed out of her lungs as she fell back into her seat. Wide frightened eyes swung towards Sophia, who looked on with concern.

It didn't reassure Morra. She trembled, realizing what could happen. They could think she was absurd, or trying to hurt them. She could lose them.

Galahad stood and kneeled in front of Morra before grabbing her chin in his hand. He scrutinized her with his gaze and her chest ached, knowing he had locked eyes with a replica of his son's.

His own eyes were clouded with pain.

"My dear, Arthur is very much dead. I know you are still grieving for your mother, but Arthur..." he trailed off.

Morra grabbed his wrist. "Please, please," she implored. "I saw him the day before my mother died. And times before that as well, often just for a second, but I know it was him, that scar right there, below his eye... I know its him. Please believe me," she begged him to understand.

Galahad stood, wiping a hand across his face. His heart was breaking and she could see it. Turning away, he slumped, walking to his desk like a man headed to the gallows.

Bleakness shrouded him.

Morra blinked, shifting in her seat. He didn't believe her, and she was going to lose everyone... No, she couldn't, she wouldn't- but what if- her breathing picked up.

"Honey," Sophia whispered to Morra gently, "you need to rest, everything will be alright."

"Please!" She tried to plead again as her voice rose. A hard bang as Galahad's fist collided with mahogany.

"We will discuss this in the morning," Galahad decreed with a firm tone. The head of the family and unyielding ruler swiftly replaced his visage of grandfatherly love.

Suddenly, he seemed very large and intimidating. The precarious position she stood in had somehow been forgotten over the last few weeks. She might be family, but Galahad only had been around her for a handful of hours.

She was a stranger in unfamiliar territory.

"We will discuss this in the morning. For now, I need you to write down everything about your father, anything you can tell me about when you saw him. Every little detail matters, even if you don't think it does." He dismissed her presence with a wave of her hand.

Morra wanted to protest, to rage and scream, to convince them she wasn't lying.

Instead, she nodded, sinking her teeth in her bottom lip as she wiped at the tears trickling down her face with the sleeves of her sweater. She looked at the picture of her parents one last time before the tears blurred her vision. When their faces turned to blobs of color, her eyes shuttered before sitting down with the notebook Sophia gave her.

Galahad and Sophia quietly whispered to each other as they walked to the desk on the other side of the room. Morra ignored them, not being able to bear hearing in case they were discussing how best to get rid of her.

Doubts swarmed her before she could attempt to compose herself. Fear swelling inside her like crashing waves causing the pen in her hand to shake. The tension in the room became thick enough to choke on as Morra wrote, ink smearing across the page as her hands shook with the force of her cries.

She just lost her family.

Again.

Words echoed in her head like roars, telling her she just ruined everything. Her unheard screams grew in silent defeat. Morra tried to focus on the task Galahad gave her; she wrote every time she saw her dad, describing the day and location. Soon the lines of two pages were filled with messy handwriting. When she couldn't think anymore, hand cramping and heart hurting, she stopped and gave into the spiral of emotions.

At some point, Galahad's brother came in as well. The three of them were pouring over large tomes, whispering quietly so Morra wouldn't hear. Galahad and Ocursus got louder. Their sharp tone and heated looks told her they were fighting, though she still couldn't hear their words.

Their attention shifted as Morra threw down the pen with a clatter. She wept, loudly and desperately unable to stand being in there she ran, needing to be alone and think without them. She left quickly, running down the hall. Sophia's voice called after her, but she couldn't, no she wouldn't stay and face them all. *Coward,* she thought as she ran. *Nothing but a coward.*

Morra needed air.

She was foolish to think she could have this. She needed to give up. It was evitable, she lost everyone in the end.

An icy breeze graced her face as she burst through the front doors. Blindly running through the garden, she glanced behind her. Seeing nobody, her run turned to a walk until she stopped at a fountain in the gardens. Icy water sprinkled her back, helping her breathe. As she calmed, Morra watched the water flow and listened to the songbirds. When her hands stopped shaking, she closed her eyes and leaned back, trying to absorb the setting sun.

The warmth didn't replace the cold dread in her heart.

Crunching footsteps alerted her to someone. She didn't open her eyes until they stood directly in front of her. Taking another deep breath, her gaze flitted up to find Kahadin. She gave him a sad smile before tracing the ground with her eyes.

"Are they angry at me?" Color filled her cheeks, remembering she fled in a sobbing mess, but it had all been too much. The heat of the room, the fire, the memories, the yelling. Morra shook her head, forcing the thoughts to go away.

"No, they are not angry; they are just worried." Kahadin paused, considering her for a moment before sitting next to her, "They are not angry at you, they just need time to process everything."

Nodding once, Morra refused to shift her gaze, so he sat, his grey eyes soft, losing the sharpness they typically carried.

"You must understand the grave situation that befell our household when Uncle passed away. The funeral was bleak. There were no remains to bury, so we buried an empty coffin. The mourning was unparalleled and nearly shattered the very foundations of our family." Kahadin had a faraway look, portraying the face of someone much older than his own years. "Arthur was not only your father, but he was also the heir to the estate. When he died, your mother, in her own grief, left. Grandfather couldn't bear that his firstborn was gone, his last reminder of his first wife."

The grief of her father's death ran deep within the family. She understood, thinking of the hole in her heart her mother occupied and the ache of her loss.

"He searched for him for years, convinced he couldn't be gone. Eventually, he gave in and let it go. He processed and moved on and now..."

She nodded, not knowing what to say. Kahadin draped his arm around her shoulders, pulling her into a hug. Tucking his chin on her head, he quietly asked with sincerity in his aristocratic face she didn't expect. "Are you okay?"

His care for her helped more than she could ever explain. Some of her fear melted, knowing Kahadin would be there for her.

"I will be, one day," she said, trying to comfort her friend, and she realized in that moment he really was her best friend. Morra hugged him back in a silent thank you. When she pulled away, she saw her cousin studying her before he pulled her back into a hug.

Leaning close, he whispers in her ear, "There are things you don't know about this family. We are special. It's why we live like we do, why it's possible for your father to be alive. I shouldn't even tell you this, but I trust you and that's not something one comes by often."

He pulled back to look at her with seriousness clouding his eyes. "I will explain as I can, and when the family meets tonight, I will push for you to be informed."

With that, he stood and started to walk away. As he reached the edge of the garden, he peered back. "You should get some sleep. Tomorrow will be long."

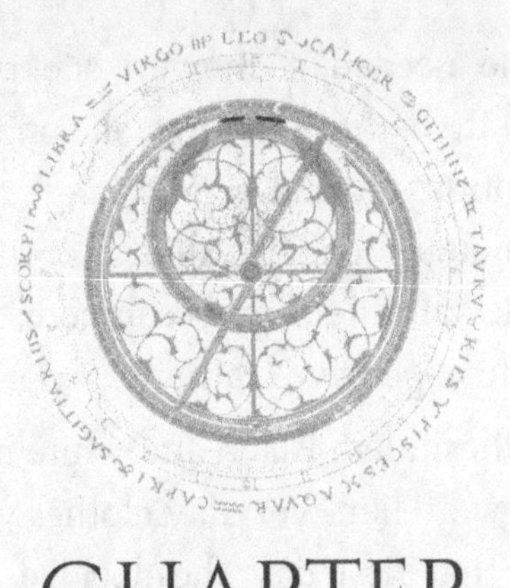

CHAPTER NINE

Strips of light peaked from the curtains, casting fractals throughout the room, blinding her tired eyes. The sun had risen and warmed the space despite the heavy red curtains. The uneasy feeling she had the night before eased with the morning light.

Morra looked around in appreciation for the first time and, quite possibly, the last. When she first moved in, she had found it suffocating. Her opinion shifted with time. The stuffy antique room now felt rich and warm. It felt cozy.

Compared to the other bedrooms, her own had been simple. They toned down the finery to make her feel more comfortable. Still everywhere had rich details, from the golden embroidery on the pillows to the leather stamped label on the trunk at the end of her bed with her name, to the crown molding surrounding the room.

Deciding she needed a shower, she padded across the room to the en-suite bathroom. First, she opened the armoire, looking at her options. It had been strange trying to dress in the clothes they bought for her. All of it oozed money, the fine cream silks, to the soft linens and cashmeres. Even the shoes were crafted from expensive leather.

At first, she hesitated. Black and white high tops, hoodies and ripped jeans were her everyday clothes when her mother was alive. After that first day she decided to wear her own clothes, intimidated by the fine fabrics that made up her wardrobe. Kahadin eventually forced her hand by burning her clothes. He laughed as she yelled, claiming he helped her.

A chuckle escaped her lips. She would never admit she liked her new clothes so much better. Morra refused to give him the satisfaction. Never before had she worn items of such luxury. Her mother and her hadn't been poor, but they weren't rich either. Most of her clothes were bought at an outlet clothing store or were thrifted.

Pulling out a short brown wool skirt, soft cream linen top, a pretty leather belt, and matching shoes, Morra folded them in a neat stack. The day ahead was a mystery. She wanted to feel prepared.

This could be her last day in the house.

Taking her clothes into the bathroom, she set them on the marble counter. Morra gazed longingly at the clawfoot tub, she wished for nothing more than to soak the ache and worry from her bones, but after running away from Galahad last night, she knew she needed to face him. Turning on the faucet, she turned up the heat. As quick as she could, she scrubbed down, got out, and changed into her clothes. Just as she walked back into her room, she heard a rapping at her door.

Opening the door stood one of her cousins.

The girl was older than her, but not by much. She had pale skin and light brown hair that fell to her jaw. With big eyes that were so very different from Kahadin and his siblings. They were softer, not as sharp, and were closer to pale bluegrey than gunmetal. Despite them being soft in feature, they hardened with disdain.

"Good morning. I see you continue to make yourself at home, cousin," she mocked, her arms crossed in front of her, "It's a shame it won't be for long." A mean smirk graced her pretty face.

Morra knew she was taunting her, but she refused to let the barbed words stick in her skin. Frowning at the pale girl, she said, "I need to check in with Galahad," she told her, trying to give her the hint to move or state her business.

The girl's arm blocked Morra when she tried to move past her. Morra looked at her with squinted eyes. This girl was the bane of her existence. Madoine had taken every opportunity to remind her she didn't really belong.

"The family is not speaking with you until we decide if you are a liability or an asset," the girl spat. In a mockingly kind tone, the girl continued, "You should really pack your stuff now. I doubt you are going to stay."

Irritation thrumming through her, and her jaw clenched as she ground out, "Seriously? Liability or asset?" Morra looked into her cousin's eyes, and she saw it... the flicker. The girl was lying. Before she could call her on it, Kahadin turned the corner barking, "Madoine."

Stiffening, her eyes glacially slid to his frame. "Yes?" she drawled, as if she was unconcerned by his presence.

"I believe you were instructed to bring Morra to the family dining room, were you not?" Without answering, Kahadin turns to Morra, cocking an eyebrow. "Let's get to it."

He turned around and started down the hall and Morra followed, Madoine on her heels.

They walked down the stairs, making a sharp right at the foot of them. Walking into the family room, as Kahadin had called it, she saw everyone gathered and swallowed nervously.

This would be the first time she had seen everyone since her first night here. Most of the family came and went as they pleased. But in front of her sat the whole family, including people she didn't recognize.

Kahadin motioned for Morra to sit down at the table. She took a seat between him and his dad, Balin. She tilted her lips, giving a half wave as Balin turned his attention to her.

"I am glad you came. We were just sitting down for breakfast. I hope you are fond of pancakes," he said jovially, as if today would not decide her fate.

Balin was a tall man, his face mimicked Sophia and Kahadin's. He had the same pale skin and icy grey eyes, with long silver hair tied back into a ponytail. Sharp edges carved his face and became highlighted by the tight tailoring of the simple white shirt, black slacks and dress shoes. It wasn't quite fancy, just high end.

The whole family looked like that. Kahadin's outfit was formal but not overly so with simple black trousers and a button-up shirt. Galahad, though, looked disheveled, and the dark circles under his eyes highlighted his tiredness. A pang of guilt shot through Morra as she looked at him. If she hadn't run away, maybe she could have given him the answers he needed, he could have slept.

The scent of pancakes, coffee and syrup wafted through the air, causing her stomach to grumble. Food came out on silver platters set gently on the well crafted table and Morra relished the distraction. A cup of coffee was pushed in her hands by Kahadin and Morra mouthed a silent thank you. Knowing today she would need it, she sipped at the dark roast for strength. The clinking of silverware and the slicing of pancakes were the only sounds for a while. Heaviness sat in the air. It clawed at Morra, but she stayed quiet.

Galahad stood up, beckoning her to follow him. She did. "We are going to the study. Please come with me." With that, he turned sharply, walking out of the room. Suddenly, Morra felt like a mouse caught by a cat with nowhere to go as she dangled on the precipice of danger. Galahad's silence intensified this feeling. They walked back down to the first floor, then down a set of long hallways.

The place still felt like a maze. Sophie had shown her around, but she still couldn't pick one hallway away from the next. After turning left and right through the halls, she began to wonder how anyone knew where they were. The pair reached two doors in the corner of the hallway. Galahad opened the doors with a flourish and gestured for her to enter. Examining the room, she realized she stood in a library.

The smell of musty paper filled the chamber, the earthy scent of old leather and fine wood permeated the walls. Oak bookshelves lined the room, and each shelf had been stacked high with ancient leather-bound books.

"Sit," he commanded, gesturing to a couch. Gingerly, she sat on the plush leather chair, distracted for a moment by the beautiful room.

The library was just as impressive as the rest of the house. The shelves and shelves of books glowed somehow from the artificial light that bounced off of strategically placed mirrors, making it feel as though sunlight penetrated through the stone walls. A black marble fireplace dominated the room. Swords, daggers, and weaponry that looked hundreds of years old framed the mantle.

Galahad sat in front of her, and for a long while, they sat in silence. Despite her nervousness, she didn't want to be the one to break it. She didn't feel like she belonged. Her gut twisted at the thought; she desperately wanted to belong.

Morra was so unsure of her place here. Galahad's grimness, the glaring from Isolde, and Madoine, calling her a liability or asset, made Morra question the people she lived with. There was an inkling that something was off about the family.

Between the home, and the farm that no one ever talked about, the way everyone looked and acted, and the bits of information she had overheard. Morra knew in her gut that they weren't telling her something. Locked doors and thinly veiled warnings were all she needed and as she looked at the old man with kind eyes, she wondered if this was why her mother never told her about them.

Maybe she was right to have run.

Maybe Morra should have run the first chance she had.

As if he read her thoughts, Galahad let out a heavy sigh. "I have a lot of explaining to do, and I would like you to listen without interrupting." He paused and looked at her intently, waiting for some sort of response. She nodded, not really knowing what to say.

"I assembled a family meeting of everyone twelve years of age and up last night," he explained in a serious tone. "The majority preferred to tell you and while I am the head of this family and make the final decision, I try to rule our lives fairly."

"When we thought your father died, your mother left. I knew she had become pregnant, but for your safety, she and I decided it was safest for you to grow up unaware of our presence."

Her jaw clenched as she listened, words hung heavy on her tongue.

Galahad must have seen it in her eyes because he raised his hand, halting her before she could interrupt.

"Your mother knew the truth about our family and wanted to raise you away from it. I told you that I am the head of this family. Tradition has placed me as such. Your father was heir, next in line, as he was my first born child. You are his first-born child, which makes you, his heir."

Galahad continued, his voice growing softer with each word. "Being heir to this family is dangerous. It's why we lost your father."

"Why?" she demanded, unable to process his words. He was acting as if they lived in the past. Heirs, inheritances, it was all ridiculous.

Galahad took a deep breath before responding. Still looking into her eyes, he uttered the words that would change her fate forever:

"Because, my dear," Galahad said quietly. "This family has a special gift, and it makes us uniquely powerful. But with that power comes danger, and I've done what I can to protect you, but I can see now it is futile." He leaned forward towards Morra. "We have the ability to time jump," Galahad told her bluntly.

Her eyes widened. What did that even mean? How could he pretend- what kind of joke was he playing?

"I know this is a lot but-"

Morra stood up, cutting him off. The beginning tendrils of anger sprouted in her at the outrageous claim. "Time jump?" she echoed, waiting for him to say 'gotcha' but it never came.

He was serious. Dead serious, he really believed it.

Galahad dipped his head, eyes solemn. "The ability is a family trait passed down from our ancestors. We are one of the only families that can do this."

Sinking back down onto the chair, her head swam with information. She wasn't sure what to think.

Galahad seemed to sense her apprehension and placed his hand on hers gently. "I know this is difficult for you to understand, but I want you to trust me."

Morra nodded warily, her body was tense, and she couldn't seem to suck in a proper breath.

"And my dad?" she questioned cautiously.

Gazing at him, Morra couldn't help wondering how mentally stable he was. Licking her lips, she glanced over his shoulder at the door. The house, with its many doors and long hallways, was intricately built and increasingly complicated; Morra underestimated her ability to find the front door from here. Fear gripped her as Galahad continued.

"He went out and did not come back, no safety precautions were enacted. I searched for him through time for ten years before I gave up."

"This can't be real!" She stood up, furious. *How could he do this,* she thought, *after everything she had been through? How could he do this and try to trick her?*

"This is no trick Morra," he replied. Morra realized that she must have said her thoughts unwittingly.

Leaning forward, Galahad took the teapot in his wrinkled fingers and poured both of them a steaming cup of tea. The hand painted cup burned her hands, but she only wrapped her fingers around it tighter. Her life had been turned on its head over and over, but this was something entirely different.

For once, she just wanted to be normal.

After a few moments, Galahad spoke again.

"Think about your childhood: You never knew about us. Your mother never talked about your father. You moved around every few years cross country, never keeping in contact with those you left behind. Your mother was not some nomad. She ran to keep you safe."

The words struck a vein of sorrow that ran deep. Memories of all the moves, of the lies and secrets. Of the dream that could never happen. Morra stood in the middle of the room, her body tense and her gaze fixed on the floor. The words still lingering in her mind, resonating in her heart like a funeral march, and when Galahad put a hand on her shoulder, she almost welcomed it. The comfort it promised was so inviting, yet something inside urged her to recoil. Staring at the offered hand, her eyes filled with questions. And suspicion.

Was it really an accident? Pain racked her body as a thought crossed her mind. *Or was it worse... was it murder?* Fury surged through her veins as visions of her mother being killed flashed before her eyes.

Because of her and this family.

First Arthur, then Adelaine. Who else would die for this?

She wanted to scream, cry, and scream again, to somehow break free of the prison of emotions that slowly suffocated her. But she only managed a whisper as the tears began to flow freely down her cheeks. "Is that why my mom died? Because of this? Because of you?" Her gaze slowly drifted to his. "Because of me?"

Galahad looked down, a pained look swimming across his face. "Yes."

Dropping to the floor, she curled her knees to her chest, trying to hold herself together. Parts of her were crumbling to the ground, and Morra didn't know if she should pick them up. Warm arms surrounded her, and she leaned into it, taking whatever comfort she could. She hurt too much to refuse his kindness.

"Listen to me, Morra." Galahads' soft voice floated to her, cutting through the fog of despair. "I am not trying to hurt you.

I am trying to explain what happened and what will happen."

She nodded gently for him to continue because what could be worse than her mom dying because of her.

"The decision to separate was hard. Your mother and I knew that for you to stand a chance of surviving, we had to get rid of the looming threat."

With one arm still wrapped around his granddaughter, he used the other to wipe her tears. Looking at her in her eyes, he continued, "I am sorry that you did not get the childhood that you deserved and I am so sorry for the loss you have experienced. My words cannot fix these things, but I can help you understand."

Morra looked at him, seeing genuine hurt at her own pain, and for the first time that night, she decided to take his words at face value. She would listen and then judge its validity.

"It is our curse and our blessing to jump through time; a power we use to influence significant events in history and prevent the future from becoming bleak. We are blessed with this power to protect the world and keep it alive."

She looked him in the eyes, waiting for a beat before finally speaking. "What are your plans with me?" she asked hesitantly, unsure whether she wanted an answer or not.

With a heavy sigh, he looked at her, loss and pain in his gaze. "I will not force you to be part of this family. I understand this burden is an unyielding one, even when you are born into it. But if you choose to stay with us and be our heir, you will have a life full of luxury and power. I do not lie to my family, or anyone, for that matter. I am telling you this because if you decide to go, you will have a hard time staying away and if anyone finds out who your father is, you will be in danger. Because of your father's position as my heir, he had many enemies, and the world of time travel is not one of peace."

They sat in silence for a long period. Doubt clouded her, stopping her from doing anything. The logistics alone didn't make sense.

"Could he really be alive?"

If he was, could he be traveling to her from the past before he died? She didn't know how that could work, how any of this could work.

"We don't know completely. We have been going over the possibilities. There is a way for us to find out, but I will need to discuss it with my siblings and with Balin and Isolde." Standing, he handed her a book, *'The Theory and Practical Application of Time Jumping' by Augustus Fahey.*

"I will send Kahadin in. I am sorry, but I must get back to the family to figure out how to go forward. You need time to decide if you want to be part of this. I will find you later." With a grim smile, he left the library.

As she clutched the book in her hands, a whirlwind of emotions overtook her. Her mother tried to give her a normal life. To live without fear and she knew there would be no *'normal'* for her here. Morra missed her mother and didn't want to replace the life she fought and died for; she couldn't shake that thought from her head. It stuck there like gum.

If all of this was true, then why was her mother killed and not her?

Would she be committing suicide by being part of this

family? Was she disgracing her mother's memory, dedicating herself to this life?

Looking down at the book, she also had to concede that her mother wasn't here anymore, and this life was hers and hers alone. The dead couldn't help her now. This was her choice and hers alone.

Kahadin.

She sighed in relief at seeing him, knowing Kahadin could help. Smiling, he reached a hand out. "Come with me. Atlas can explain better than any book written two hundred years ago."

Dazed, she did not question him.

She just followed.

CHAPTER TEN

Morra's insides twisted like she had been spun around on a carnival ride. The world she had once known shattered... glass on the floor, ready to cut unsuspecting bare feet. She felt like an opened wound following Kahadin, silently stuck behind the crumbling wall of what she thought she knew. Steadily, they climbed the spiraling staircase until they reached a heavy oak door. Turning the latch and giving a bit of a shove, Kahadin stepped into the astronomy tower escorting her in. Stained glass windows cast light across the floor of the spacious room. Tower was an appropriate name, she thought. Tall stone walls curved into a point, like a keep from an old castle. Her breath left her body as she stood in awe.

Shaking his head, Kahadin caught her hand pulling her forcefully from the sitting room into a room off the left. The large hexagonal room resembled a house after a tornado.

Papers, news articles, and opened books coated every inch of available space. In the middle of it all was a figure leaning over an impressive amount of papers, scribbling furiously, muttering to themselves.

Morra watched as they quietly murmured in a language Morra had never heard. The tall figure hadn't noticed the pair yet. Looking over at her cousin, a smirk lodged on his face, he gave her a conspiratorial wink. "Atlas!" he shouted.

The lanky figure at the desk jumped with a yelp, hitting their head on the cabinet above them. The person spun around while rubbing at their goose egg. "Kahadin, I thought I told you not to sneak up on me."

Morra's breath caught in her throat as she gazed upon his face.

The boy who had pulled her from the forbidden room appeared even more lovely in the daylight than she remembered. The stone corridor's light failed to capture the true extent of his beauty, his tall frame was adorned with bright green eyes and warm bronze skin. Although thin, he wasn't without muscle. She could see them rippling under his shirt.

Averting her eyes, a blush bloomed across her face like roses opening in spring. His brown hair seemed to glow as the sunlight drifted in from the large window behind him. A goofy grin spread across his face. It must have been contagious, as Morra's own face slowly mirrored his. A strange excitement fluttered in her chest as she gazed at Atlas. He wore a loose-fitting black shirt and dark pants, and he moved with a simple grace that caused the breath in her throat to catch.

A small cough cut the tension, forgetting that Kahadin stood next to her, both Atlas and Morra, startled by the sound. Kahadin stood, his feet planted, arms crossed, with a predatory grin. In the gleaming light of his perfect teeth, Morra groaned. She knew at that moment that her cousin and best friend would never let this go. He was like a dog with a bone when it came to gossip.

"Should I leave or?" A fist collided hard on his biceps.

"Hey! What was that for!? I can't help it if your mutual crush is that obvious." Morra's hand throbbed. It would have been softer to hit bricks, but it was definitely worth it. It didn't matter that his words rang with truth.

With red cheeks and more than a bit of embarrassment, she shot an icy glare at her cousin before raising her eyebrows in an effort to refocus his mind on more urgent topics like time travel. She knew it needed to be discussed, even though she couldn't take her eyes off his face or the scar that spider webbed from his left temple to his right eye.

"MORRA?" Kahadin looked at her expectantly. She had been staring again. Red deepened across her face. Thankfully, her darker skin could hide some of it, but she could feel the warmth, nonetheless.

Luckily for Morra, Atlas was staring at her as well, just a tad more discreetly.

Kahadin led the introductions before moving on to the real reason they were there. "Grandfather told Morra about the family, and I thought it would be helpful to talk to you rather than read this drabble," Kahadin said, throwing the book on the desk, causing papers to scatter.

Her heart dropped as she scrutinized him, looking for any trace that he was family. The first boy she likes and, of course, he is part... no. Everyone looked similar, even her, despite not having fair skin. No grey eyes, everyone had grey eyes. Her torrent of thoughts rattled in her skull; the dull roar almost overshadowed the boy in question's next words.

"Your part of the-"

Atlas quickly stuttered, "Oh, no. Galahad and Sophia took me in when I was young and since I am not blood, I can't time jump, but I became in charge of the family records. I help research and then catalog every mission and every finding. I am kinda the family historian," he rambled, giving her a small sheepish smile, causing his eyes to crinkle, tugging at the scar.

Kahadin rolled his eyes, a smirk on his lips. "Atlas, she doesn't need to know your every life detail," he jibed.

Atlas threw a wadded piece of paper at him before turning back to Morra. "I take it you have questions on time jumping?"

"Is it real?" she asked softly. Despite being sidetracked by the boy answering her questions, her whole world felt like a lie. Her whole being, her family, her mom, it was all a lie.

"Oh, very much so. It's hard to believe at first, but it is very real."

Perched crossed legged on a chair Atlas had dragged over for her, she leaned in. "How? How is that even possible? And why can only our family time travel?"

"Well first," he said, pushing his round glasses back up his straight nose, "it's time jumping, not travel. It's not possible to break the quantum time space barrier. With Einstein's description of relativity, he says we could time travel but we could never come back. But what they didn't know is that time and life are not linear."

He pulled out papers as he talked, shoving them her way. Glancing at Kahadin as he flipped dramatically on the bed, he caught her eye as he mimed Atlas talking. While the boy talked a lot, Morra found it incredibly endearing, even if half the words were foreign to her.

"See, if it was then time travel would make sense and we could move through time, but our lives would not."

"What?" she asked, not knowing what his words meant.

"Okay, so if we were to break the barriers of time and space, it would only allow us to travel through time, but our bodies could never cope with the speeds. Instead, we use a special energy that allows us to break the boundaries of time and space without damaging our bodies or killing ourselves." He started writing on the board in his usual messy script. She watched as he wrote on the whiteboard next to him. Getting a moment of silence to think about everything. She looked around. What she saw in front of her was possibilities. Her best friend, a cute boy, a family that wanted her. *Or at least most of them,* she thought scathingly. It was a chance to have kinship, a family when hers was all but lost. A chance to have a father.

This could change her life.

She watched Atlas talk with such ardor that Morra's own face flushed with a smile. He was rambling again; she knew he knew it but he couldn't seem to stop. It was adorable.

He glanced at her, giving her a sheepish grin as he gestured to the whiteboard. "The math just isn't there yet."

"So, how is it done, then?"

"Oh, yes!" He scrambled to sit down. "Time, we found, is not linear. That's why the math doesn't work. It's more similar to a stack of paper and in certain areas the paper is weaker than each layer in that area throughout time."

Demonstrating, he grabbed a bunch of loose papers, in the same spot on each piece he used an eraser to thin the page for the first fifteen pages. "See, so it has weakened this one spot for many years, meaning it is thinner until…" Taking water, he drips a single drop on the thinned area. "This water represents your family. It will easily soak through the weak paper until it hits the non-weakened paper where it stops flowing through." Showing her the dry paper sixteen pages down. "Your family goes to these places and can jump into them."

"So, we time jump through time that is weakened and stop falling through time when the time stops being weakened?" Morra reiterated.

"Essentially, but also not."

Morra tilted her head, confused. She didn't quite understand, but she learned more than she would from a dusty old book. Focusing on the boys, her eyes softened. She was thankful Kahadin brought her here. Gazing at Atlas, his green eyes glittered with excitement, and Morra realized she was thankful for more than one reason.

"It's not actually a weak point."

"The deeper the history, the deeper the energy." Kahadin chimed in "Its why we use monuments or important landmarks."

"Your family can jump into that time space. It is easy and without huge effort. But to leave it is a monstrous task."

"Okaayy," she drawled, trying to keep up with the theory. She really wished she paid more attention in science class.

Continuing to try to explain it, he waved his arms. "Okay, so by manipulating this, what we call Aossílùth, in your blood you can shift the time-space barrier."

"So why us? Why can't you?"

"Because others simply don't have Aossílùth. Their energy is not strong enough to break the quantum time rift. They can't jump, it would rip apart their bodies. The force without the buffer your genetics provide would shatter a human to dust."

Understanding dawned on her. While his equations were nonsense, she began to grasp the theory. Sitting for a moment, Atlas paused to give her time to respond.

"Can we travel to the future or just the past?"

Kahadin pipes in, "Just the past."

"Why?"

"Well, the future isn't written down. It is not a solid thing. Nothing exists until it does. You can't travel into a void. We can go to the past but not the future."

"How do you know what time you would land in?" she fired back at him, smiling at the ping-pong conversation.

"For that, you need a map of time. We have one that shows where to go and when you will land. If there isn't a 'weak spot' at the location you need, but at the time you need, you then have to find normal transportation." Kahadin jumped in, "Like a horse and carriage."

Morra's head spun with everything the day brought her. She no longer knew how long it had been since breakfast, but she knew the girl who ate pancakes with Balin was not the same girl who sat in the astronomy tower with Kahadin and Atlas. A part of her still didn't believe this life was even possible. Her heart raced just thinking about the implications. It felt like a baffling dream, one she didn't want to wake from. Morra now had to decide if she wanted to be a part of this family, this life. As soon as the thought crossed her mind, she knew the answer.

Goosebumps rose on her skin, and her bones trembled with the truth. She wanted whatever this life had to give her. Kahadin lips tilted at Morra as he nodded slightly at her, as if he also noticed the moment she settled into the reality of his world.

Morra had one last question she needed answered before she could tell everyone her decision. "Have you figured out what happened to my dad?"

"I have a theory, but I am not sure yet." His words were marked with hesitance.

"Please?" she supplicated, leaning forward almost close enough to touch, "please."

He wavered under the pressure of her pleading. "So in between each paper is a space where the atoms don't touch, imperceivable but still there. I think that somehow your dad got lost in the in between. I believe it made it possible for him to travel to different times at will but unable to move planes onto the solid fabric of reality."

This was all so... insane. The more Morra listened, the more entranced by it all she became. Atlas seemed just as passionate. His love for *time travel* became infused with every word and fling of his hand, and it was infectious. Atlas, and by extension, Kahadin, answered every question she had. While she still didn't quite understand everything, she deeply appreciated somebody finally being honest with her.

Leaning forward, with the softest of touches, Morra brushed against Atlas as she grabbed the book Galahad gave her. Smiling at him in lieu of an apology, she thanked him with as much sincerity as she could.

"For what?" he asked, cocking his head to the side causing his glasses to fall askew.

Morra grabbed his hand, squeezing it briefly. "For telling me, for explaining in a way I understand. Recently everyone has tried to keep me in the dark about my life. But the two of you," she said, including Kahadin, "have been honest with me. So, thank you both."

Kahadin just nodded with his signature smirk, but she knew he appreciated her words. The softness in his eyes couldn't hide it.

Atlas, on the other hand, just beamed at her, cheeks flushing red.

Exasperated at the two, Kahadin rolls his eyes before poignantly staring at Atlas and Morra's still joined hands. "Come on, you two, let's go see if the others have found anything."

"Will they even tell us if they do?"

He shrugged as they headed down the spiral staircase leading away from the tower. Smiling slyly, he, in a hushed tone, said, "In this family, you learn how to snoop. One cousin is bound to know something they should not."

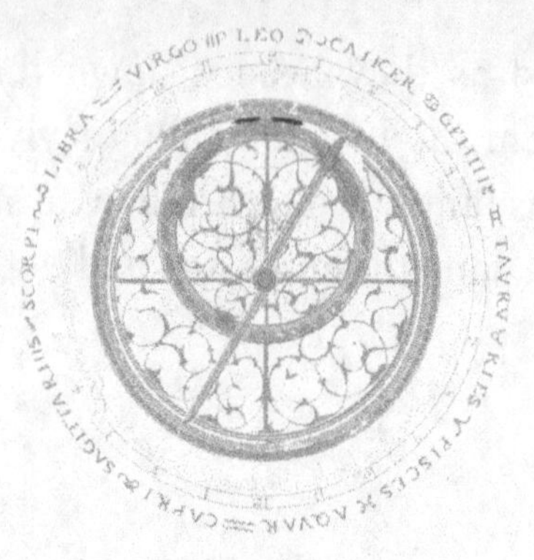

CHAPTER ELEVEN

❖

Footfalls could be heard through the hall as the trio bounded down the stairs. They laughed as Atlas and Morra stumbled, all the while Kahadin stayed as polished as ever even while running. The three burst into the gaming room with the theater as a movie played in the background as they collapsed, breathless, into a pile with everyone else.

Morra discovered that this is where most of her cousins, or the ones she liked, hung out. If they weren't there, they were in the courtyard training.

Which, as she thought about it, made way more sense. Time jump training. The next time she saw Galahad, she would ask. Hopefully, he would allow her to learn more. If she was to be the heir of this family, then she needed to be prepared.

A nudge from Atlas pulled her from her thoughts. Smiling gratefully, she paid attention to Pallas, who was talking to Kahadin.

"Anything?" Morra asked, as she scooted closer to them. Atlas following suit.

"Still nothing, just like yesterday and the day before, and the day before that," Pallas mocked.

"Actually," Ladianna strolled into the room, interrupting them. Father finally caved and told me something. I think he knew we were going to find out one way or another."

"Well?" Kahadin prompted her impatiently.

"Well... they are currently going through old writings from hundreds of years ago, which of course have to be in extinct languages. He told me when they have movable intel we would be informed."

Everyone's eyes shifted to Atlas, who ducked his tall body sheepishly. He raised both hands in surrender. "If I knew, I would have told you already."

"So," Morra said, her voice breaking the silence, "what do we do now?"

The others glanced around at each other, but Kahadin spoke first. "We wait. Hopefully, we'll get more information soon."

Morra sighed, dreading the wait. She liked having a plan and being able to move forward with it. But there was nothing for them to do at the moment.

Atlas laughed quietly and nudged her in the side. "Come on, Morra, you know how it is here. Nothing ever moves too quickly. We have all the time in the world." His words softened her impatience slightly, and she smiled gratefully at him before turning back to the others, who were still talking.

"I need to do something. I have been stuck here for weeks without going out. What about training? Can we do more of that?" Morra asked, hopeful that she could do something other than sit around and read.

"Oh, trust me, there will be plenty of time to train. Training and studying will be all you do here soon,"

Ladianna told her in a conspiratorial whisper. "Can we just, I don't know, go do something fun and act our age for once?"

They all took one look at her and turned to Pallas, giving pleading eyes. Pallas was older than the rest. Ladianna was seventeen, as was Atlas. Kahadin was sixteen like her, but his birthday came first. A point he loved to remind her of.

But Pallas was twenty-two. He had his own car and plenty of access to others. If he handed over the keys, they wouldn't have to ask. Or being told no.

"Where would you even go?" he asked, exasperated, yet he still rifles through his pockets. Pulling out a silver set of keys to a black Audi, he dangled them mockingly at them. "The mall downtown, nothing too wild, I promise," Ladianna promised him. She, of the group, was the most trustworthy. Morra didn't know why, but Ladi carried an air about her. It almost compelled you to confide in her.

"Fine, but you didn't get them from me." He tossed the keys and Kahadin caught them, much to Pallas' dismay.

"Ohhh no, not you, not after last time." When the sheepish expression crossed Kahadin's face, Morra nearly squealed in joy. That was perfect leverage if he dared to make fun of her tiny crush.

He gave the keys over to Ladianna.

Morra looked over to Kahadin, a vicious grin spreading across her face. "Last time?"

He groaned as Ladianna hooked arms with her. "I will tell you in the car."

The teens eagerly got out of the black SUV. Midday fell upon them with the sun in the sky shining heavily on their bundled faces. The mall sat nestled downtown between busy streets, their home was perched on the outskirts of the city but it only took an hour's drive. The mall itself was large, with four stories of shopping and food and fun. All tall windows and classic steel reflecting the midday sun.

As they walked inside Atlas peered around contemplative. "Let's go to the arcade first."

Morra, eager to try something new, walked into the arcade wide-eyed. It was incredibly loud, games pinging and kids laughing. Black carpets with bright neon shapes coated the floor while everything else was bright red. It clashed horribly and Morra loved it.

Kahadin led them in, and it didn't take long for each of them to find something they enjoyed playing. Morra chose an old school pinball machine. Sleek black with red buttons on the side and while playing, she couldn't help but think of her life now. The dings of the machine drowned out the ambient noise cocooning her in a world of her own. Here she was playing, goofing off with people she considered friends and family. Back when her mom was alive, she didn't get the chance to make genuine connections. If she was honest with herself, Morra knew the fault lay at her own feet. Never let anyone in, then you never have to leave.

But here, she finally could stay... if she wanted.

After a while, they regrouped for some pizza and soda before splitting off into pairs with plans to meet up later. But before Morra could decide who to go with, Atlas grabbed her hand, pulling her towards the air hockey table. His circular glasses framed his joyful eyes, and Morra couldn't help but grin. The game started, and Morra scored within seconds, while Atlas huffed and tried to concentrate. Morra laughed as she won three out of five matches, and Atlas conceded that she was the better player.

As the hour wore on, they all met up at the virtual reality area, where Morra put on her headset and stepped into another world. Focusing on shooting the groaning pus-filled zombie, she never noticed Atlas sneaking up behind her, tickling her sides causing her to let out a screech of surprise.

"Rude," she grumbled with no heat to the words and a smile she couldn't shake.

Morra bounced on her toes as they left, filled with giddy excitement. The bright orange halo of the sun dipped behind the trees as the breeze, cool and crisp, skirted across her skin. Gazing over at Atlas, whose soft brown hair was gently tousled, she traced the shadows the sun cast on his face with her sleepy eyes. A shy smile blossomed on her face.

Her heart pounded and with shaky hands, she decided to act on the butterflies that had been filling her since she first saw him that night in the basement. Reaching over, she took his hand in hers, boldly linking their fingers. Whipping his head in surprise, his eyes locked onto hers and then dropped to their linked fingers. A soft look graced his face as he gently squeezed her hand in return.

Later that night, the group went to the movies. Nerves filled Morra as they found their seats. Atlas had to choose a horror film. Part of her thought he wanted to see her shriek again. Warm popcorn was pushed into her hands as darkness swathed them. She couldn't remember the last time she had sat in a theater.

Finally, the movie began with full force, causing Morra to jump in her seat and bury her face into Atlas' shoulder. He immediately wrapped his arm around her, and she couldn't help but giggle with excitement. Her face still nestled in his arm, she weakly slapped at him as a warm blush spread across her cheeks. Morra could sense Atlas hesitating for a moment before he reached out and tucked her curly hair behind her ear. His chapped lips lightly brushing against her forehead.

His fingers cradled the side of her face, caressing her with a featherlight touch. As if by a mysterious magnetic force, Morra's eyes were pulled up, only to find darkened green irises staring intently at her. She kept herself there, captured in his spirited gaze, unable to turn away.

A current ran through her and without a second thought Morra leaned in as Atlas greedily met her back with the same intensity. Finger wound through her locks of wavy brown hair.

The screen behind them faded into nothingness. The hoots and hollers of the other movie-goers went unheard to the young pair. Lost in each other's embrace, they found themselves unable to break away from the comfort of their closeness. With a gentle sigh, Atlas leaned in to meet Morra's lips with his again. This time, his kiss was slow and passionate, full of hope; the reckless young kind of hope. The kind that bubbled into more if given a chance.

The heaviness that creeped over her hung on her like a noose seeped away, leaving her lighter. Weightlessness and warmth, his warmth, surrounded her. Suddenly, Morra was no longer the girl with no parents. She was not the girl who could time jump and had a destiny to change the world. With his lips on hers, she was just a girl who liked a boy. Morra never thought she would want that cliché.

Slowly, they pulled away and Morra let out a shaky breath. Grey eyes met green ones. A smile crossed her lips as she laid her head on his shoulder. She forced her eyes onto the screen as she bathed in the warmth imbued in her heart. "Nice," Ladianna mumbled under her breath next to Morra. She laughed as Morra threw the now cooled popcorn at her.

Once the movie ended, the group decided to go home. Darkness had encroached during the movie, the air was now brisk with cold wind, causing them to shuffle to the car with renewed purpose. They knew a surprise trip to town would be begrudgingly tolerated, but a missed curfew would not.

Morra felt, for the first time since her mother died, alive and happy. They all piled into Pallas's SUV, eager to get home and rest after such a peaceful day.

The winding road and night sky soothed Morra into a comfortable lull. *Things were finally looking up,* she thought, catching the toothy grin from Atlas as she peered in the back to see Ladi and Kahadin asleep. She knew no matter what happened next, they would all face it together with courage and determination.

When his hand sought out hers, holding it delicately the whole ride home, she knew things would turn out okay.

The four of them stumbled bleary-eyed into the home minutes before curfew. With little stealth, they separated and went to their rooms. As Morra walked up the stairs to her room, she touched her lips, remembering chapped lips and green eyes blanketed by soot colored eyelashes. Even though they had not spoken of their kiss, Morra remained hopeful. She had never been interested in any boy before. There had been one girl, but it never really went anywhere.

Part of her thought it was because she knew she would have to say goodbye. But once again, she was reminded she didn't have to.

Crawling into her soft warm bed, she couldn't help worrying about Atlas. She liked him but what if he didn't like her that much. He didn't seem like the kind of person who would kiss her just to kiss her but still. The thought turned her stomach, but she knew she had to consider it as a possibility.

A knock at the door caused her heart to beat wildly. Rushing, she opened it, Atlas stood head down and shoulders hunched.

Glancing up under his ruffled hair, he smiled sheepishly.

"I know it's late, but I just wanted to maybe talk about…"

"Oh, okay yeah, do you want to come in?"

"I actually was wondering if you would..." trailing off, gathering the nerve to finish his sentence, "If you would take a walk with me?"

Butterflies took flight in her stomach as she gazed at his offered hand. Morra hid the vengeful fluttering. She didn't want him to know she was the nervous one.

"Okay," she conceded, slipping her hand into his.

The temperature outside had dropped significantly as they had readied for bed. Goosebumps raised on her skin as the sharp breeze bit through her thin pajamas. But Morra refused to complain as Atlas tucked her close to his side, shielding her from the harsh cold with his warmth.

Darkness spread across the estate, blanketing the gardens they roamed through in shadows. The only light came from the glowing stars and the warm yellow shine of the moon. Fingers linked, they wandered out of the gardens in silence, basking in each other's presence until they reached the lake. Moonlight danced on its surface, casting a glow on them. The wind picked up and Morra could hear the echo of the crickets singing, the breeze rustling through the trees.

Atlas guided her to a grassy knoll. Trembling slightly from the wet grass seeping cold into her, she closed her eyes, breathing in the atmosphere. Out here, the air was crisp with the heady smell of nature. Perfumed flowers were starting to decay mixed with damp earth and driftwood.

They sat there for quite some time until Morra couldn't take any more silence.

"I-"

"Did-" They both chuckled.

"Go ahead," she told him, tilting her head towards the older boy.

His eyes glowed as the moonlight reflected off the lake, illuminating them from within. "I like you. I know we don't really know each other, we haven't spent a ton of time together, but I don't know, you feel like... home. And I can't ignore that, but I can't lie to you." He ran his hand through his hair frazzled, almost upset.

"Atlas, what are you talking about?" Worry clawed at her throat as she observed him. Panic grew in his eyes as Morra watched him.

"Galahad made me promise I wouldn't tell anyone," he whispered, pulling her in between his legs. Atlas wrapped his arms around her torso and pulled her close to his chest. Shaking his head lightly before resting it on top of hers, he explained, "I am not from here. All the family knows is that my parents were friends with Sophia and when they died, she took me in, but that's not true."

He took a moment to collect himself before he continued.

"I am actually from France, well, technically Egypt. My parents owned a little shop in Egypt and when France invaded, my father was killed." Atlas sighed, shoulders slumping as he closed his time worn eyes. "Before the nightmare that ensued there, some general fell in love with my mother when he laid eyes on her. When the French left Egypt or were forced out, he proposed marriage."

Heart-wrenching grief shone in his eyes, a sorrow that she felt deep inside her bones. The loss of family left a deep wound in the soul, as if a meteor had struck its unyielding toll. Nothing could fill the abyss. Only time could mend the fractured soul.

"You don't have to continue," she told him, reassuringly, turning to hold his face in her hands. "I will still be here."

"I know," he told her. "I want to." His eyes regained their focus. The soft glow they once carried changed. They were now that of resolve.

"We didn't know the French Revolution would happen. They were both killed. But a friend took me in and that's when I met Galahad." As he continued, it dawned on Morra. Her brain blanked as she listened. He wasn't from here, and she understood where his story was going.

"Things in France just got worse. Sir Damus asked Galahad to take me. He knew about the time jumping, and with luck and a fuck ton of hope, I was the first person without fae blood to ever jump."

"Atlas, I am so sorry that's horrible that you had to live through that. Nobody knows?" she asked. Without waiting for a response, Morra pulled him into a hug. Burying his face into her shoulder, warm tears soaked through the thin satin as Atlas trembled.

"Why?"

"It goes against everything the family has been taught, messes with the law of time, and if they knew the leader of the family went against that for me, well, they would have their own expectations."

Galahad protected him by forcing secrecy, just like he did with her. Nodding to herself, Morra embraced her solemn duty to keep his secret hidden, just as he had done in defense of their family. She gladly carried the burden of her choice and wouldn't break the trust placed in her hands. It started and ended with her.

"Why tell me?" she asked. He barely knew her, and to share this secret with her was a leap of faith. With a confused shake of her head, she waited for him to gather himself.

"Because you are the heir to the family and because I like you. Where I come from you don't wait, time is not on your side." He gave a watery chuckle. "My parents married after only meeting each other once; trusting you seems small compared to that."

Morra ran her hands through his hair, tangling her fingers in his dense locks and using them to tilt his face. Eyes shining, she leaned in, softly kissing him. Their lips met in sweet, brief touches.

Ever so gently, she pressed her lips into his again, relaxing into his hold. Morra poured every ounce of comfort she could into him. The kiss was a show of support, telling him he didn't have to carry all of it on his own.

Morra pulled away and looked him in his eyes before they slowly scanned his moonlit face. "I am glad you were in a time where I could meet you. Atlas, I am glad you are here."

Eventually, they got up and headed back inside, stealing kisses as they walked back when the air got too cold for the teens to bear. He linked their fingers, and she knew her smi le matched his.

A thrum of worry pulsed inside her as she stared at the way his smile pulled on his scars. She was not good at keeping people at a distance; it was always her downfall.

"I should go." He stared at her, his gaze piercing her soul. "I need to do more research. Galahad might have an idea on how to save your dad."

She nodded gratefully.

With a groan, he pulled away from her, and Morra slipped into her room as he turned the corner.

CHAPTER TWELVE

Hues of red, purple, and green peeked from the gentle layer of snow that blanketed the gardens. Winter began to slowly creep into their fall weather. The petals that still held on with the stubborn hope for warm weather had icy dew. Morra stood overlooking the mirage of color and gazed at the lake behind it. Taking a slow breath as the sun slowly rose, she wrapped her thick knit cardigan around her before pulling her brown wavy hair into a bun on the top of her head.

As she stood in the quiet of the late morning, she contemplated her life. She couldn't believe it had been months since she stood on the balcony of her apartment in Chicago. Noise echoed through that city like a constant stream of consciousness. It seemed to be carried on the back of the air currents like an unwanted crow surfing on the spine of an eagle. For miles it echoed, never sleeping and never dimming.

But here, the wind held no sound that didn't already

belong to the land. No, instead it carried the sounds of the lapping waves of the lake, birds singing, deer rustling, and the sound of her friends' laughter. It smelled of wet dirt and gently decaying plants. It evoked memories of leaves falling from trees and warm summer sun gracing her face. As Morra stood there, she knew she couldn't live without the wind of this place ever again.

Maybe this was the real reason her mother always ran. Maybe she was never running but always seeking, Morra thought. Seeking the kind of wind that filled the soul. For her mother, the wind wasn't the absence of sound. For her beautiful mother, it was the sound of her father's laugh.

His voice. His love.

Her wind carried his love for her on its back. And no matter where they went, her mother could never find peace, for he was not there in the breeze.

She stood there, wishing for her to feel it one last time. Her heart broke again knowing that her mother died before she found the tranquility that coated Morra only moments ago. It had been too late for Adelaine, so Morra vowed, there in the silence, that she would take up the search in hermother's stead. She would keep searching for more winds like this for both her and her mother.

Galahad walked onto the grey brick balcony, interrupting her melancholy thoughts.

"Did you enjoy your day out yesterday?" he asked slyly as he stood next to her, taking in the rising sun.
Glittering light fell through the tree line, bouncing off the lake's dark surface, casting a golden hue on the rest of the

world. Morra refused to miss a second of so instead she nodded, keeping her eyes on the horizon.

"You disappeared again." The accusation in her tone was harsher than she intended but she wouldn't walk it back. He kept leaving, it shouldn't matter but it did.

"A hazard of the life, I'm afraid." He sighed showing his weariness. "Morra, I hope you want to stay here, but I will understand if you want to go."

"I at first felt like I would be betraying my mom's sacrifice if I stayed," Morra explained, quickly glancing at the older man before shifting her eyes once again to the sun. "But I don't think she would begrudge me finding a home here. And I have... found a home here." Gazing back at her grandfather, a smile played at his lips and his eyes twinkled as she continued, "If it's okay with you, grandpa, I would like to be your heir."

Beaming, Galahad pulled her into a hug before kissing the top of her head. As they both gazed out at the land, he replied in a watery tone, "Everything I have is yours, Morra. That is, everything I have left."

"And if it works for you, I would like to help you find my father."

Adjusting the thick reading glasses, his eyes misted over. "Nothing would make me happier."

"God, I miss him so much," Galahad lamented, before chuckling and wiping at the tears pricking his eyes. "But now is not the time for sadness. Today we celebrate."

With plans to gather the family to tell them of Morra's choice, he moved to go inside. He wanted to inform the staff to call everyone back to the house.

"I have one question though," she interrupted, making him pause. "Atlas had mentioned something about fae blood. I hadn't asked about it because it seemed irrelevant at the time." She trailed off, skirting around the truth. She refused to break Atlas' trust.

"You want to know if it's true?" he guessed.

Morra nodded.

"Atlas explained the math, I'm sure. He chuckled at the exasperation on her face. "The truth he leaves out is most of it is just magic. Oh, now don't look at me that way. How is that any less believable than time travel?"

"Well, I guess it's not."

Before Galahad could answer, his phone rang. "Sorry dear, I must answer this." He peered at her apologetically and she just nodded and waved him off.

Later that day, curled onto the antique couch near the unlit fireplace, Morra explored the book her mother gave her. She didn't know why, but melancholy clung to her like an old sweater. Morra ran her finger down the spine of the faded yellow gold cover. The embossed letters faded over time, the gilded paint barely clinging on. The pages inside turned yellow with age, but the bindings still held strong. It seemed ancient and beautiful.

Cracking it open, a puff of air surrounded her. The smell was nostalgic of bedtime stories and the chamomile tea her mother brewed every night. Clasping her eyes shut for a moment, she soaked it in. If she tried hard enough, she could almost hear her mother reading aloud.

Turning through the pages, she began to read. Her mother had minor notes in the book, not on the page but attached delicately with paper clips. Morra let herself explore the writing, fingers tracing the wispy swirls of her mother's penmanship. She didn't know how long she sat there when someone knocked on the door.

It creaked open and, to Morra's surprise, her uncle Balin stepped in. "Hey wanted to let you know the family is back for the-" with a tilt of his head a fond smile spread across his face. "What are you reading?"

"Oh, this was my mom's." She held up the book, showing him the cover.

"Did you know that came from the library here?"

Surprise swept past her before she realized her mother must have got it from Arthur. She highly doubted there were many first editions and she knew how extensive the Manors library held many first editions.

"It also is riddled with wrong information," he added.

"They are made up stories, none of it is right. Arthur wasn't an actual king."

Balin hummed, cocking his head to the side. "Did my father tell you much about the time jumping?"

"No, we started to talk about it earlier, but he got a call."

Nodding he continued, "We have all been worn thin trying to find out anything we can about Arthur. Regardless, I know that those books," he said, gesturing to the book laid discarded next to her, "are an inaccurate version of history because they hold stories of our ancestors."

The blank stare shouted Morra's doubts to her uncle. "We are related to King Arthur?" she questioned suspiciously, not believing it until it hit her. Who's to say this, too, wasn't real?

"Oh, no not Arthur," Balin clarified. "Actually, I guess we are, but most of our lineage comes from Morgana Le Fay."

"The high priestess of Avalon, that Morgana Le Fay?"

"It's where your name came from, Morra."

"But she's a fairy, right?"

"In modern terms, she is a Fae. Her blood runs through us and it gives us the Aossílùth we use. Originally, we also carried her name, but after a time, many people knew of the legend and knew of the name, so we changed it to Fahey and then to Seelie. Do you know what a Seelie is?" Morra shook her head, indicating no, so he continued, "It's a Scottish term for Fae."

"What does any of that have to do with anything?" Scrunching up her face, Morra crossed her arms. She felt unsteady, like she was bracing for an impact she just didn't know what would hit her.

"To fight a war, you must know your enemy. Are you familiar with yours, Morra?"

Not understanding the question, she replied "No."

"We are related to Arthur Pendragon because he is Morgana's half brother. He is not Fae because Morgana's father was Fae and the King of Avalon. Fae have unique features, one being their blood, and while that has been diluted over time, we can still tap into it. Our blood lets us travel, but it lets our enemy travel as well. We call them the Enemies of the Past. They travel through time and try to throw off the balance of time. They want chaos and evil."

"Evil?" she asked seriously.

Solemnly, with no levity his face usually carried, he agreed. "Evil."

Dumbfounded, she sat there, impressed. Once again, her worldview shattered. It felt like falling and while it was terrifying and caused her heart to jump in her throat; she began to feel comfortable in the terror. Then the reality hit, "How am I able to help? I'm just sixteen. I am a kid. I can't even drive yet," she said, overwhelmed by the magnitude of the situation.

Balin smiled slightly, causing the crow's feet hugging his eyes to crinkle as he put a reassuring hand on her shoulder. "Being part of this family is damning. It takes away your chance of normalcy, your chance to live a regular life, but the reward is far greater than I could even explain. At ten, we ask our children if they want to live this life. We ask only once. If they do, then they train. Combat, anatomy, physics, and history. They learn to walk, talk and act like they belong to different times because if they don't, the past will kill them. That is, if our enemies don't find them first."

"Ten is so young."

"It is, but this life makes you grow up quicker because people's lives are at stake. So you can help by training, studying, and healing. I have a feeling you are more important than we know, but this life is yours to live. I know Galahad asked, but now I will again, and know this is the last time we will ask you this; Morra, do you want a normal life or do you want to change the world?"

Morra loved that he bothered asking. It made her feel more at home here, knowing people cared. She could see where Kahadin and Ladianna got their empathy, even if Kahadin would rather shove needles in his fingernails, then admit he had emotions. But she couldn't help but wonder. "Why are you asking?"

"My dear, you are family. Arthur was my brother and for my whole life he taught me and guided me. While sometimes he would guide me astray," Balin explained with a fond smile and a memory in his eye, "he was always there and when we thought he died, I promised him I would live in a way that honored him." The smile on his face turned bittersweet. "I know if he were here, your dad would be asking the same thing. Since he isn't, I will do it in his stead."

Tears welled up in her eyes and she pulled a surprised Balin into a hug. "I think he would be thankful. I know I am," she told him.

Morra followed Balin to the formal dining room where a feast had been spread across the large table. Galahad happily announced Morra as his official heir, and almost everyone was overjoyed.

As Galahad spoke, Morra couldn't help swinging her eyes across the table to find Isolde. There was a certain smugness that Morra couldn't hide. Her aunt and her daughter had nearly terrorized Morra during their time when everyone else was thankful to have her and those two acted as if she usurped their rightful position. At some point, the deep sadness of rejection had burned into a fury that they would have rather had every reminder of Arthur dead and gone. All so they could carry on the family legacy for themselves.

A disappointed sigh of resignation passed Isolde's lips as they pursued. She didn't seem to hold much anger over the decision, but Madoine had a different reaction. Fire burned behind her eyes. "HER? HER? This nobody who barely has etiquette is expected to-"

Isolde promptly shushed her, but it didn't stop her from continuing. "I have been trained since Arthur got himself killed." and say what you want, but he is dead. And you should be too-"

This time Galahad cut her off. "Enough. You will respect my decision and hold your tongue." Madoine opened her mouth like she was going to argue. Galahad must have noticed because he shot her a glare before quietly barking,

"Room. Now."

Madoine turned to her, lips curling back to bare her teeth. Morra quirked her lips into a tiny smirk, eyes flashing. She'd have to keep an eye on that one, she thought.

As her cousin was shown out of the room Morra decided to ignore the outburst as everyone began to discuss her dad. So far, nobody had figured out how her dad was alive, and it filled Morra with relief that they believed her. During the discussion, never once did anyone tell her she had imagined it despite Madoine's words.

The snow fully settled in as winter came in full force. The last of the blooms had died, and the lake had frozen over. Hours turned into days, and days to months, but the family

continued to search tirelessly for her father. Morra trained with them, learning new skills and honing her current one. Kahadin and Ladianna helped her the most with this. Their knowledge of the outside world became irreplaceable. Pallas and Lucan had also been a great help in her training, always offering their encouragement and guidance.

Surprisingly, the most helpful in combat was Madoine. She never tried to pull punches. Sometimes Morra was actually concerned she was trying to kill her, but it made her learn fast. She discovered that she was decent with swords and guns but terrible at hand to hand combat or anything up close.

Lydia, Kahadin's mom, taught her about navigation and language. Isolde, though, was the bane of her existence, as she was in charge of both her history and cloaking lessons. They spent hours going over history and timelines and how to use her knowledge and looks to win people over. Really, it was a fancy way of manipulating people, Morra thought.

Then she trained her not to be seen. She was vicious. Most days, she had to walk away and cut their training short.

Today was one of those days. Isolde would inevitably tell Galahad that she walked out, again, but it didn't matter.

She slunk up to the astronomy tower to find Atlas. Taking slow steps, Morra's whole body was wrecked from training the day before. Large, mottled bruises covered her left side, where Madoine had kneed her during their training. It had knocked the wind out of her and fractured two ribs.

She had not cared.

While Morra laid prone on the ground, Madoine attacked. Ruthlessly flipping her on her stomach, she grabbed Morra's hair in her fist and pulled a knife to her throat. Madoine was still upset that Morra was the heir, but Morra gave as good as she got. A smile crept up her face as she reminisced about her face that night at dinner. Morra didn't think Madoine's nose would ever be straight again.

It sucked trying to get the blood out of her hair, but it was worth it, she thought.

With the grin still on her face, she opened the door, promptly sighing with disappointment. Atlas wasn't there, but as heaviness filled her limbs, she decided sleep sounded nicer than scouring the Manor. Instead, she just crawled into his bed and laid her head on the cold pillow. Thoughts of their first kiss played in her head as sleep lulled her into the place between sleep and wakefulness. Morra couldn't help but think Atlas was the kindest person she had ever met. As her eyes shut, she wondered if this was how her mother felt about her dad.

Sometime later, Atlas barreled into his room, flopping on the bed, jarring her awake as the pain in her chest flared. An apologetic look crossed his face as he asked, "Hey you, training go okay? Was Isolde angry about Madoine's broken nose?"

"You have no idea," she said with a chuckle. "What about you?"

"Well..." he said, gently maneuvering her to rest on her chest.

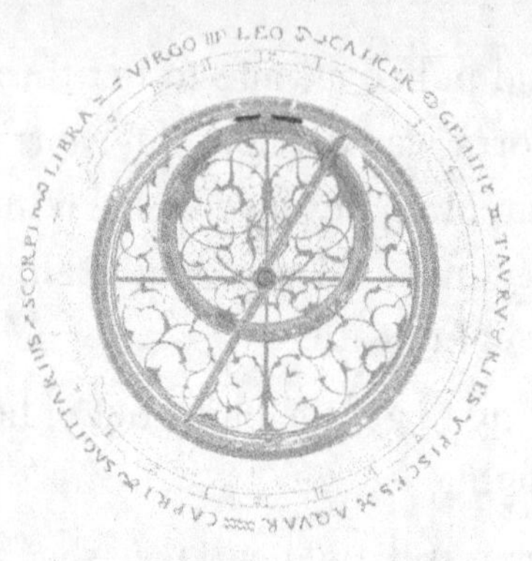

CHAPTER THIRTEEN

Morra sat in her grandfather's office, which now closely resembled Atlas' room than Galahad's prim office. Every surface became obscured by piles of papers, books, and notes.

Living in the house for months now, Morra had formed strong bonds with her newfound family. Despite her best efforts, she still struggled to refer to Galahad as "Grandpa" and Balin as "Uncle", preferring to remain formal. Even after all this time, Morra had yet to address Isolde as her aunt. It was petty, but Morra thought her aunt needed to act like a grownup.

She desperately wanted to spend more time with Galahad, but the search for her father had taken up the bulk of his time. Every day he seemed more strained and exhausted, dark circles forming beneath his eyes.

Kahadin mentioned that he searched for ten years. Losing her dad had caused cracks in the family that ran deep. The search for Arthur turned fruitless. Eventually, the adults requested their help. The Manor was full of books that had been in the family for centuries, methodically searching for information in each became critical in their hunt for answers.

Sitting on a leather couch, with three books in front of her and a stack on the side table, she looked down at them, exhaling. "I don't think these'll have anything," she uttered aloud to no one in the quiet room.

Galahad pinched his nose, nodding in understanding. "I know, but we must check anyway."

Morra walked over to him, sighing again as defeat crept up on her. "Could we perhaps-"

Atlas burst through the door, breathing heavily with his hands on his knees, cutting off her next words. Through his heavy panting, a grin spread from ear to ear. "I- we have something!"

Galahad stood, taking the paper from Atlas' outstretched hand, eyes locking with the boy. "Nostradamus?"

Atlas nodded, vibrating from the adrenaline of the breakthrough. Morra glimpsed the scrap of paper.

"It's not complete, but it's a start," Atlas informed him. Galahad turned to Morra. "Would you like to go to France?"

"France?" she parroted back, confused. Neither made sense; the confusion could be seen on each face. Balin and Isolde stood behind her along with most of the cousins who all rose with Atlas entrance.

"Yes," he explained, "to Nostradamus."

"What do you think you will find there?" Balin asked, the excitement in his voice obvious. After sixteen years, everyone had lost hope.

Isolde scoffed, "Besides the word of a senseless man who claims he is a prophet."

Ignoring his daughter, he turned towards Balin. "Maybe an explanation, Nostradamus is known for his visions of the future. If anyone could help us, it is him," he answered. "This is part of a prophecy, but it's incomplete, so we need to know the rest of it." Galahad's face was ashen, and he became breathless with hope.

"What does it say?" Morra asked.

Atlas and Galahad shared a look she couldn't read. Her lips pursed as irritation consumed her. "Don't you dare start hiding things again," she demanded, ripping the paper from his hands. She studied it, narrowing her eyes at the words.

Daughter born under the horned goats setting sun

Orphaned by the future and the past

Seek for the bone of the loved

Until-

"It cuts off after that," Atlas explained, rereading over her shoulder.

"And you think I am the child of this prophecy?" Morra's eyes widened in stunned disbelief and her skin broke out in goosebumps. "This is some wizard shit. This can't be real."

"Morra, we are literally descendants of a fairy," Kahadin drawled. She wasn't fooled by the lax tone he had stood, body tense like they were on the training mats.

All eyes were upon her, full of expectation, and she felt a chill slither up her spine. The responsibility of saving her father may just fall upon her shoulders.

"I don't know, dear," Galahad replied. "But I do know that Nostradamus will. And you have yet to jump. I believe it's time."

Doubts clawed her insides to thin, red bits of fabric. She had studied it, understood it in theory, but actually time jumping was a completely different matter.

He then turned to Atlas and asked, "What time point should we jump through?"

Pulling out a thick leather-bound book, he quickly scrolled through it. "Well, there are a few times you can go to, but none before 1549 after he moved to Salon-de-Provence."

He scratched his head and rifled through more papers. "I don't have much in this notebook regarding times. We will have to go to the cartography room."

An astrology clock hung from the tall ceiling of the room, spinning gently. The room itself was quite large and decorated with beautiful old maps that captivated Morra.

Graphite drawn maps hung next to old watercolor ones. Others were crafted with more precise pens, and some with quills that depicted monsters. All revealed the world from different angles, perspectives, and times.

A table housing a large antique map dominated the middle of the room and, with a light touch from Atlas, it lit up.

From it rose holographic monuments across the world. Dates hung above, wrapping around pulsing red lines that connected each piece. Morra didn't know what they meant, but as lights danced around her, she became awestruck by them.

"This is the current time point." Atlas pointed out the line that ran through France; specifically, Salon-de-Provence, where Nostradamus lived. "1549. But I think you shouldn't jump that far, with it being her first time." Morra could see worry shadowing his face dimming, the bright eyes and voice becoming rough. She didn't comment. There wasn't a point, so she focused back on the map, scanning the virtual lines connecting the monuments.

"Do you have information where Nostradamus was before 1549?" Morra asked, looking up from the hologram unable to meet Atlas' distressed eyes. Part of her heart blackened with unease, something about it filled her with trepidation.

"We do. Nostradamus is one of our relatives, so we kept his whereabouts in time," Galahad explained.

Dates filled the air as his fingers danced over the screen. Births, deaths, important events, everything and anything now hung above her head. The chaotic mess suddenly, with a flick of Atlas' wrist, snapped into four neat boxes.

"What are you searching for?" Morra asked, when nothing seemed to be happening. Atlas and Galahad were intently staring through the lines, almost in a trance. Balin stood shoulder to shoulder with Morra lightly bumping her.

Despite the tension, he seemed younger than she had ever seen.

"We need to know where he was, so we aren't forced to wait to find him while in the past," Balin told her quietly, not wanting to break the focus.

"Found it," Atlas voiced cautiously, "but you're not going to like it." Only ragged breaths could be heard as the unease in the room rose to an unbearable level. Morra held herself in a fighting stance on instinct, hand curled into loose fists as Atlas glanced at Galahad hesitantly.

With a deep sigh and a flourish of his hand, Galahad motioned for him to continue. Atlas' eyes slid to hers, causing butterflies to erupt within her. His pinched eyebrows and soft eyes spoke to her soul before he shifted his attention again. "Place de la Révolution, 1789." Beside her, Balin cursed under his breath.

Galahad nodded grimly. "Well then."

The shoe finally dropped and with it her heart into her stomach. "Isn't that when the revolution if France began?" Fretting, her heart pounded as she remembered all her recent history lessons. The date and place were highlighted in bold, glowing, blue letters that glinted slightly as she stared.

"Yes," Atlas said in a shadowed whisper as Galahad riffled through some book. He was intently listening, even as his hand flipped through the papers, causing the thick red ruby ring on his finger to catch the light from the projection.

"And isn't that where the guillotine was used? Executions?"

"Yes," he said, throwing her an apologetic look as worry swirled around his face. The tightness in her shoulders wouldn't ease, Atlas clocked it. Walking to her, he pulled her into a warm hug and finally Morra could breathe. With gentle strokes to her hair, he whispered, "If there was another point that you could jump through, I would have you, but..." he trailed off.

"It was used to execute more than 3,000 people. Wasn't Nostradamus at a different place or time?"

Galahad cut in, answering, "Yes, but we know the prophecy was written down during that time. If we go back earlier, he may have not had the vision yet. We need him to know about the vision, so maybe he can help in the search for your father."

Before taking a step back, Atlas rubbed his nose against hers, stealing a quick kiss. "I need to prepare for your trip." Morra didn't want him to leave, she wanted him to wrap his arms back around her. But before she could speak, Galahad pulled her from her thoughts.

"And I need to speak with you," Galahad informed her, standing, pulling himself away from the book. With a quick "come find me later." Atlas left the room.

Galahad walked over to her, offering his elbow. "Come, Morra, let us discuss a few things." He guided her, deciding to take a walk outside. The frost had fully settled outside, and the wildlife settled with it. The cold wind and the wisps of snow caused shivers, but with it, the last of her tension eased.

"I must apologize for my... inattention," he said morosely, knowing how consumed he had been as of late. "I brought you into this family and then abandoned you to it. It's understandable if you are angry with me."

"You are forgiven."

The pair wandered through the gardens until they came upon a bench under the large willow. Sitting on it, she faced him and continued, "Losing my mom and never getting to see her body was one of the worst things I have ever felt. I can't imagine what it would be like to lose a child. You don't need to apologize. I would do anything to see my mother again. And I will do anything I can to make sure you can see your son."

It had been a day that was already too long, and the sun hadn't even set, and Morra wanted nothing more than to crawl into a warm bed and cuddle. What she didn't want were the words Galahad uttered quietly, with puffs of warm air curling around the statement like knives stabbing her armored underbelly.

"Are you afraid to meet him?"

Nausea overwhelmed her as her gaze fell sharply to the ground where her feet shuffled, causing a small cloud of dust to kick up. She pondered the question before she spoke. In truth, she didn't know; she worried that he would be disappointed in her. What if he disliked the daughter he had been so excited about? Or worse, what if he liked her and Morra failed him? Or even worse, what if she failed and never got to know what her parents thought of the woman she was becoming?

A heavy arm settled around her shoulders, pulling her in for a hug. Her doubts must have shown on her face. "He will love you as much as the rest of us do."

A smirk worked its way onto her face. "I sure hope he likes me better than Isolde."

Galahad laughed, head back and eyes closed, losing some of the weight he had been carrying. The pair sat for a while in content silence before he turned to her once again, seriousness etching lines on his face. And Morra, guessing where the conversation was leading, clenched her jaw painfully.

"I told you that the business of time travel can be a dangerous one, and that is true. We are leaving for France and the time of the French Revolution." The pinched look worked its way back on her face. Seeing it, Galahad reached over, cradling her hand in his. "It's a dangerous time for anyone, especially women. You are sixteen and in the past you would be of marrying age. This can be useful but also dangerous. You must be ever vigilant."

She nodded, trying to understand the importance of his words.

"You are smart, a decent fighter, cunning, well educated, and you are extremely beautiful. This can afford you many things, but it can also get you into trouble, especially in 1789 for anyone associated with the highborns. People will assume you are a part of it."

"That sounds dangerous."

"It's deadly, my dear. Do you understand? When we step in there, no longer do you have the protection of the twentyfirst century."

He looked so serious as he warned her, and it made Morra smile. It was time she let go of her reservations, this was her family and they wanted her to be a part of it. It was time she let herself.

"I understand, Grandpa." Morra watched as Galahad's eyes lit up. It was the first time she called him that.

"We will leave for France in the morning and jump from there. Promise me that you will listen and heed my warnings. Nonetheless, remember that this isn't a time for fear but action. If you have questions or need anything while we are there, lean on me. It is my job to protect those I love and even if it's at the cost of my own peril. Do you understand?"

Morra's gaze drifted to the old man's face, and she studied the delicate wrinkles that framed his gentle eyes. His eyes seemed to beg her for understanding, yet his face was solemn, displaying the weight of his many losses. Morra knew she had to do whatever it took to bring his son back; she wanted to show she was worthy of the love and family he had so generously given her. She nodded and assured him, "I understand, and I promise to listen to every word you say."

"Good," he replied.

Morra stood as she thought on his words, something he said didn't sit right. "But I won't let you die for me or for anyone, I promise." She left before he could respond.

Morra tucked herself into Atlas' side, his strong lean arms holding on to her tighter than ever before. The moon shone through the window, casting shadows on the couple as Atlas lazily stroked her skin in silence. Neither spoke as a blanket of worry covered them.

It was by far the first time Atlas had prepared for someone he loved to jump, but that night, with its cold wind and dark storms, something different hung in the air. Morra didn't know if it was her lack of knowledge and skill, the pressure to find out information about her dad, or going to a place steeped in violence; she wasn't sure, but the worry that tugged on everyone felt palpable.

After dinner that night, she knew sleep would evade her. She spoke her farewells to Kahadin, who refused to admit the worry she could see in his eyes. Morra forced a hug on him and, despite his stiffness, he wrapped his arms around her, squeezing tightly. Ladianna threw herself into Morra next, her blond hair suffocating her slightly.

When her goodbyes with her cousins were done, she climbed the steep stairs to the tower to find Atlas. He didn't hear her come in, so for a moment she leaned against the doorjamb and watched him. The night's wind blew the curtains, rolling them like waves of a dark sea and Morra watched as moonlight fell across Atlas, leaving shadows dappled across his olive skin.

Again, Morra reveled in his presence as she pulled him into the bed. The way his arms tightened around her almost made her change her mind. They had given Morra no guarantee that she would come back from trying to find her father, whether that meant tomorrow or a month from now. She had been trained, been briefed, but still, she may be giving this up.

With silent understanding, Atlas cradled her in his arms. No words were spoken between them as hands gently traced up and down. Morra became lulled into an almost sleep by Atlas' slow, rhythmic breathing.

Dawn light streamed into the room, pulling them from the cocoon of warm sheets and body heat. Moving slowly, Morra packed her things. Neither spoke, afraid the noise would cause the proverbial clock to tick faster. Atlas offered her his hand, and she took it without hesitation. Their fingers stayed locked all the way out of the Manor and down the cobble street to the plane she arrived on only a few months prior.

Ignoring the noise of the rotors revving to life, Morra turned to Atlas. "I -," she paused clearing her throat. She decided to wait on those words instead she said, "I am not sure how long we will be gone but I will try to make it quick, yea?"

"It will only be a few days for me," he lamented with a sad smile gracing his face, a shadow of worry in his eye. With a shake of his head, he pulled her into a hug, holding on as if she would disappear into smoke. Atlas had become a home to her, a place she could call her own, and as she breathed him in, she knew she would always come home to him. With a deep inhale and a firm kiss, lips lingering, they released each other.

Boarding the plane, her nerves of flying had seemed to disappear. Apparently, her new fear outweighed floating in a tube in the sky. Finding a seat, she turned her gaze out the small window to see Atlas standing a ways back on the landing strip. Deep concerned eyes were framed by a stoic face. Atlas slowly mouthed; *I will miss you.* Unable to look anymore, she turned from him, closing her eyes as the rumble of the engine gently vibrated her.

Glowing orange waves of gilded light cast shadows onto the city of Paris as the plane slowly descended through the clouds to the ground of France. As the wheels touched French soil, Morra felt calmer and more anxious than ever. It warred inside, making her dizzy. She knew France had started the turn of democracy, but the Revolution had brought nothing but death.

Stepping off the plane into light rain, Morra threw up her hood as Galahad turned to her. "My dear, we are staying at a hotel near the Louvre. I have already arranged for someone to take our belongings to the room."

"Okay," she agreed, preoccupied staring out the window of the black SUV that picked them up. The city held beauty in a dark sort of way. The buildings themselves were old and stately, but in them held an undercurrent. Something she couldn't name, something almost sinister in its recognizable unfamiliarity.

"We will go to Place de la Concorde in the morning, my dear. But tonight, we rest. I want to take you to my favorite restaurant and take a stroll around town."

"I would like that," she replied.

Dawn arose and with it the weight of the day. Morra had given up on sleep long ago and now, under the fluorescent yellow glow of the hotel bathroom, she gazed at herself. The image wasn't a pretty one. She looked young, too young to face what had happened. Too young to face what was coming, b ut nonetheless there she stood, white-knuckling the granite

countertop trying to find some sense of peace. Fear swam in her eyes, and Morra didn't want to acknowledge it.

The jump didn't scare her. Losing another parent did, the immutable thought became unavoidable. It ate at her, sharp teeth and heavy-handed. Trying to shake the feeling, Morra adjusted her bodice, what Galahad called a caraçao, she had to dress for the time. Not too nice making her a target, but not too cheap either. She winced when Galahad explained it.

Being a woman sometimes sucked.

A knock on the bathroom door startled her. "We must get going, my dear."

"I can do this," she whispered in the reflection.

They arrived at Place de la Concorde. It was massive.

Paved with smooth stones, the streets were polished to a shine by the boots of thousands of people each day. White marble adorned by grand arches and intricate carvings dotted the buildings in stone like drawings on a map.

The past echoed through the square and, as Morra's gaze flitted around, she marveled that it still existed. She had never seen something this old. Despite her travels with her mom, nothing had come close to this.

"It is quite impressive. Even the events of the past couldn't destroy this beauty. You will learn that Frandce is a hardy place," he surmised, seeing the familiar place through his granddaughter's eyes.

Nodding, she took in the sights. The crowds were bustling, going about their daily lives. People were buying and selling things from open-air markets, others simply enjoying the sun's warmth as they chatted with friends. Galahad made his way to their destination, Morra followed absentmindedly to absorbed in the atmosphere of the city.

Walking towards an older building that proudly held the French flag. A gilded plaque hung on the side, tucked between tall cream pillars: *Hôtel de la Marine, built in 1774.*

"So, how does this work?" Morra asked.

Suddenly, a tingle worked up her spine, and she understood. Quietly, Galahad guided her to the side of the building, out of the view of the tourists and their flickering cameras. A quick glance behind her showed a proud Galahad, almost reverently asking, "You can feel it?"

She nodded. It was almost like a slow moving current. "What is it?" Lifting a tentative hand, she hovered above the cold stone, stopping just short of touch.

A barrier laid between her hand and the wall, a tangible layer that couldn't be seen but she could feel it. Pushing and pulling, a layer of something older and more complex than she could comprehend. The invisible force rippled like the wrong sides of magnets being pushed against each other. One side pulling away, yet the force of the opposite sides pulling together.

It felt inevitable.

Galahad regarded the building with an awe still present in his eyes despite having jumped a hundred times. "I could be scholarly and tell you but the simple truth," he softly chuckled, "is that it's magic. Some things in life don't need explanations, they just are. This is one of those things."

A thrill ran through her veins as she beheld the grand edifice, a peaceful warmth surged through her fingertips, as if it were inviting her to join its embrace. Golden visages of light rippled across the barrier and deep within an ancestral right filled her veins like something lost had instantly been reclaimed.

Morra's slightly pinkened lips pursed as she cocked her head to the side. Raw untapped power coursed through her like high tides. "How do I control it?"

Galahad's shadow blocked out the light as he moved behind her. "Think about the time we are going to capture it in your mind and feel it. It will be disorienting, but you must focus. We will stay connected during this jump, just in case. Hold my hand sweet granddaughter and when you are ready, let the magic overtake you."

Hand in hand, she closed her eyes and surrendered to the pull. Gold and silver dust clouded her vision, blinding her instantly. Her wavy hair spun as rushing winds began to swallow her trembling body. Sensations, thoughts not her own pulsed through her, hopes, dreams, fears, and pleasures of those who once lived here intertwined inside her.

Reaching out blindly, air rushed through her fingers like a softly rolling wave. Desperately she reached out, searching for something to cling to, a shred of reality as she plunged into madness. Her stomach dropped as her lungs spasmed, unable to draw in the breath she desperately needed.

Morra's palms and knees connected to the hard floor under her, cutting in with sharp stones, forcing a gasp of air to fill oxygen starved lungs. Time chaotically shifted through her; seconds and hours had no difference, just emotions and lives spent rushing through her.

Like ghosts.

The dominion of Time seemed to pulse around her for an eternity. Soon the gold and silver faded to a chill that spread over her body, like jumping into an icy lake in mid-winter. For a moment she doubted she would ever feel warm again, but just as soon heat returned to her numb limbs and her breath evened out before she opened her eyes. Slowly, the world came back into focus.

Galahad tightened his grip around her shaky hands, helping her up. "Well done, my dear. You will get used to the disorienting feeling quickly."

Hauling herself off the floor, she caught her breath as the last vestiges of dizziness faded. When the floor stopped swaying under her, she looked up and saw pride in her grandfather's eyes. She was proud of herself as well.

Adrenaline had surged through her veins as she jumped and even after it had worn off; she felt a lingering giddiness. Blinking, the scene unfolded before her. The Hôtel de la Marine glowed with renewed splendor in a kaleidoscope of colors. No longer were the people of the square consumed with their phones, just commoners walking through the square.

Turning to Galahad with a smile playing on her lips, she asked, "What now?"

"Now, we go to Versailles."

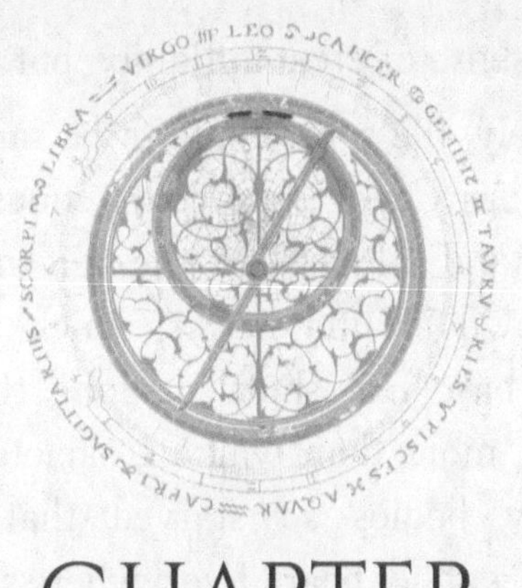

CHAPTER FOURTEEN

"**B**onjour!" the driver of the coach exclaimed as the pair climbed on. The open carriage had been there waiting for them and as Morra settled into her seat, she wondered how they knew to meet them. The intricacies of time travel were still so unknown. Just thinking of it made her head throb, causing black dots to swarm her vision.

Slowly blinking, the world righted itself enough for Morra to look around as Galahad exchanged words with the man in front. Catching sight of the horses, a dull sense of wonder filled her at the strangeness of what had just occurred. Time travel was a funny thing. She had been warned about the differences. They explained the clothes and the food, even how the air smelled, but never did they speak on the horses. The palfreys were smaller than most horses she had seen before and blinding white; a white that only the lack of color could produce.

It gave the sense of great antiquity, but not time worn.

Unfortunately, the same couldn't be said for France, she thought as her stormy eyes explored the square. An unbearable stench of soot and filth filled the air and clung to the surrounding crowd around her, so thick it hid their skin beneath. Filthy bare feet shuffled along the ground. Their owners, nothing more than walking skeletons, with sunken faces and bony bodies so starved that Morra felt an uncomfortable tug at her heart. Everywhere she looked, lifeless faces drifted around, all oozing a hopelessness so great that it seemed to suffocate each of them in their own individual reality.

Her own world was so far removed from the dark abyss these people lived in. A pang of guilt shot through her as her eyes drifted to a waifishly thin girl sitting in the lap of her mother. The girl's eyes were hollow, framed by sharp cheekbones. Tears pricked at the brutal poverty surrounding them. Their world was on the brink of collapse.

The Parisian air held a palpable tension.

"Galahad, what's happened to this place?" Morra asked quietly, as if her voice could destroy the thin bubble separating peace and violence. She had never been a superstitious person, but raising her voice seemed like a bad omen, giving light to the active shadows.

"Sadly, this is what life before the height of the revolution. It's the reason this is a volatile time. Hunger and anger are powerful antagonists." He explained with a sad but resounding tone.

The horses nickered, hooves scraping the ground as the carriage began to move, jostling them in their seats as they moved down the rough cobble. Her eyes were locked ahead until a commotion behind her gained her attention. Whipping her head around, two men began fighting, punch after punch. Her stomach twisted at the sight. As the carriage turned around the bend, Morra saw a piece of silver glinting off the sun and a woman screamed. Swallowing hard, she faced forward and leaned into Galahad's large frame, protecting herself from the harshness of the land.

"Everything will be okay, Morra. I won't let anything happen to you. Just remember what we talked about," he told her gently, tucking his arm over her shoulder.

He was right: *It wasn't a time for fear, but for action.*

Morra saw the world they were now in with clear eyes as all romantic machinations dissolved. It was dark, cold, and it was cruel. Eyes clamped shut, she tried to breathe and count to five as the anxiety pooled around her like a shadow of a hand firmly wrapped around her throat. She felt the cool spring air, much warmer than the cold winter breeze of home, and heard hooves clopping on the cobblestone streets. Wind whipped around them and Morra listened to the noise, begging her mind to focus. Tapping into that sense of calm, she let her eyes flit open.

Morra vowed to be brave and move through the fear of becoming what she needed to be. There was no alternative. Promises had been made to her mother and to her grandfather.

Nonetheless, she still scooched closer to Galahad, not wanting to be far from his side.

The ride to Versailles was a short one, less than an hour. Once inside the city, Galahad and Morra quickly arrived at the Palace. It was gorgeous and grandeur and somehow pomp oozed from the grounds and the people walking around them. A stark comparison to the pain and suffering of the Parisians outside the gates.

Morra jumped down from the coach with the help of Galahad and immediately could feel the creeping tingle of eyes tracing her frame. Looking towards Galahad, Morra noticed an odd focus marring his face, pensive.

Catching his gaze, a raised eyebrow silently questioned him, "I can't place what day it is, and I fear Nostradamus may not be within these walls. It poses a worry as tension rises here in this nation." There was something unnerving about hearing Galahad's usually confident voice waver.

"Can we help those people?" Morra asked him, carefully walking past the first set of gates onto the graveled road lined with white pebbles that kept tripping her in the heels she was forced to wear.

Leaving people to suffer didn't sit right, and she knew it wasn't her right or responsibility to fix the past, Galahad imparted on that heavily, but still. She was afforded a gift, and her cheeks reddened at the thought of squandering a chance to fix it. The shame twisted inside her, but the question went unanswered as her attention shifted as a group of women walked past them.

They were adorned in extravagant dresses, composed of layers and layers of heavy fabric. The sun hung high in the sky, warming everything its light touched, so very different from the weather they left behind. It was unseasonably warm

for early March. Sweat prickled on the small of her back as she tugged the tightly laced top. Her own light yellow outfit, one modified for comfort, still hung too heavy and warm over her frame. She wondered how they did not die from the heat a nd then shook her head
as if trying to unthink the thought,
knowing the answer was probably grim.

Speaking softly and laughing, the group's voices were heavily accented with French. Morra stared at them rudely as she cocked her head, listening and somehow understanding the language they whispered to each other. Noticing Morra and Galahad, the women carrying parasols to shade them from the beating sun ceased talking to openly assess the pair.

Her head tilted up defiantly on instinct. It seemed the lessons Isolde had beaten into her helped. Some passed with awe and others glared with fire in their eyes. Morra's complexion, and her noticeably foreign features, made her look like an outsider. She had been warned outsiders were unwelcome.

Ignoring them, she followed Galahad through an ornate door and into the first corridor of the castle. Bright eyes followed the spiraling staircase as it weaved to the second floor,disappearing. An intricate chandelier hung from the landing above, casting dotted light with a warm glow.

The ornate building stood tall, almost grotesque in its opulence. The sun glinted off the domed roof that crowned the building. Warm creams and blinding whitelimestone wash adorned the pillars, sculptures, and statues that flecked the grounds. Even the two guards near the entrance were dressed in the finest velvet and plush hats.

Before they could pass through the second set of doors, one guard stopped them with a clipped halt. "State your business." The man eyed Morra up and down, distaste gracing his face. The image caused a weird sense of nostalgia, Isolde often wore the same look.

"We are here to have an audience with the king and queen," Galahad informed him sternly.

The guard scoffed. "Take your complaints elsewhere. The royals are not holding court."

"They will for me." With precise and firm words, the man continued, "tell them Sir Seelie has arrived."

Morra couldn't help the small smile that graced her lips. Never had she seen him like that; in the carriage, she rode with her grandfather, the man who brought her a milkshake when she needed it. But now, the man in front of her was a different person. Galahad Seelie was the head of the most prominent families across time, and it showed.

Embodying absolute power that would not back down and would not ask twice, he spoke with a voice that demanded to be heard. His word was law in the family. She now understood why.

The guard's eyes widened and immediately turned and walked into the second set of doors without a word. He returned in less than a minute. "Apologies sir, their highnesses will meet you in the parlor."

Galahad did not acknowledge the guard as he followed at a brisk pace, forcing Morra to walk behind them. A wobble slowed her movements even more, but to others her pace must have been dutiful. The powder blue high heels were killing her feet, rubbing the back of her ankle bare as the corset poked into her ribs, shortening her breath.

Suddenly, the history and etiquette lessons she had endured over the last couple of months seemed justified. It was important to blend in; she knew that and could feel that as the tension ran higher through the country. Bringing unwanted attention could be a death sentence. Feeling the weight of the time, her conversation last night began to make sense.

Rapping on the door alerted Morra of Galahad's presence and with a sigh, she hauled herself out of the soft bed. The glowing light clicked to midnight. Sleep had escaped her as thoughts churned like swelling waves. Every time she attempted, the torrent of thought ate at her. Trudging to the door she swung it open without missing a beat, she turned and dove right back into bed.

"What's up?" she groaned with a yawn, now firmly under the covers.

"I just wanted to go over a few things before tomorrow. When we jump to a new time, it is our duty to protect the people of that time's illusion of life," he cautioned as he sat on the edge of the bed.

"I have no idea what that means, gramps," Morra grumbled, exasperated at the cryptic words.

Galahad's broad shoulders shook with a silent laugh. "I don't think I have ever been called something so informal. I think I like it.

You are such your father's daughter." She grinned viciously and full of pride.

"What I mean is, only a small few will know who we really are at   each point in time. Typically, it is reserved for those in power who will aid us. But many will know our family name as a strong and influential line. Keeping up with this façade is how we cultivate. There will come a day when these relationships save your life. I am advising you to be careful, do not act first and if you are unsure what to do or say, turn to me. You will be seen as a Lady of the Court. We have to act lik e we belong to this time. Understand?"

Morra, at the time, hadn't understood what he was trying to tell her, but watching the guard bristle reflexively gave her clarity.

White-gloved hands turned a gilded knob, granting them entrance. The room within was warm and smelled of heavy perfume and swimming with the soft hum of voices. Morra looked around as the smell burned her throat and decided it was the definition of garish. She wavered between impressed and horrified.

Giant paintings, gold leaf framed mirrors, sculptures, and bronze statues decorated the large space. Its intensity strained her eyes, causing her to blink rapidly. Focusing her gaze, she noticed the two towering chairs centered on the back wall, elevated slightly on the dais. They, too, were outlandishly adorned. The room, the whole palace, embodied the phrase fit for a king.

The commoners living outside the wall gripped tightly to their hate of the privileged ignorant ?people living behind the guarded gate. Morra couldn't fault them. If her children's faces became hollowed as they gripped their aching bellies while those deemed good enough got to live in the richness of the castle without worry, she too would want to burn it to the ground.

The worry of those in the square haunted her and the extravagant room left her mouth ashy, the distaste almost visible on her face. Stiffly, she walked farther into the room behind her grandfather.

Galahad whispered her name. It was a sharp warning and quickly her mask of neutrality was rebuilt. The eyes of the people already in the room were fixed firmly on the two of them. All conversations ceased the moment they stepped in, leaving only the sound of her heels tapping against the black-and-white marble floor to fill the silent room. Morra continued to look ahead, pretending not to notice the glances and subtle murmurs that began to pass between the others there. She was a prominent member of the court, Lady Morra Seelie, and she refused to lower herself by paying attention to those around her.

The thought made her mouth twitch into a smirk—and another gasp echoed from somewhere to her right. Did they frown upon smirking in this place?

An announcer broke her thoughts as an antechamber door was held by another man in white gloves. The king of France stepped out. As one the whole room bowed, Morra, a moment behind the rest, bowed as well.

Peering at the man who had absolute rule over the nation, Morra was stunned. As a child, thinking about what a king looked like, Morra always thought they would be imposing.

Someone who would stand tall and proud, battle tested and strong, but the man before her....

He embodied softness.

Slumped shoulders and a soft chin add to the meek demeanor. Even his clothes screamed his lack of hardship. Lace and ruffles adorned the man's velvet red coat. The crown atop his head wobbled, his flabby neck unable to bear its weight. Morra scrutinized the man, seeing only weakness emanating from him.

The king didn't know hardship, not like the people in the streets of Paris. Her lips curled slightly in disgust. It was hard for her to find sympathy while looking at a man who would be beheaded in less than two years.

The woman walking behind him was different though, and Morra became thoroughly intrigued. Her presence ignited rippling commentary. Morra heard only bits and pieces, but the vitriol in their words became clear.

"I heard she's barren..."

> *"Did you hear she's having an affair with her own brother?"*

"No, the king would execute her!"

> *"Who's to say she isn't having an affair with her own sister?"*

"I saw her the other day with a servant, a boy."

> *"Everyone knows she's a witch."*

Despite the despair clear in Queen Marie's eyes, she stood proud with defiance. She held the look of a woman who knew what awaited her, unable to do anything. All the queen had was that glimmer of perversity, and those in her court demonized her for it. Something inside Morra set aflame.

Not a single person bowed to the queen as she walked in. Morra, making a split second decision, took a step forward to stand shoulder to shoulder with Galahad. Catching the queen's attention, she curtsied deeply. In jerky movement her legs bent, but the message was clear.

The queen's eyes softened slightly.

Awkward tension filled the air as everyone watched the interaction until the king cleared his throat, "Sir Seelie, it is wonderful to meet with you at last."

"Thank you, sire. It is my honor to present Lady Morra Seelie, my granddaughter." Tilting her head in deference, Morra acknowledged him.

"A pleasure," he drawled offhandedly with a flourish of his wrist. "Come, we have much to discuss."

They ended up in an antechamber that led to a grand sitting room. Large windows covered the room, causing the light to bounce off the parquet flooring and be absorbed by the large tapestries. Chairs and benches in contrasting fabrics littered the room. The king sat at the far end of the room, allowing Galahad a private audience while the queen tended to her children.

Morra sat quietly in a hard ornate loveseat, not wanting to disturb either party, but when a woman came to take the children, she decided to speak with the infamous Marie Antoinette.

"Lady Seelie," the queen addressed her with a nod, "I admire your bravery to deviate."

Morra gave the woman not much older than herself a sheepish grin. "I hope I did not offend."

"It was a kind gesture," she said softly. "Those do not happen often within these walls."

History didn't do the woman in front of her justice. The stories she heard growing up about the wretched extravagant Marie Antoinette who spent money and let the common folk starve did not match the petite, polite woman in front of her.

The only thing it got right was her beauty.

Marie Antoinette sat gracefully. Her ash blond hair twirled upwards into an artistically disheveled updo that highlighted her doe-like blue eyes and milky skin. Unlike the other women in court, Maire wore a simple white chemise belted with the same blue ribbon that embellished her hair. She didn't wear the extravagant clothes of the time, nor did she wear much makeup.

"You're not what I was expecting," Morra told her cautiously, taking stock of the queen. She remembered history class in school and learning about the woman who now sat in front of her. The two images didn't mesh.

The queen of France huffed out a bitter laugh. "What did you think of me? Were you seduced by the vitriol those of the court spew?"

Shifting her rigid body, she created space between them, and immediately Morra felt bad. Poking the woman's biggest insecurity, great, just the impression she wanted to make. Silence hung between them as Morra floundered on what to say.

"Honestly, my queen, I thought you to be young and..." choosing her word carefully, she continued, "petulant. Much to my dismay, I must admit, I thought some of it to be true."

Both women sat quietly in their own thoughts as stillness overcame the room. Galahad and the king talked quietly in the corner, undisturbed by the moment of tenseness between the others. Sunlight streamed in, and Morra watched as motes of dust swirled through the gilded room. The silence made her cagey, as wrong words hung stiffly in the air. This foreign exchange tugged at her, making her unsteady.

"I am sorry," Morra apologized softly, turning to her. "I won't make that mistake again."

Her pink lips curved into a tired smile. "You are forgiven. Most here don't like that I refuse to lean into the extravagant life anymore. I did it quite often when I was younger. I had thought it was expected of me, but when I realized what was happening, I-" her words came to a sudden halt as she turned away, eyes fixed on the bright light drifting from the windows.

Something about the queen sparked a deep instinct inside her. Morra didn't know if it was her ironically innocent eyes of a woman stuck in an obedient role without the advantages Morra was raised with. Or if, simply, above all else, she hated a bully. Whatever it was, the need to help this poor woman became intense. She might not be able to help everyone outside these walls but maybe she could help her.

"You can continue if you want, Madame. Your words will not be repeated."

Pale features stared at Morra for a long moment, considering with a shrewd look in her eyes. Shifting nervously at the intense stare of a ruling monarch, Morra patiently waited, hoping the queen would let her help.

Making a decision, the queen elegantly slid over, the white chemise gently swaying as she did. "After the birth of our first child, we went on a royal procession. We witnessed the struggle of the people that we were now in charge of, and I decided to change my ways in solidarity with them."

Marie gave a small rueful laugh, the tinkling sound drawing the attention of the men across the room briefly looking before fixing their attention back on each other as Maire continued. "It only isolated me from the court. They thought I was rejecting their way of life, and to the small folk, it was not seen as proper despite my intentions. I continued despite it. I have never been one to back down because of the gossip of others."

Pity swelled in Morra for the young queen. The sadness she carefully hid behind soft words and a demure expression didn't fool Morra. The aching loneliness that encompassed the queen was akin to Morra's before she met her family.

"Do you like it here?" The question held no pleasantries or levity as Morra's dark eyebrows pulled in. The muscles in her face began to ache at the near constant pull. The past was much sadder than she expected.

Marie patted her hand placatingly, "I am alive. I take my joys where I can."

"Is it not better to remain optimistic? Isn't it possible for the unrest to stop?" Morra could no longer hide her intent from the pained tone and soft smile. Her heart broke for the woman illuminated by sunlight, for she knew it as well.

The truth was plain in her body.

"No," Maire declared. "I know what will become of me. There is no place for optimism in war. My children will be prepared, though I will be dead at least I know they can survive on their own. I am more optimistic for them than I am for myself."

Biting the inside of her lip, Morra barely held her composure. Marie didn't know, and Morra couldn't tell her. Warm saliva gathered at the back of her throat as her eyes shuttered. Looking up, she saw Galahad, still in quiet conversation. Her heart clenched, turning her back on him, she quietly whispered to Marie, "Do you know who I am? Who my family is?"

"I do know of your family. France has always championed behind your family so when the dauphin becomes king, they are told of the importance of lending a hand with those of your name."

"Well then, you know I could help-"

She cut Morra off before the younger girl could continue.

"Dear, I have learned sometimes it's better to let things be."

Morra grabbed the delicate wrist of the pale woman. With a gentle yet firm squeeze she pleaded, "Please..."

"I don't intend to start a revolution," her expression turned to stone as the muscle in her jaw clenched, "nor do I intend to stop it. It is not either of our place to step in."

"I apologize, my queen. That wasn't my intent," Morra recused, knowing she overstepped.

Morra trailed off in silence, content with trying. Galahad may have been upset if he knew she tried to change things, no he would be angry. Then again, his machinations were the same; he, too, was trying to change things. Why could he, while she stood by and watched a good person die?

The thought got pushed down as guilt immediately swelled. Galahad was trying to save her dad. It had to be different, right? More justified. Unable to answer that or unwilling, Morra focused on the present.

The queen said nothing for a moment, then stood, her thin dress falling delicately around her curvy frame. Pulling out a worn book, she walked over, sliding it to Morra with a quick glance at her husband.

"It's called the Rights of Man, written by a French reformer named Mercier. He has... revolutionary ideas. But Morra, be careful with it. The king outlawed it. Most of his suggestions cannot be executed unless there is a change in the French government. I advise you to be cautious. Your family name will not protect you." With a meaningful raise of an eyebrow, the queen stood.

A breath caught in her throat and Morra knew she was supposed to let history be, but the pull inside her wouldn't let her leave without trying. Maybe this was a way to fix things for everyone. Before she could talk to her anymore, both Galahad and the King came over to them. Morra stood, curtsying slightly at the king's attention.

"Lady Seelie," he addressed her directly, "I would like to invite you and your grandfather to dine with us."

"Thank you, sire. It would be our pleasure." The French rolled off her tongue smoothly but speaking like a rich posh kid, in a way Kahadin perfected, seemed foreign.

The thought made her smile as she wondered how he would do in this situation or if he had ever jumped before. "I must take my leave," Marie said, "until later."

"Until later, Madame." Galahad bowed.

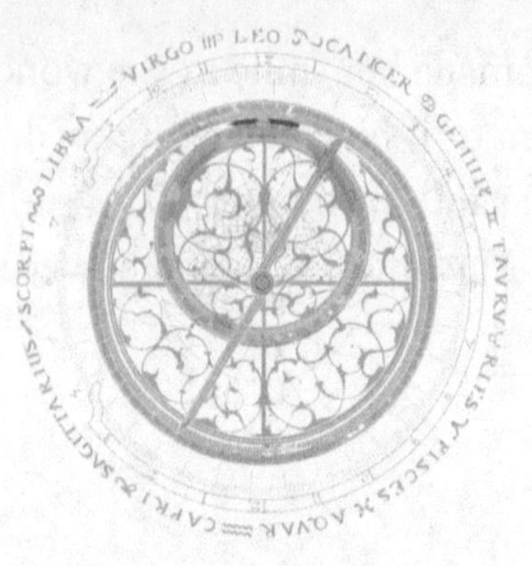

CHAPTER

FIFTEEN

***

Standing in the hall, nervousness filled her as she watched Galahad's large frame disappear, leaving her with a short, beady eyed servant. Alone, in the past. Of course, they couldn't stay together. These people would never let that impropriety stand. But as she followed the servant, she wished he could be closer.

Opening a door, the man let her into a suite. They were lavish but not overtly so, full of marble and high ceiling, mirrors and soft green fabrics made the room both fit for royalty, but comfortable as well. Her trunk rested at the end of the bed, the inside filled with the finest clothing of the time. Pulling out an over dress, she slipped it on. The dress clung to her torso before flaring at the hips over the weird cage these people wore. She missed pants. A chuckle escaped her as she imagined walking around the castle in a pair of trousers. She'd kill someone from shock.

Busying herself, Morra perused the room and numerous bookcases, before selecting a padded chair and settling down.

She cracked open the spine of the book Marie had given her. By the time there was a knock on the door, she had a plan in mind. Galahad stood at the entrance in fancier clothes than usual and Morra couldn't help the giggle, "I like your kitten heels."

Pursed lips and a blank, unamused stare was all she got back. "It is the fashion of the time." He sized Morra up as she stepped towards him, adorned in her own mess of frills and lace. Sheer yellow fabric, coated in rose embroidery, draped delicately over her frame. Morra lifted her dress to show off her own pale yellow heels that matched the rest of her outfit perfectly.

After an approving nod, she tilted to her head and waited for Galahad to follow her. The balcony had a view of the gardens and she looked over them as she asked, "So, what did the king say?" She aimed at a nonchalant tone. Already she missed everyone back home, but there were things to be done here.

He sighed before replying as he ran a hand over his face. "Nostradamus isn't around; he left a few days ago. We could be here for another week or two until he returns."

Morra breathed out in relief, her shoulders slumping forward, before quickly trying to recover. "Is this normal? To be gone weeks at a time in the past."

"It is not unusual. There have been many times I have been in the past for years," Galahad explained, looking over the garden's eyes, glossing over with memories. Shaking it off, he turned, offering his arm, "Ready for dinner?"

Brushing off the invisible lint on the dress, she nodded, letting him guide her through the windy halls. By the time they arrived at a grand staircase, Morra was out of breath, ready for bed. No endurance training could have prepared her for walking around in heels and a cage that they called a dress.

Her heart pounded as reality sank in, this was her entrance to high society. It would seem if she could save Marie, she had to be perfect. With shaky steps, she descended the stairs.

An announcer dressed in fine silks welcomed them into the austere room. Morra looked around, appalled by its lavishness. The walls were lined with exquisite tapestries woven in deep blues, reds and golds, long tables adorned with silverware and platters of food.

The entire room seemed to stand still as they entered, all eyes on them as they made their way to the head of the table, where King Louis sprawled. "Your majesty," Galahad exclaimed, bowing before him, "It would be our honor to dine with you."

The king nodded in reply, smiling at Morra as she curtsied. "Your presence is most welcome. The Seelie's have always been cherished friends to the crown."

Beckoned to sit by the king, whispers broke out as Galahad perched next to him in a large armchair. Morra moved to sit in the empty seat next to the queen. This chair had no arms, just an equally lengthy back. As Morra sat down she gazed around the room. The chairs seemed to change to benches the further they sat from the royals. She looked at the queen and gave her a small smile as the servants came out with more food.

Morra bit the inside of her lip. The sting prevented her from thanking the footman for serving her meal. Her mother's voice berated her lack of manners.

Dinner was intimate and austere. France wasn't quite what she expected; it felt more like her normal life than she would expect. A pang of nostalgia wracked through her bones as she gazed at the tiny pheasant on her plate. It reminded her of Thanksgiving meals with her mom.

After everyone had eaten, the dancing began. The courtiers were dressed in their finest clothing and twirling gracefully across the room. As they glided, their intricate costumes caught the light of the chandeliers and sparkled with gold and silver sequins. A cacophony of strings, brass, and woodwinds all played together in wonderful harmony as Morra twirled around the floor.

Soon, the large group retired to the salon. Morra, exhausted and windswept from dancing, sat down as some of the other women gathered around her.

"Lady Seelie, it's a pleasure to meet a young member of the Mists. We thought you didn't exist." A woman with unabashedly artificial red hair, perfectly coiffed, leaned across the table as three more women sat down.

"Mists?" she questioned.

The pretty waif of a woman on her left leaned against her. With a slight hidden roll of her eye at the redhead, she confided in a whisper, "The dolt of a baroness was trying to demean your station. Instead, she just reminded everyone here," she gave a pointed look to the women who shrunk back slightly, "your name is old enough and well revered to be a Mist of Time."

Morra's jaw ticked at the moniker and the woman noticed, "Do not worry darling, it's what we deem those whose status is so high no one alive knows how it happened. I am Lady Dupont."

"It's a pleasure," Morra replied, "I am just honored to be here and be given such time with the queen amongst her struggles." Waiting to see if the women would take the bait, she grinned as everyone leaned further in.

"Why would she have struggles?" scoffed one woman in the group.

"Oh, you didn't hear?" Morra asked, eyebrows raised in feigned surprise. "She had to condemn her whole family back home in Austria. She had written to them begging for support and help, and what do they do in return? They go to war with the country, trying to help us. It's a pity, but she did the right thing by telling that brother of hers off."

Everyone in the group broke off into whispers. It starkly reminded her of school, all gossip with no substance or fact checking. Morra was thankful that nobody seemed to care about the truth.

Galahad stared at her across the room, watching his granddaughter command the attention of the group. She flashed him a toothy grin.

"Who is that?" Morra asked the group of ladies beside her.

The person in question stood tall, hands tucked behind their back. Their face remained partly hidden in shadows as they gazed out the window to the gardens below. It had become common at court not to recognize someone, with names often slipping from her memory. However, this person stood out.

Their attire differed from the extravagant garments she was accustomed to seeing. The clothes were intricately tailored, exuding a sharp and edgy aura amidst the more flamboyant French fashion. The fabric itself possessed subtle shimmering details adorned with silver and gold embroidery on the cuffs and neckline. A fashion she hadn't seen amongst the French.

"Charles d'Éon," Jeanne Rousseau mock whispered, voice shrill enough to cause the dogs outside to howl. The woman hadn't become any more pleasant, Morra thought subversively.

Weeks had passed since her arrival in France. Morra swiftly became one of the queen's ladies. She was unsure if it was due to their budding friendship, Galahad's intervention, or her own surname, that afforded her this opportunity.

Regardless, she didn't question her good fortune.

The downside was having to deal with pitiful people, like Lady Jeanne Rousseau, the same woman who tried to demean her in front of the other women. She was a mean homely woman who believed others were below her, and she made sure they knew it. Her skin looked like someone had pulled it too tight over her skull. The white powder makeup she fancied only highlighted the frightening details of her face. The redhead often liked using her status to get what she wanted, even though everyone around her often outranked her.

Morra firmly believed that status didn't mean anything about a person. But she did believe the baroness was one of the worst people she had the displeasure of meeting.

Unaware of Morra's internal musings, the bitter woman continued, "Do not associate with him. He is.... not our kind of people."

Lady Dupont leveled a look at the woman. "Lady Rousseau, I do believe you know better than speaking ill of a woman in a higher position that your own, do you not?"

The statement piqued Morra's curiosity and her eyes bore into the side of her face until Louise Dupont turned to her, forming a circle. The women stood huddled in one of the quieter halls of the main palace. Morra leaned against the hard surface of the wall, thankful for the smooth, cool touch as she shifted uncomfortably in her warm dress. Around them, the empty hall seemed to echo with their hushed conversation. The high pitch whine of the baroness bounced off the tapestries, which were so faded they were nearly indistinguishable from their background.

"Her name is Charlotte d'Éon, a knight of the Sun King's father. She had been in England for a long time but must have come back recently," Louise whispered.

Morra turned a stony gaze to Jeanne, "Why did you address her as a male?" She had an idea, but if she was being honest with herself, she wanted to make the dolt say it out loud.

Not catching the hint of steel in her tone, Rousseau continued flippantly, "Well, until recently, d'Éon was a man and we do not associate with those people. If he hadn't been favored by the king's grandfather, then he likely wouldn't be alive."

The other woman who stood with them pursed her lips. She was older than the others, a highborn widow who happily lived off her late husband's money. Morra adored her scathing wit and nonplussed looks; the one she was shooting the baroness right now. "Yes, we are thankful laws have become more lenient, especially the ones on adultery, are we not?"

Rousseau's face turned as red as her hair.

"Well, I am going to go introduce myself."

It was Louise that stopped her, this time with a delicate hand on her forearm. "Are you sure that is wise?" Morra eyed her hand, the look on her face must have been unfriendly because she quickly continued, "I only mean that while most of us welcome her here in court... befriending her may," she paused trying to find the right words, "It may affect your social standing in this court."

Morra sighed, frustration only growing as Louise continued, "You are one of the queen's ladies, associating with the likes of her could get you demoted."

"You do realize there is more to life than these four walls. Even if the walls are enormous. I understand this is how you live, but I will speak to whom I like." With that, she stormed off.

The baroness' voice echoed to her ears. "Looks like a spot is opening up, ladies." The smug smile was evident in her tone.

Morra ignored her as she marched down the hall to the mysterious woman. Clicking of heels alerted the woman to her presence.

"Good day, mademoiselle," the tall woman called, turning from the shadows as Morra approached. Her voice was all soft notes and melodious tones; an air of grace and confidence oozed from her every movement. Morra couldn't help be awed by it, and she quickly understood why Rousseau, who currently watched them over her beak-like nose, would want to undermine her. Lady Rousseau couldn't compare to the woman in front of her.

"I couldn't help but notice your attire. It's quite different from what we're used to seeing at court." Morra spoke hesitantly, hoping the woman would take the compliment as it was.

Charlotte smiled, a small quirk of her lips. "Yes, I have acquired a unique style from my many travels."

Morra looked her up and down. "I enjoy it and admire your bravery. Some days, I feel like a wrong curl could jeopardize one's status."

Charlotte's smile widened, revealing perfect white teeth. "Ah, the perils of court life. But I suppose it's all worth it for the sake of fashion, hmm?" She gave a small chuckle, "Though I must admit, my attire has caused quite a stir among the courtiers."

Morra raised an eyebrow in curiosity. "Would you like to join me for a walk in the gardens? You can tell me all about it."

Huge white columns stood erect under a clear blue sky dotted with clouds. Light pink cabbage roses with hints of yellow in their petals hung from each archway, their sweet fragrance assaulting the senses. A soft breeze blew with the faint aroma of lavender and honeysuckle past as they walked down the stone path to the center of the garden. Morra found herself enraptured as Charlotte described the rolling hills of her homeland and recounted how she had joined a battle on horseback, her armor reflecting the red and orange hues of the waning sun. Charlotte's eyes lit up with enthusiasm as she told stories of faraway places and revealed a cleverness beyond that which came from fighting alone. As their feet wove down the many paths, Morra couldn't help but notice the weight of judgmental gazes leveled their way, but she didn't much care. Let them stare.

"I heard you have made friends with Charlotte d'Éon." Marie paused with her needle hovering over the delicate lace fabric, eyes scrutinizing under her thick eyelashes. Attempting to understand the meaning behind the vague yet conversational words, Morra studied the queen's face. It was frustratingly blank.

Morra had been bestowed the title of the queen's ladyin-waiting in the early weeks of her stay and since then, she had spent her days beside the regal woman as she waited for Nostradamus's return. They would often explore the gardens and read books together, even having tea parties with the royal children. In those moments, Morra felt a connection forming between them. She would like to think that she knew the woman well. And yet she still couldn't decide what the blank look and deceptively mild tone meant. She only hoped Marie wouldn't disappoint her now.

"Yes, I have," Morra replied mildly. "She's an interesting person and I quite enjoy her company."

Marie raised a delicate eyebrow. "Some say she's not fit for this court. That she's not proper."

Morra sighed heavily. "I know, but I don't care about that. I'm not going to let the opinions of others dictate who I associate with."

A smile crept its way onto Marie's round face. "Good. You've always been headstrong, haven't you?"

Morra laughed, relief flooding her. Marie had indeed reacted the way she had hoped. "Yes, I suppose I have. I think I got it from my mother." A pang shot through her as the words left her lips. It hurt terribly, but as time passed, it became more bearable to speak of her. Pleasant almost.

"You were close?" Marie asked, needle point abandoned.

Morra nodded. "Very. She was my confidante, my friend. I miss her terribly."

Marie's eyes softened. "Morra, I'm sorry; I do not know what that is like, to be close to my mother, but my father and I were inseparable. I miss him every day." They sat in a shared silence, both knowing what it was like, and Morra felt more seen than she had in months. Her family was kind and loving, most of them at least, but they just couldn't understand how she felt.

Marie did.

After a moment, Morra cleared her throat and rested her hand on her friend's arm. "Being here at court and making new friends... its helped ease the pain a little."

Marie nodded in understanding. "I'm glad to hear that. And if Charlotte is one of those friends, then I trust your judgment."

Morra's heart swelled with gratitude. "Thank you, Marie. That means a lot to me."

Breaking the tension, the queen smiled and leaned in, giving Morra a conspiratorial whisper, "In full confidence, I adore Charlotte."

Morra smirked, "Careful, if the Baroness Rousseau overheard, she would have you demoted."

Both women laughed until their stomachs ached.

"I truly dislike that woman," Marie said as she watched over her children dancing in the bright green grass. April had come quickly, as they waited for Nostradamus, and with it steady fair weather. They were sitting under an enormous umbrella relaxing in the shade of the garden at the Petite Trianon. The other ladies had departed some time ago, when the children had come back from their governess, Marie Angélique de Mackau.

Morra hummed softly, a smile tugging at her lips as she watched the children play. Their laughter and shrieks of delight echoing through the palace garden. She had gotten to know more of the women of court over the last month and a half. Besides Rousseau, Dupont, and Dubois, Morra was introduced to some of the other ladies. The Princess d'Hénin, who had a no-nonsense attitude, but she still managed to be kind; Vicomtesse de Castellane, who was cold and distant with the other ladies yet seemed almost fond of the King's wife; and many more she couldn't hope to remember.

"Lady Rousseau, that is," the queen clarified, pulling Morra from her rambling thoughts.

Morra nodded, "I had assumed. I do believe I would have died of shock if you had a soft spot for the woman," she said with a smirk.

"Not after what happened that July," the queen murmured. Morra could tell it was a thought not meant to be spoken out loud, and she knew she shouldn't ask. Should have left it go unaddressed, but as Marie's eyes glossed, her will to keep quiet slowly slipped away.

Marie was open with her, but kept her secrets close to her chest. It was understandable, in Morra's opinion, but she wished she could get closer to the woman. Cursing softly, she asked, "What do you mean?"

Marie jumped slightly and looked at Morra with a sheen in her eyes. "Oh nothing, it is of no consequence now."

Reaching over, Morra grabbed her hand, squeezing it gently. "I am your friend, Marie. You can trust me."

"It's not something I can speak on," the Queen muttered, her gaze unfocused, as if she was lost in a distant memory.

Taking a deep breath, Morra squeezed Marie's hand again and said, "I care about you, Marie and I may be one of the few people here not looking to raise my status. You can trust me."

Marie's voice quavered, "two years ago, I lost my daughter." She directed a vacant gaze at the shrieking children, as Morra silently closed her eyes in sympathy for the usually cheerful queen. "My little Sophie," Marie uttered a sorrowful chuckle, "such a chubby baby and yet the best physicians couldn't save her from tuberculosis. After her death, I was inconsolable for months. My family tried to tell me she was young and had yet to grow attached to me." Tears trickled down her face as she continued, "But I couldn't help thinking of how she would have been my friend."

Her teary eyes turned hard; a look Morra had never seen shadowed the young queen's face. "In the midst of my grief, I walked in on Rousseau telling some of the other ladies that *'the princess was lucky to be spared the tolling weight that is the queen's friendship'.*"

Morra looked at her in outrage. "That bitch!"

"Morra," she gasped, "you mustn't say that aloud. It could be dangerous for both of us." Marie's voice was low and urgent, her eyes scanning their surroundings.

Morra wanted to roll her eyes but instead conceded with a nod. "You're right, my apologies. But she's just so despicable. How could she say such a thing?"

In that moment, she realized she truly viewed Marie as a close friend, and Morra had a horrible penchant for breaking rules for the people she cared about.

It was time to talk to her grandfather.

CHAPTER SIXTEEN

Galahad knocked on the door to Morra's room before letting himself in. "There is a small ball being held tonight in the honor of Estates General next week. We are to attend." His unexpected entrance startled her and caused her to look up from the book she was reading. The one Marie had given her in the sitting room weeks ago. "Grandfather, how much longer do you think we will be here?"

"Anxious to get home?" he asked gently, sitting across from her. "It has been six weeks, it's not unexpected to be homesick."

"Six weeks already? That would mean I'm seventeen." Her brows furrowed. "How do birthdays work because I will still be sixteen once we are back home?"

Galahad smiled, "Birthdays become arbitrary after eighteen. Most of the children do not jump for enough time that it matters. Our blood gives us the ability to age slightly longer than everyone else and once you hit my age, dear, you don't tend to keep track." He leaned back in his chair and continued, "Is that why you asked?"

She looked down at the book. It was leather bound, and Morra ran her fingers over the embossed letters and title before sighing heavily and shifting in her seat, "No. I miss home, but that's not why I asked either. I just feel like I'm not doing anything useful here. I want to be out there, making a difference, helping people." Flashes of the Queen's brokenhearted face swam in her vision.

He looked at her with a sympathetic expression, yet Morra felt like he was mocking her. "It's not our place to change things. We are tourists, dear, not architects."

Morra looked down at her book, a strange feeling growing in her chest under her grandfather's kind gaze. "What if we did... change things, that is?" she asked hesitantly.

"What do you mean, Morra?" Galahad leaned in; his interest piqued.

"I mean... what if we used our position here to advocate for the people? To make a difference in their lives," Morra explained, speaking slowly, trying to articulate her spinning thoughts. Her face became drawn with the weight of her question, her lips pursed as she waited for his reply.

Galahad frowned. "That could be dangerous, sweet girl.

We must tread carefully while in the past."

"But we could do so much good!" Morra argued, passionately begging him to listen. "Think about all the people who are suffering under this oppressive system. We could make their lives better." Why shouldn't they help? Sure, France deserved their freedom, but Marie didn't deserve to die. Why couldn't both happen? Revolution could happen without bloodshed, couldn't it? Did she have to die?

Galahad sighed. "You have a pure heart, my dear. But the world is not that simple. We cannot waltz in and change as we see fit. We aren't gods."

Her gaze fell to the book in her hands, her grandfather's kind eyes staring at her with such expectations. Longing and failure held her body in a subtle curve as she slumped in on herself, smoothing out her dress again. Dust motes floated through the air in the space between them and Morra knew disturbing them with her arguments would be useless.

He spoke as if letting it go was an option. But what kind of person would she be if she didn't try? A tiny part of her wondered what kind of person he was if he didn't see the worth in helping.

The queen beckoned Morra to her chambers, not the Petit Trianon but her actual chambers in the palace. Standing in front of the wooden door, waiting for the obligatory *'enter'* she rocked back and forth on her heels. Nervousness filled her as the queen called out and the servants opened the door.

She entered the room cautiously, surprised to find the queen looking distressed. In her hands she held a small blanket, pale pink in color with lace frayed at the end, clearly worn from endless rubbing. Stitched in delicate white thread Sophie Hélène Béatrice swirled on the edge.

Marie looked up at Morra, her expression desperate. "Do children die of tuberculosis where you're from?" It was the first time Marie acknowledged her abilities.

Morra gave her a sad smile, sitting next to the queen and foregoing any pretense of status; in this room, she was just helping a friend who was grieving the loss of their child. Still, Morra felt taken aback by the question.

"No. Well, yes." The queen looked up, confused. "People still die of it and some of them are children, but in my time there is..." Morra tried to think of a way to explain it to the woman who most likely had no clue how an immune system worked. "There is a shot that a physician gives in the arm of children, and it makes it so they don't get it. In the place I live, they have stopped giving the shot because it is so rare."

Marie bowed her head, lip quivering. "How long?" she asked, "how long until mothers do not have to feel this pain?"

Morra didn't know, so she just shook her head. "It's not something I ever learned."

The queen seemed to find some solace in her response, as if it provided a glimmer of hope that others wouldn't experience the same kind of pain she was feeling; even if it was false hope, it was something.

Bile rose in Morra's mouth at the thought of the queen's pain and the loss of her daughter. It rose even higher as Isolde's voice rang clear in her mind, *'One dies at seven, another at ten. Her only surviving child is her eldest daughter spent years in prison before being married off to her cousin.'*

Marie smiled unconvincingly. "Are you ready for the ball this evening? It's at the royal opera house."

The ball was grand and lavish as all things were in Versailles. Chandeliers hung from the ceiling, and flower arrangements adorned every table. Morra had dressed in her finest gown, a deep ruby red that accentuated the undertones of her hair. As she walked into the ballroom, she couldn't help but feel nervous as her gaze scanned the crowd. The nobles were dressed in the most exquisite attire, and the jewelry they wore was worth more than the home her mom had bought in West Virginia.

Morra saw multiple men try to lock eyes with her, but she turned her head, playing dumb. She wasn't interested in dancing with any of them. She was here for a purpose.

The women were all adorned in extravagant gowns, their hair piled high on their heads. The men were dressed in fine suits and jackets, their powdered wigs and perfume filling the air. Morra and her grandfather played their parts well despite the flutter in her stomach as she stepped off the last step of the grand staircase.

Spotting Charlotte in the crowd, she broke off from Galahad, who had already made eye contact with some of the noblemen. She made her way towards her.

"You look lovely," Charlotte complimented her, twirling a lock of her hair around her finger.

Morra's laughter echoed over the ballroom floor as she scanned the crowd. Her eyes locked on the powdered wigs perched atop every nobleman's head. Charlotte joined in, but her voice was soft and musical, like a lute played by gentle fingers. "I'm just glad I don't have to wear one of those powdered wigs," Morra told her. "I'd be sneezing all night."

Charlotte chuckled, her eyes fixed on a group of nobles huddled in a corner. "Yes, I don't think they're very practical," she said. "But they make the men look quite dashing, don't you think?"

Morra shrugged. "I suppose," she said. "But I'm not really interested in the men here." Charlotte's eyebrows lifted in surprise and Morra laughed gently, swatting at her friend. "I am not interested in the woman either. I'm more interested in finding ways to help the people of France."

Charlotte's face darkened as she spoke. "It's a noble cause, Morra. But be careful. The nobles here aren't exactly known for their kindness to the common folk."

Morra nodded, scanning the room for any indication that their conversation had been overheard. She knew that venturing into this world of silk and wine would require a deft touch and keen intuition.

They chatted for some time more before broaching the subject on her mind. "I am still fairly new to court and would love a.... précis of who is who."

Charlotte smiled slyly, her blue-green eyes glinting in the candlelight. She hadn't been a renowned spy for nothing. "Of course, my dear. Let's start with the Duke of Orleans," Charlotte began, her voice low. "He's been known to support the people, but he's also been accused of corruption and embezzlement. He's a dangerous ally, but a valuable one if you can gain his trust."

Morra listened raptly, mind racing. "What about her?"

She nodded to a woman she hadn't been formally introduced to, but she had heard of her; a close confidant to the queen once upon a time. "What about the Duchess de Polignac? Is she worth knowing?"

Charlotte's face twisted in distaste at the mention of the Duchess. "Ah, she's a tricky one. She's been known to influence the queen in ways that benefit her own interests. But be careful, she's a viper. She'll turn on you in an instant if it means saving her own skin. She was once the queen's closest friend, but it seems she has since fallen out of favor. However, she still holds considerable influence in court, especially among the ladies."

Morra nodded, filing away the information for later use as she watched the ladies of court flock her way. Rousseau leading the charge, hugging the woman like old friends.

Interesting.

"Who is-" The sounds of fanfare splitting through the air cut her words short as the king and queen entered the room. Morra and Charlotte curtsied deeply, as did the rest of the court. The queen's face was tight with a forced smile until her scanning eyes locked on someone in the crowd. It was barely perceivable, but for a brief moment, relief flooded the queen.

Following her gaze, Morra asked Charlotte, "Who is that?"

"Oh, that is Axel Von Fersen, a Swedish Count, and a colonel of the Royal Suédois regiment of the French army. He's been known to be a close confidant of the queen."

"So, he is fully in support of the functioning monarchy?" Morra followed him with his eyes. He was talking to a group of men, but his eyes continued to drift to the queen.

Something in his face spoke of more than friendship.

Charlotte was just about to answer when a voice, coated with disdain, interrupted them. "Ah, Chevalier d'Éon, it's... a pleasure to see you in court." Lady Rousseau stood in front of them, dripping in a yellow gown that was extravagant in all the wrong ways, and clashed horrifically with her hair.

"Oh, is it?" she replied in feigned surprise.

The redhead pursed her lips and swung her gaze back to Morra. "Well, I see you chose not to accept my advice." She side-eyed Charlotte. "I was hoping you would have wised up and found a more suitable companion for the evening."

"Ah yes, and I had hoped you would have found a more suitable dress for the evening," Morra retorted with a smirk, her eyes flickering over Lady Rousseau's garish gown. "But alas, it seems we're both disappointed this evening."

Charlotte stifled a laugh as Lady Rousseau's face turned red with anger and she spun on her matching yellow heels and stalked away. Morra knew she would pay for the comment, but it felt quite good.

Charlotte muttered under her breath, "Bitch."

Morra looked at her, a vicious grin spreading across her face. "That's what I said!" They both burst into laughter, enjoying the small victory, but music cut their conversation off. People dispersed from the dancing floor as the king and queen made their way down.

"Excuse me, ladies," a deep voice interrupted them. They turned to see the Duke of Orleans standing behind them, a falsely charming smile on his face. "I was hoping to have this dance." He bowed slightly before extending his hand out to Morra. She hesitated for a brief moment before placing her hand on his. She had heard the rumors about the duke even before Charlotte, but she also knew the power he held in court. Saying no to him could be dangerous.

"I would be delighted," she replied with a tight smile. "Excuse me," she told Charlotte, whose eyes narrowed. The question was obvious, but Morra just winked at her friend, whose shoulders relaxed.

As they made their way to the center of the dance floor, Morra could feel the beady gaze of the duke boring into the side of her face, tracking her movements. Like a beast of prey looking for the weak spot.

"You're quite new to court, aren't you?" he asked, his voice low and smooth. It raked her nerves.

"Yes," Morra replied politely. "I'm still trying to navigate my way around."

The duke chuckled. "Well, I'm sure Charlotte has given you quite some information, and I have heard you have gotten quite close to the queen."

"I have." Morra hesitated for a moment, considering Charlotte's earlier warning about the duke's tendencies.

"Your grandfather is here as well, if I am not mistaken," he asked, still twirling them across the dance floor. His dark eyes scanned the crowd as if searching for the man.

"Indeed." An undercurrent of tension ran through her. He seemed to want something. His grip tightened slightly as he spotted the older man. A sigh a relief passed her lips as the violins crescendo to an end and everyone around bowed before parting.

"I sure hope he is on the right side of the upcoming détente."

"I wouldn't presume to talk for him, nor would I know the intricacies of men's business, now would I?" Morra stiffened but tried to keep her tone neutral.

The duke chuckled again, a sound that sent shivers down Morra's spine. "Of course not, dear. But it's always good to have powerful allies in times like these, wouldn't you agree?"

Morra forced a smile, unsure of what to say. She, of course, knew of the upcoming political upheaval and tensions between the monarchy and the people; it was all anyone would talk about. What she didn't know was that Galahad was a part of the Estates General, he never spoke of it. Her mind raced, searching for a way to end the conversation.

"Excuse me, Mademoiselle Seelie," a deep voice interrupted them. She turned to see Axel Von Fersen, dressed in a deep blue intricately designed waistcoat, bowing deeply.

"May I have this dance?"

Morra breathed a sigh of relief as she placed her hand in his. "I would love to."

As they moved to the center of the dance floor, Morra relaxed slightly at the count's kind yet distant smile. This was reaffirmed as he whispered low, "The queen asked me to come rescue you from the duke."

Morra chuckled, of course she noticed. "You are quite close to the queen?" She kept her tone light, making sure no judgment entered it. It didn't work. Axel pulled himself straighter, chin up as if he were a soldier marching in a parade. His eyes scanned the room, searching for someone, anyone firmly keeping his eyes off her. The muscles in his jaw bulged as he ground his teeth and she quickly continued,

"As am I. She has been so kind since my arrival here." He relaxed minutely. "She is quite a person, isn't she?"

Axel's eyes seemed to shine as he finally looked back at Morra. "Her Majesty was also kind upon my arrival in court."

"I've never met anyone quite like her," Morra replied, a smile spreading across her face. "She's compassionate and wise, yet also determined. I respect her tremendously."

Morra swayed gracefully, her feet gliding across the marble foyer as the Swedish count guided her. The lilting waltz drifted around them, and Morra let her mind drift to the looming political unrest in Marie's country. She knew all too well what it would mean for her friend and her children if civil war broke out - had she the courage, or even the means, to save them? As they spun in circles, Morra found herself gazing into the count's deep blue eyes and realized he may have a way.

Charlotte's words alluded to it but even if she hadn't, Morra could see Axel loved Marie, but before she mentioned it, she would speak to Galahad. He specifically asked her to talk to him before she did anything of importance.

As the dance came to an end, Axel bowed politely to Morra before excusing himself. "I must attend to some business, but I hope we can continue this conversation soon, Mademoiselle Seelie." He disappeared into the crowd, leaving Morra alone with her thoughts.

She made her way over to a server carrying a glass of wine while scanning the room for Galahad. Spotting him, she strolled to him. "Excuse me, gentlemen," she said, interrupting his conversation with a group of men. "May I have a word with my grandfather?"

Galahad turned, face softening at the sight of her. "Of course, my dear. What can I do for you?"

Morra wrapped her hand in his elbow, gently guiding them to the balcony. The music from the ballroom played loudly, drifting out of the open door, merging with the crickets and frogs from the nearby pond. The air had a hint of jasmine and honeysuckle drifting from the courtyard below and the wind whipped around them, messing her hair from the tight curls they had once been in.

"So your cover this whole time was the estate generals?" Galahad's expression turned serious as he looked at Morra. "Well, yes, it makes sense that I have come early to prepare. Our name is old and ancient. It would be perfectly reasonable for me to attend."

"This is awesome," Morra exclaimed. Galahad looked at her blankly and she sighed. He seemed lost, so she explained, "You are going to a meeting where your opinions matter. You could advocate for peace. The nation can be democratic, and the royals could keep their heads."

"Child, I told you we do not intervene. We are here to speak to Nostradamus and to leave. This is about your father not saving a country that has already gone to war and re-built itself," Galahad replied, his voice low. Morra's brow furrowed at him, and silence settled in around them. Everything seemed to be still for a moment. The music from the ballroom reached onto the balcony, wavering in and out of the silence.

"Well, what happens if the king calls on you for your opinion?" she demanded, hands on her hips.

"I will just tell him that I have been out of court life and need to get a grasp on the full situation before I can advise him."

"What if he gets mad, and it jeopardizes our standing in France?"

"My dear, it doesn't matter. The king will be dead in a few years; let him be mad. Now I do need to get back."

Reaching out before he could turn away from her, Morra grabbed his forearm. "What happened to *it's not a time for fear, but for action*'? It sure seems like you're scared," she spat. Anger swirled in her at his lack of empathy for the people here. She couldn't believe that Galahad, a man she respected and loved dearly, would be so dismissive helping people.

Galahad whipped his gaze down sharply before forcing his arm out of Morra's grip. And Morra, at the moment watching his retreating form, made a decision.

Darting through the dancing couples, Morra searched the room. When she spotted him, she quickened her pace, her heart pounding in her chest. The air around them was heavy with anticipation as she grabbed his arm.

"Axel," she said urgently, desperation tingeing her voice. "I need your help."

He looked at her in surprise, his brows furrowing. "What is it? What's wrong?"

The clinking of glasses and conversations muffled by laughter filled the air as Morra glanced furtively around the room before leaning in close to whisper, "I'm going to try to save Marie," she said finally. "But I need your assistance if

I'm going to do it. Can you help me?"

He searched her eyes cautiously, unsure of what she was proposing. She took a deep breath before launching into her plan in a hushed voice. A brief silence hung between them before he finally nodded slowly.

"Yes," he replied firmly. "I'll help you."

It didn't take long for a meeting to be set. With Morra's knowledge of who was for and against the monarchy and with the Count's connections, it was easy to assemble a party of people who might set a different course for the country.

Morra couldn't do the talking. It would not be beneficial to have a woman interject her ideas. She wasn't delusional in thinking they would listen to her. However, she had Axel by her side, a seasoned negotiator who had traversed the elaborate labyrinth of court politics for years, mastering its intricacies. Trailing behind the Axel, Morra's presence stirred a mixture of bewilderment and simmering resentment among those gathered.

The room exuded an air of opulence in the fading evening light. Adorned with dark wood paneling and tapestries showcasing intricate designs. Mahogany and velvet furniture, embellished with delicate golden accents, graced the space. A plush red carpet blanketed the floor, leading the gaze to a large fireplace emanating a comforting warmth from the far corner.

Seated around the table were the formidable figures, the key players in this high-stakes endeavor.

They spent nearly an hour debating who should or should not be invited. They chose to invite Marquis de Lafayette, Emmanuel Joseph Sieyès, Jacques Pierre Brissot, Maximilien Robespierre. And, to her reluctance, Napoleon Bonaparte.

As they entered the room, Morra could feel the tension in the air. All eyes were on them as they made their way to their seats. The Marquis, Lafayette, greeted them with a nod, while Napoleon Bonaparte gave them a haughty stare. Morra could feel her palms getting sweaty as Axel took the lead, allowing Morra to fade into the background.

"Gentlemen, thank you for coming. As you know, the situation in France is dire. We are on the verge of collapse. The people are suffering, and our government is severely flawed." A current of tension went through the group. The words could be considered treason, but the count forged on, "I know this topic is the essence of the Estates General tomorrow, but I believe nothing will be amended. Unless we can find common ground."

The meeting was strained, with various sides arguing their positions loudly. Morra stayed in the background, observing the interactions. Axel, on the other hand, was right in the center of it, articulating their plan with precision and passion.

As the natural light of the sun began to fade, Morra lit candles and poured wine to soothe the mounting tensions, but she mostly kept to the shadows. They had gone over the plans for hours the night before, perfecting each detail. She was sure the staff would start rumors.

Finally, at the tail end of sunrise, an agreement was reached. The men had decided the monarch could stay, heads intact but the true power could no longer remain with the royals. It belonged to the people. While it was not quite the victory they planned it was enough for them to begin working towards something greater.

"That went better than I thought it would. I was unsure they would be agreeable to a democratic monarchy," Axel confessed as the last person left the room. He drained the last drop of wine from his glass, as did she.

Morra's eyes sparkled with gratitude and happiness. "Thank you so much for everything Axel, your help and support have been invaluable. Without you, I don't think I could have done this."

Axel smiled warmly at her and lowered his head in appreciation. "It was my honor," he replied candidly. "I'd do anything for the Queen."

She grinned widely, knowing that Marie was now in excellent hands with Axel's support. Now she could focus again on discovering Nostradamus and rescuing her father.

Finally, she felt relieved.

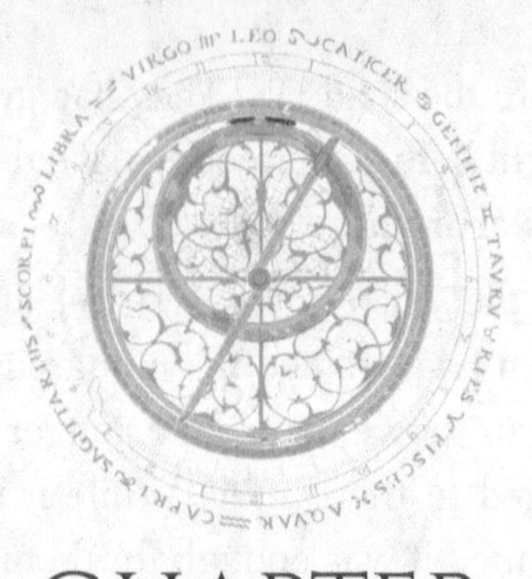

CHAPTER SEVENTEEN

The relief didn't last long as Marie stormed into her room. Her face blushed with anger. "What have you done?" she demanded, her voice biting. "You had no right to make decisions in my name, and I had to find it out from Yolande de Polignac. Do you know how that makes me look?"

Morra stood still, much like a deer hoping a predator will pass them by, as she formulated what to say. "Your Majesty," Morra began, her voice barely above a whisper. "I thought-"

"You thought?" Marie cut her off, her eyes flashing with fury. "You thought to meddle in the affairs of this country. *My* country. All without my knowledge or consent? Do you have any idea what kind of danger you have put us all in? The danger you put Axel in?"

Ah, she thought.

"You love him?" Morra asked softly.

Marie's angry expression softened slightly before shifting back, "That is beside the point, Morra. I trusted you and you went behind my back. You could have ruined everything."

Morra took a deep breath, steeling herself as she rose to her full height. "Your Majesty, with all due respect, everything was already ruined. I couldn't stand by and wait for you and your children to be executed."

She paled slightly, taking a half step back. "There was a plan-"

"To flee Paris? It failed," Morra said, harsher than she intended. She grabbed the queen's hands, gathering them in her own ink-stained hands praying she would listen. "We did what we did because we believed it was the best course of action for France, its people, and for you. Axel knew the risks, but what would happen if we didn't intervene was a bigger risk that neither of us were willing to take."

Marie's eyes softened, and she sat down on the edge of her bed. "I know," she voiced. "But you have to understand that my life, the lives of my family, and the life of every person who supported us are at risk because of your actions."

A silence sat between them as Morra nodded her understanding, realizing they were at an impasse. At the moment, she would have to accept the queen's dislike, and, in turn, Marie would have to accept her decision to take the matter into her own hands.

The two sat in an almost comfortable silence for a few moments until Marie made a noise of remembrance. "I initially came to let you know that Nostradamus has arrived with an envoy from Italy."

As the moon rose high in the sky filtering in glittery light, Morra found herself sitting at the little desk in her chambers. She stared down at the ink dipped quill, watching as the dark ink splattered the stark white page. She missed home, Kahadin, Ladi, and, most of all, Atlas.

Writing notes in the past for someone in the future had been incredibly complicated. It may be a moot point. Or, she thought, staring at the half filled parchment, Atlas had read them already. The logistics made her brain ache.

Her words were delicately designed. If someone opened it in between now and then... she shook her head at the implications as she scratched more words. The pages quickly filled with her stress and complaints, her laughs and fun moments, and most of all, the incredible love she had for him.

Them.

Her nose crinkled as she hastily included everyone else back home, not yet ready to say what she felt, especially from two hundred years in the past. The letters became a daily ritual while they had waited for Nostradamus' return. Each day it started the same, staring daggers at the paper lit by glowing candlelight. Each day it ended the same as frustration overwhelmed her while she tried to word the letter without telling him those three small words.

It had been seven weeks since their arrival, seven long weeks awaiting Nostradamus.

Nostradamus had returned to the castle the day before with the Italian envoy, and Galahad had arranged a meeting with them both after the Estates General.

I should be home soon, she wrote in a scratchy handwriting before she folded the letter and stamping the fresh wax with the family crest.

The next day, she made her way to the sitting room where they would convene. She rounded the corner, only to find Nostradamus standing there. His eerie gaze rooted her in place. He just stood there as if he had been waiting for her.

The man towered above her, thin as a blade but with a face like a hammer and unfocused eyes that burned into her soul. Stopped in her tracks, she watched him for a moment. Like a doe caught in the gaze of a predator, her muscles tensed, ready to run at any twitch. Time dragged on as she tried to quell the icy fear that rose inside of her.

She knew she should turn back, but something made her pause. Maybe it was curiosity, or maybe it was fear. Either way, she stayed put. Dread overwhelmed her senses as they locked eyes. All at once, his presence seemed to fill the hall, engulfing both of them in its thick, oppressive silence. Fearfully and unsure, Morra took a step to the side, before quickly recoiling away as his eyes glazed over with a pearly white sheen.

His deep, hollow voice engulfed the hall. Faintly his words were echoed by voices not his own, "You are troubled child, rushing off to war without knowing the cost. Innocence and arrogance interlaced." For a moment he seemed to gaze into some distant abyss, his voice now an ominous whisper:

"Daughter born under the horned goats setting sun
Orphaned by the future and the past

Seek for the bones of the loved

Until the drip of time caught up

The present time together with the past

Two will rise in distant lands

Two powers that must be kept apart

And she who was proscribed will return to the kingdom

The one who will play the bravest parts

For times good for evil, the sweeter for the bitter

Sacrifices shall return again, and blood shall be spent

Until ancestors and forebears come forth through the depths,

Lamenting to see thus dead."

The flicker of flames in his eyes faded, and he turned back into a normal man. She stood there, a heavy silence enveloping them.

"I have no control over the visions. I apologize." Morra looked up at his slumped shoulders, regret seeping into his form.

"No apologies needed, sir. That was what I traveled here for," she said in a choked voice, trying to remember and make sense of his whispers. Swaying back and forth, Morra replayed the words. Galahad, she thought, she needed Galahad. Stumbling backwards, rough stone hitting her back.

"What do you mean by bones of the loved?" her voice shook.

Pity clouded his features. "I will not tell you, even if I did know, I am already bound to secrecy. If not by God, then by the love of her who gave me my powers," he whispered vacantly. "But I can tell you the cost of war is more than you think, and it's too late for the bones are already wrapped in flesh."

Colors swirled in her vision as she tried to find a wall to steady herself, but instead she collapsed forward. The prophet quickly caught her before she hit the ground, holding her to his chest.

"Lady Morra! Oh, please not again."

Morra woke up with a gasp, feeling searing pain and a pounding headache. She swayed, still feeling dizzy and disoriented. Despite it, she looked around and couldn't help but smile. There, sitting on the couches next to the hearth, sat Galahad, Marie, and her children.

Galahad noticed her awake and rushed to her side. Examining her, he touched her head, gruffly saying, "You had us all very worried." Maire perked up, but stayed by the fireplace with the kids.

A breathy laugh escaped her as Galahad guided her into a sitting position. "Yeah, apparently Nostradamus can be pretty intense."

"That he can. I talked to him, and he had the information we needed. He will be here later to talk to us. Then we will go back home."

"When will we leave?" She looked over his shoulder at someone she had gotten very close to. Her heart panged at saying goodbye. A squeeze of her hand caused her to look up. Galahad had a sad smile of understanding.

"Tonight. I must say my goodbyes to a few people, including the king." He kissed her head, "say your goodbyes. We will leave when we get back."

Marie made her way to Morra after Galahad had excused himself.

"Morra, I never got to say thank you." Dropping the mask, the older woman so fiercely held onto, she smiled, "Impropriety be damned." She threw her arms around Morra. "You truly are what this court needed; I am so glad to have known you." She pulled away, giving Morra the sincerest look, she had ever seen from anybody in this place.

Tears fell from her eyes as she looked at her. Wiping them away "I apologize your majesty I just... am going to have a hard time saying goodbye."

She pulled her into a hug and, against her ear, she whispered, "I will miss you too."

Reality hit Morra, and she felt her heart tear at the thought of never seeing the Petit Trianon with Marie and her children ever again. This goodbye was final. Tomorrow, when she was back at home, Marie, her children, and everyone she met would be dead.

She broke into sobs.

"Oh, der Schatz, it will be okay." Marie continued hugging Morra tightly. "Live and be happy. I will never forget you. And I want to thank you for the kindness you have shown me and my children."

Morra just couldn't hold it in anymore. "I don't want to let you be executed," she croaked pleadingly, not knowing if what she did would be enough.

"And I do not want my children to see me die, but it is a reality we must face. One day we will all die; it is the natural order of things."

"I wished I could have helped more. Done more." Morra did what she could, she only hoped it would be enough.

"You did more than you think. The Estates General went far better than any of us hoped. It has shifted opinions." Morra pulled back in surprise, hope flashing in her eyes as

Marie continued, "Silly girl, you may have just saved us yet." Tears welled in the queen's eyes, but she blinked them back. "Thank you." She gave her one last hug before gathering her children and leaving.

Morra cried more, heartbroken by the weight of the world and time on her shoulders. A knock on the door and Galahad's deep voice rouses her. Behind him stood Nostradamus.

"I apologize for my earlier behavior. I was just overwhelmed." She told him once they all were seated. Galahad had helped her stand and walk to the chairs near the now unlit fireplace.

Nodding his understanding, "Most are after the first time they meet me." Switching subjects, he continued, "I think I know of a way to stabilize your father enough to pull him back into the proper space and time. There is a device I have heard about." Pausing hesitantly, he pushed forward, slumping in his seat. "The pieces have been broken up and scattered by our family."

Galahad ran a weary hand through his salt and pepper hair. "Why?"

"It's thought to be only a single use device that can do more than pull someone from a time vortex, and that is a power much too large to let everyone have access to it."

"Does that mean we shouldn't use it?" she asked, distressed.

A long pause held space between their words before Galahad spoke up, "If we weren't supposed to use it, he wouldn't have informed us about it." Giving Nostradamus a hard look, he demanded, "Will it work?"

"I cannot say." His voice became gruff. "It will be risky to find the pieces. You are putting your lives in danger. You won't be the only ones wanting to get their hands on it."

Stoically, Galahad sat there on a white and gold damascus chair, staring at his weathered hands. "What does this device look like?" Morra knew from the contemplative look that Galahad would risk everything if that meant he would get his son back.

"It's an astrolabe infused with magic by those much older and stronger than us. I do not know where the pieces are, but many people die when knowledge of these parts gets out."

"Thank you," Galahad told him, breaking the etiquette of this time by pulling the startled seer into a hug. After releasing the man, Galahad turned towards Morra as Nostradamus bowed, leaving the room. "We are leaving soon." She nodded, feeling the tears threaten to fall again.

"I need to go now," Morra said, voice cracking.

"Okay dear." He nodded, petting her hair soothingly.

A million thoughts ran through her head as she got into the carriage that took her back into Paris. Watching fields go by, she just hoped her time made a difference.

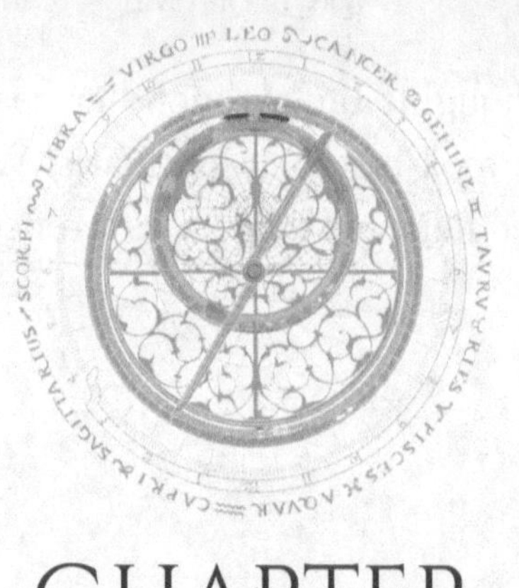

CHAPTER EIGHTEEN

Narth Carolina's uncharacteristically frigid winter blanketed the ground with snow and brought a chill that killed the crops, but Morra didn't care.

Snow and ice crunched beneath her boots as she walked up to the house. Even in the winter months, it was exquisite. The Manor stood tall, with walls made of stone and a large wooden door inviting her in. A smile graced her face. She had missed the place, not fully realizing it had become home to her.

A true home.

Pushing open the door, she stepped inside, absorbing the warmth. The sadness had retreated on the plane, leaving just a pang. Hearing voices from another room, Morra paused before deciding to ignore them. She desperately missed everyone, but first she had to know.

Her room looked the same as she left. Clothes were strung on the floor and her mother's book was open on the end table. Curling up on her bed, she grabbed her phone and began browsing some sites about Marie Antoinette. Waiting for the history website to load, she bounced up and down excitedly, her curly brown hair wetting her shirt where it touched.

Morra quelled tears of excitement as she read:

'Marie Antoinette died peacefully in her sleep at the age of 83, being survived by three of her children...'

She skimmed through the rest of the article, learning about the day after they left.

'The king and queen attended a meeting that included representatives of the military and the common people. With the queen's aid in negotiations, a treaty was signed which would remove the monarchy from having absolute power. This treaty was said to have prevented what was to be one of the bloodiest revolutions ever. With the help of Napoleon Bonaparte, who was one of the elected representatives of both the people and the military, the royals were able to garner alliances with other countries. This helped the financial recession and brought aid to thousands of people.'

Morra fell back onto her bed, sinking into the soft red silk comforter with a sigh of contentment. She closed her eyes and for the first time truly took in the feeling of being back in her own bed, the feeling of having accomplished something truly extraordinary. The gravity of what she had done, of having saved the lives of her friend and her children, suddenly bore down on her. Morra smiled, understanding finally what Galahad and Balin had meant about how rewarding being a Seelie could be.

A knock on her door pulled her out of her musing. Sitting up, she yelled, "Come in!" the smile evident in her tone.

Galahad entered her room. Morra excitedly opened her mouth to tell him about the queen, but stopped seeing the expression on his face. The color had been drained, and he refused to look at Morra with his red-rimmed eyes. Her gut dropped. Something was terribly wrong.

Peering out listlessly, he slumped on the bed next to her. "Grandpa?" she asked softly.

Without turning, he blindly reached over to take her hand. She wanted to ask, but the words wouldn't come out.

Instead, she sat there hands shaking, waiting.

"It's-" He went to speak, but abruptly stopped. Clearing his throat, he tried again. "It's Atlas, my dear. He is sick." Galahad's cheeks glistened with shed tears and his throat bobbed convulsively as he tried to keep from breaking down.

Without a word, she leapt off the bed and ran.

Her feet threatened to slip on the tiled hallway floor, but she managed to stay upright and skidded around the corner, slamming into the wall. She kept running without looking back.

The dull thud of a failing heart and hitched gasps of air filled the house like a dull roar as she descended the stairs. Her unheeded steps echoed through his room like thunder in a cave as she barreled towards his side.

Her gaze fell upon his brittle skin.

Hiss.

The rattle of air pushing between gritted teeth was as loud as the machines that he was connected to. Morra stopped breathing; her lungs suddenly unable to hold air within their chambers. They took no oxygen, reserving it for him. Shuddering with a sob, she reached for him with desperate, involuntary movements. When her palm touched his frail arm. His dull face shifted her way, but his eyes didn't meet hers.

His flesh, muscles and skin twisted and contorted, almost snapping his bones in its force. Clench jawed; he breathed out slowly.

Without a shirt covering him, she saw the blackness.

It ran through his body as if a spider had encased his veins from the inside. The sickly color traced its way from below his heart outward. Clawing at his neck, slithering down his arms and entwining him in a battle and the inkiness was winning.

Wetness streaked her cheeks, cascading over her nose. Silence embedded itself into the walls and every tear that fell became audible. She choked down the scream as fear seized her heart and, for the first time in years; she prayed.

She knelt, the air around them heavy.

Her finger, pale and shaking, reached out, touching his skin, a cold, colorless canvas. His eyes were glassy and distant as she took in the sight of him. There was a faint smell of antiseptic in the air, but beneath were hints of death and decay. The sickly sweet smell clung to the room, making her stomach churn.

Her trembling fingers cradled his icy hand as she closed her eyes and continued her whispered prayers. After pleading with every god she could name she found green eyes boring into her own. The corners of his mouth moved, trying to complete a smile, and her heart shattered.

His clumsy touch wiped the waterfalls on her cheeks away.

"Please, *please* live," Morra begged, silent tears escaped her lips. She didn't know if her pleas were meant for him or the universe.

"What happened?" Morra asked Kahadin without taking her eyes off of Atlas. She refused to take her eyes off him for even a moment, but she knew he would be in the room. He wouldn't leave his best friend.

A strained voice rasped against her ears. "Time poisoning."

Before she could ask what that meant, Atlas tried to speak.

"Mor-" blood spluttered from his mouth as his eyes scrunched in pain. Letting out a small moan, he tried again.

"Morra, I am sorry."

"Shh, ssh." She pushed the wet mop of hair from his forehead, telling him to save his strength.

"Life with you would have been enough for me." The words came out, muddled through blood tinged lips. "I know you don't believe in gods, but mine let me live my life with you. And when I prayed, they answered," he spoke, grasping her hand weakly, his voice like sandpaper on freshly cut skin.

"They let me see you one last time."

She shook her head, pain swelling inside her until she could no longer gaze at him. Her head fell forward, and her body shook with the weight of her cries.

"I just need you to know you were worth all the pain and struggle in my life. Loving you was enough for me and I- I can die knowing a love like ours."

"You bastard. Stop talking."

Quiet footsteps sounded behind her, quiet sniffles and murmurs, but she paid them no mind. She knew everyone must be there, but she refused to focus on them, only Atlas.

Morra shook her head, too grief-stricken to speak, but before she could back away, Atlas reached out with a weak hand and grabbed hold of her.

"No, I can't." His throat bobbed painfully as the poisonous inky tendrils dug its fingers in until all he could do was gasp for air. The blackened ichor of blood trickled from his ears and nose.

He pulled her down, so that they were eye level, "I love you, Morra." He barely managed to get through those three words before a coughing fit wracked him. But it was enough; it was almost too much.

She knew that this may be their last moment together, and she fought back another round of tears threatening to fall from her eyes so that she could look at him one last time.

Touching his face gently, she memorized every line on it, trying to imprint it in her memory. Her thoughts and feelings didn't matter, only letting him go mattered. She didn't get to say goodbye to her mom, and she would be damned if she didn't tell him.

Morra mustered up a smile.

"I love you too," she whispered, as she gazed mournfully into Atlas' beautiful green eyes for one last time. She leaned in and pressed a gentle kiss against his lips. Tears streamed down her cheeks as they parted ways, and she watched him slip away until there was nothing left but an empty shell in front of her.

Morra fell into him and let his lifeless body hold her as she sobbed into his still chest, "I love you."

She pulled back and gazed at his face for the last time, and refused to look away or move. Morra became frozen, unable to speak, move, breathe.

Her chest had been cleaved open and Morra didn't know if her heart was still beating, frankly she did not care if it was. As Morra blankly stared at his lifeless green eyes, she hoped it had. The world around her went grey, and she understood her mother in a way she never wished.

Numbness radiated from her body, and her mind, blanketed her senses and her vision. The chaos became quiet, the turmoil cooled, and she was submerged in a dark sea. Waves of guilt and anguish splashed on her and left her body wet with their salt. Maybe that was just the tears.

Morra was nothing but a shell, a hollow building, with no sunlight shining through it. The only sensation was the itchiness of Atlas' drying blood on her hands. Morra didn't want to wash it off. The last piece of him, his kiss, viscerally stained her lips and after it was gone... so was he.

Closing her eyes, she listened to the conversation outside her bathroom door. Hands had pulled her away from his body some time ago, but she paid no attention to their maneuvering nor to the words.

"How long has she been like this?" The muffled voice was rough, tear stained.

Another replied, deeper, older than the first, "Since we pulled her off Atlas after he passed."

"Pulled her?"

"She wouldn't let go." Kahadin.

The crack in his voice made her eyes close. Not wanting to hear the muffled conversation, she flicked the tap all the way on. Morra didn't want to step in, but as the numbness filled her now empty heart, she couldn't find the will to care.

Nothing seemed to matter now.

Steam billowed from the curtain, and she got in, not minding the burning water. At least she felt something. The blood turned the water red, swirling around the drain. The dirt and grime washed from her body, but no force of water could wash away the pain.

Finishing up, she dressed in clothes someone laid out for her. Probably Kahadin. Adorned in sweatpants and a flannel button up that belonged to Atlas, she wrapped her hair in the beige terry cloth towel and once again peered into the mirror.

The eyes staring back at her weren't the same ones that had been there hours ago. No, the eyes gazing back at her held no laughter or joy, didn't show the heart that was always too big for her body. They were dull and lifeless.

Unable to look, she moved away, pushing the heavy cedar door open. Leaving the bathroom, her bare feet sounded heavy as she walked towards the voices.

Balin, Kahadin, and Galahad stood there waiting for her. Their faces hung, aged with grief, eyes red from their own tears. She wasn't the only one to lose someone she loved, but she couldn't ask, she couldn't speak.

Kahadin moved first, reaching for Morra, and pulling her into his arms, breaking his usual icy shield. He held her together with a strength she didn't possess. His warm sweater smelled like cedar and patchouli, and tears streamed down her face at the smell of home. She had missed him so much, but that heaviness seemed like a flicker of a shadow to the pain she now felt. How she wished she could go back.

He let her cry in his arms as she clung to him as if he were her lifeline. After a moment, he gently guided her away from the others and out of the room they had been standing in. Morra stayed in Kahadin's embrace as he led them through the Manor, but she paid no attention to their destination or the hallways they traveled down. She could hear muted conversations following far behind. But she chose to ignore them in favor of losing herself in Kahadin's warmth and steady heartbeat.

Eventually, they stopped outside a large wooden door. He opened the door to reveal a dim room, filled with dark furniture and small tables with books. There was a large comfortable couch with pillows. He guided her to the couch and helped her sit, never once leaving her side.

When everyone had sat down, Isolde addressed the family,

"How did that *boy* get time sickness?"

Morra expected vitriol to run off her tongue, but with a tone that complimented the mascara stains across her cheeks, Morra knew her heart had been broken as well. Her lips, normally made up in a perfect red bow, now quivered. His death devastated Isolde, and for the first time, Morra felt something towards her aunt.

"I do not know," Galahad croaked as raised a shaky hand, wiping his face. "It must have been the Enemies of the Past," he muttered under his breath. The family gasped, quickly talking while Morra sat lost, not understanding.

"What do you mean?" she questioned, looking up for the first time since being sat down.

Every family member was present, huddled together on a sea of red leather couches and chairs. The fire blazed in the hearth as sparks of vengeance danced dangerously between everyone in the room. It went unnoticed as the heavy snowfall blanketed the earth, but Morra could see it.

Atlas had been deeply loved by each person in the room, and now each face had gritted teeth and watery eyes, desperately wondering why he had been taken away from them.

"Time sickness happens when the past is changed beyond repair. When a moment of time is changed too much, the world lashes out on us. We have to go back to our own time, or it kills us. Atlas took a one-way trip. He couldn't go back." Voices of confusion rung out as Galahad told them how Atlas became a member of their family, but Morra heard none of it. Instead, a voice replaced Galahads, one that echoed loudly in her head. The colors in the room swirled around, sweat pricking on the back of her neck as she listened to the haunted voice.

Rushing off to war without knowing the cost...Seek for the bones of the loved...Until the drip of time caught up.

Her heart began to race as she realized the terrible truth. Looking down, Morra saw blood embedded under her nails as her hands shook. *I killed him, I killed him* , she thought as her throat tightened like a noose. *I changed time, and he died a slow, painful death. I killed him.*

Suddenly a hand touched her, making her flinch. Concern shone in Balin's eyes. "Are you okay?"

She couldn't reply, couldn't even lift her head to look at her family as shame filled her. And understanding.

Kahadin spoke next, "I think we sho-"

Before he could finish, Morra bolted out the heavy doors, running to the cartography room. Eyes crazed, she ransacked the room throwing paper as she went, searching. Searching for anything that could tell her how she fixes what she had done.

Creaking caused her to whip her gaze around. "What are you doing?" Kahadin stood, wide-eyed, staring at the mess. Morra shot an icy glare at his cautious words. Ignoring him, she went back to her frantic search. A warm hand wrapped around her biceps, pausing her movements. "Morra?"

"Leave," she said coldly, grinding her teeth together.

"Just tell me what's going on." Morra ripped her arm from his grip.

"Please?" he begged. Concern, frustration, and grief swirling around in his voice like a tornado. Ignoring him caused the twister to hit and he raised his voice, "He was my friend first now you will tell me, or I will go inform Grandfatherabout what ever the fuck this is."

Scowling at him, Morra hissed through gritted teeth as salty tears streamed down her face, "I am fixing this. I killed him," her voice broke. "I have to fix it."

All of her anger disappeared like a flash of smoke, and she dropped to the floor, sobbing. She cried at the unfairness of the world. She kept losing everyone she loved, and each time, it was her fault. Her mother died because of her, and so did Atlas and Morra couldn't do it again.

She couldn't lose another person, not him.

"Morra, please." Kahadin sat in front of her, tears gathered on his long eyelashes. It made her feel like a monster.

"Don't cry," she whispered, scooting closer and wrapping her arms around him. Her heart couldn't handle him crying. Not Kahadin and his stoic predictability. She couldn't watch him break too. "I am so sorry; I will fix it." Morra whimpered, silently begging him for forgiveness.

They sat like that for some time, but eventually he looked up at his cousin and friend. "I do not know what happened, but I am coming with you." His hardened gaze gave no room for argument. Nonetheless, Morra resolutely told him no, this was her fault, and it was her time to make it right or die trying. She couldn't watch his body be lowered into the ground and keep on living knowing she put him there. "You can't stop me," he informed her.

"You don't know where I am going." Neither did Morra, but she had an idea.

Nostradamus.

He would have the answers, but he refused her once in the 18th century, so she knew she had to go back farther. She couldn't jump from anywhere else, so France it was. Her guess was during the rule of Henry II, Atlas said something about a jump point. It was all she had.

Kahadin, lips pressed, called her bluff, "You don't know where or when. You have only jumped once. Do you really want to do this on your own?"

Morra couldn't take it. Silently she stood, leaving Kahadin sitting in the wake of her mess. He couldn't come. She refused to drag others into this. If she lost another person... Kahadin coming would be putting him in danger. Closing her bedroom door, she took just a moment to sit in the terror before getting to work.

Shoving clothes into her backpack only took minutes and when it was done, she headed towards the door, knowing what she needed to do next.

She felt sick staring into the empty room, Atlas' room. His body had been removed at some point. Papers and books still were scattered around just like that first day, but now if she looked closely, she could see dried red dots coating some of the pages. Closing her steel eyes, she willed her feet to move and after a moment of utter despair, they did.

Research hung pinned to a corkboard by the window. Slowly, she moved towards it. Pictures of an astrolabe sat in the center. Times, dates, pieces, and scribblings were pinned next to it. Blindly, she gathered it all as the air became heavier and the bile creeping up the back of her throat became unbearable. Shoving it into the bag, Morra decided she would deal with it once she was back in France, but before she turned to leave, her eye caught against something on the table.

A red wax stamp gleamed in the little light leaking through the blinds. It was old and broken, but she recognized it. Her letters lay on the table and paper clipped to each one was another letter with scratchy handwriting. Morra picked them up with reverence and folded each one neatly as numbness filled her shaking hands. After safely tucking them in her backpack, she turned to give the room one last look before leaving.

Traveling back to her room, she decided to climb out the window. She couldn't be stopped now.

The trellis wrapped up the side of the house like the waxy green vines that lived on it. Peeking her head out the window with her leather bag weighing on her shoulder, she shook the metal, making sure it wouldn't crumble under her weight. Shutting her eyes, she gathered her courage. The climb from the fourth floor was trying, the metal slick from ice and snow.

Finally getting to the ground on shaky knees, she sucked in a deep breath, the cool air soothing her tattered lungs and steadying her heart. Morra took a minute sitting in the wet earth, the soil parting under her prying finger. This would be what would encase Atlas if she couldn't save him. She wanted to scream at the injustice of it all.

Taking in the cool night air, watching the stars twinkle in the sky, she laid her head against the house, tears welling in her eyes. All she wanted to do was punch something, but despair grew in between the anger, the pain, and the guilt. It grew like weeds out of concrete. Given time, they would take over her heart. Morra almost wanted to laugh at the sick irony of her life. When she first moved in, she had planned to run away and now she was actually running away. Things had changed so much.

A foot lightly tapped her, breaking her from her spiraling thoughts.

"Come on."

Opening her eyes, she gazed at the familiar face, the one she yelled at. Wiping her tears, she stood, brushing mud off of herself. In a small voice she asked, "Where are we going?"

"France," he said simply, tiredness coating his frame. "1556."

Morra fell into him, wrapping herself around him, hoping he understood the words she couldn't say.

CHAPTER
NINTEEN

It felt like free falling straight into a void. It might have only been a few seconds, but the sticky blackness of the fall kept Morra trapped for hours, days.

Suddenly she was in a murky pool, drowning, tendrils curled around her into an unkind hug, a bone crushing pressure. Every breath felt like she was inhaling inky fluid. When she landed, she laid on the dirty ground, trying to orient herself. This jump was different, darker. She didn't feel the hopes and dreams or people around, just shadows and despair. There were no gold or silver lights this time, just blinding darkness.

Morra could still feel the pressure and every breath burned. Opening her eyes, she stared at the stars, actual stars. They were everywhere, as the light of the day had yet to make an appearance. Cold air breezed past her, causing goosebumps to scatter across her skin, making a constellation like the night sky. It cut through her nausea and gave her the strength to pull herself into a sitting position.

She hadn't fully thought this plan through and now, back on French soil, she questioned herself. Kahadin had fleshed out a plan; it wasn't the best, and it stood on a lot of hope and 'what ifs' but it was all she had.

The last time Morra meddled, it got someone she loved killed, but she knew she couldn't stop. If nothing else, she needed time away from the faces destroyed by grief, the anger everyone had at the world, and the knowledge that she caused it. Bile rose in her throat when she thought about the pity in their eyes. The poor girl who lost the boy she loved, they would think. She had wanted to scream at them, yell, throw things, but she didn't because she didn't want them to know what she had done.

"Oof." Kahadin tumbled to the ground, managing to tuck his body in a roll on the impact. He unfurled gracefully into a sitting position. Standing, he dusted off his jacket and looked down his stupid, perfect nose at her disheveled form.

Smirking lightly, he raised a single eyebrow.

Morra made a mocking face at him as she got up. Compared to him, she looked like she got trampled. A thin layer of grey dust covered her now torn jeans and her simple black long sleeve shirt. Her once tame hair was now knotted and had bits of gravel fall out when she shook it in an attempt to subdue it.

Reaching down, Morra grabbed her equally dirty bag. It held up well during the travel. Despite the thin layer of dust, the cinnamon-colored leather was untouched. She knew she would have to change soon, so they didn't get caught before they even started. Kahadin must have thought the same thing as he ushered her to a corner of the building, hiding her in the shadows with his tall and lean frame.

Kahadin had truly thought this adventure through more than Morra. He grabbed the clothes from the wardrobe, appropriate attire. Pulling out a dress, he showed it to her. It was beautiful and immaculately detailed. The dark velvet gown had a rounded neckline and a small ruffle necklace bordering the dress. On top was a kirtle, an overlay lavender colored skirt contrasted with the velvet below. Flowers and leaves embroidered the fabric with silver thread.

Kahadin took pins from her hand, helping pull the messy waves into a delicate mountain of swirls and braids. He wrestled her tresses until it felt like strands of spun silk, a soft, luxurious texture. With the last pearl pin delicately placed in her hair, he changed to be presentable for court. Dressed in a suit to match, they made their way down the street. Her dress was extravagant, but to garner the attention of the court, and to be allowed to stay without fuss, Morra had to flaunt wealth. During the redeye flight to France, Kahadin told her about the wedding.

The marriage of Mary Stuart, Queen of Scotts, and the French Prince, Francis Valois, would be a monstrous event that gave them the opportunity to be seen.

The women in Marie's court had taught her many things. They always been one upping each other, spending either daddy's money or their husbands. It was how you gained attention and earned status, and Morra was willing to play any of their games to save Atlas.

She would play better than the rest and do whatever it took.

Adorned with the finest fabrics and jewels, she took Kahadin's elbow as they walked towards one of the many empty chateaux that belonged to the family.

They arrived at Notre Dame at the same time as most of the procession. Morra looked down, taking a shaky breath as she fiddled with the exquisite beading on her gown, the same from the morning. She had traveled to France before, but this time, the rush of excitement never came. Worry filled her heart as she thought of Atlas dying in her arms, the image was burned in her mind, the scream she heard when he took his last breath. The scream she knew she created still rang in her ears like a phantom banshee following her every move.

The last jump had no real consequences. Of course, she wanted to help her family get her dad back, but this, she thought biting on her nails, would determine if she would get to see the love of her life again.

She felt Atlas' death like a soldier missing a limb. The pain cut her insides like a dull blade being dragged across her flesh. Viscous blood spilling out as gore splattered walls and stained the floor.

Tears welled in her eyes as she blindly looked out of the carriage at the cheerful faces. It surprised her they weren't staring at the rot that escaped her chest; it must have been noticeable. Morra smelled the reek of death palatable in the air. It seemed to follow her wherever she went, and with each death, it grew. Those she loved always died. The scythe of the grim loomed above her. As she looked over at her cousin, she knew the longer he was around her, the more likely his fate would end blood-soaked like the rest.

Piercing grey eyes pulled her from her thoughts. "Don't. It will not help and if this works, then what we went through will be prevented." Kahadin's brows knitted as he reached over and grabbed his cousin's delicate hand. "I am here."

As the ornate carriage gently rocked to a stop in front of the cathedral, Morra hung her head as she really saw him for the first time since they left. Dark circles framed his dull, almost lifeless eyes. Guilt rushed through her. She lost the love of her life, and he lost his best friend.

"I'm sorry. I should have asked about how you are doing." This person was supposed to be her friend, yet she had not yet checked on him once. Shame swelled underneath his unwavering scrutiny.

"It doesn't matter how I am feeling," he said, mouth pinched, eyes boring into hers with a seriousness she had never seen on his face.

Angered, she argued, "Yes, it does." She staunchly refuse to dismiss his emotions, even if he wanted to.

Defeat swam in his eyes as his shoulders dropped, his posture softened his words. "It only matters if we can't bring him back." He turned away from her. "It only matters if we fail. Now pull yourself together." Sitting tall, he prepared for his entrance, a stony mask firmly in place.

Following his lead, she pulled her shoulders back, extending her neck as she took a deep breath. She could do this.

The carriage came to a halt; the door swung open, and a gentleman clad in a suit bowed as Kahadin made his way out. Reaching a glove clad hand in, her cousin offered his help. She stepped out in her gown and high heels, the announcer proclaimed their names to the rest of the courtiers. Morra hid her surprise, raising an eyebrow to Kahadin in a silent question as they regally walked down the rolled out carpet.

Her eyes were drawn towards the large stained-glass window as they made their way into the cathedral. The wedding decor was beautiful, nothing less than the best for the marriage of the Queen of Scotland and France's own Dauphin. Kahadin and Morra had planned for this moment in time, where dignitaries and nobles from all over the world gathered to celebrate. The presence of the Seelie family would not be unexpected, considering their presence in French history.

The late April day seemed so calm. A time when birds were still fattening after winter, and the air was thin with early spring. Despite the beauty of it all, there was an invisible cloak that seemed to suffocate the rapidly brightening earth. Morra didn't know if it was the ostentatious event or the fear clawing at her throat. She did her best to not let either notion show on her face.

As the pair found their seats in the balcony section, they watched the other nobles and guests walk in. The air was thick with anticipation for the royal family. Morra sat back as far as her gown would allow when the church bells started ringing. All of Paris and all of France would know with each ring that the moment had come. Everyone in the cathedral stood as the king took his steps inside. On his right was a woman much older than him.

"Who is that?" Morra boldly asked the woman next to her in a hushed tone.

She raised an eyebrow at her. "That is Diane de Poitiers, the king's mistress. You must be new here."

Morra nod absentmindedly while staring at the official French mistress. Dressed in a lavish black and white gown, her hair was twisted in an up-do fixed in place with pins that matched. The king himself wore black and white as well.

The next person who walked in was a stark comparison to them. The king's wife, Catherine Medici, wore an emerald green gown accented with gold buttons and lace. Her golden locks cascaded down her neck to rest on her shoulders. A few strands had escaped her control and fell onto her pale cheeks. She walked with her head high, looking the noble straight in their eyes, daring them to make a comment.

She was the woman who hired Nostradamus and who they needed to get an audience with. As if he read Morra's thoughts, Kahadin leaned towards her. "She is the one we need to meet."

A chill ran down her spine as she watched the woman glide through the church. The room became alive with whispers. Someone murmured of her flights with the dark arts, others spoke of her prowess.

Morra carefully looked down from the balcony to see the Dauphin with his father. The king refused to acknowledge his wife Catherine de' Medici's presence as his mistress fawned over him like a child.

Kahadin's elbow connected with her ribs, and with a wince she smoothed the disgust that slipped through her mask. She looked around, hoping nobody saw her. Thankfully, everyone seemed to be distracted by the Cardinal dressed in blood red walking his niece down the aisle. The sickly boy who would become king await them on the dais.

Mary was indeed beautiful, dressed in a lily white wedding gown that buttoned to the neck with pearls. Attached to her gown was a velvet grey train that glided across the polished floor. Adorned on her head was a crown sparkling with jewels that proclaimed her status as a queen in her own right.

Glancing around, all eyes were glued to the couple except one; a pair of steel-grey eyes peered at her. The stranger, catching her eye, tipped his head in acknowledgment. Nudging Kahadin who was also scanning their new environment, alerting him to the man looking at them. Familiar eyes set on an unknown face, Morra continued to study the stranger, nodding gently to him. It must have been enough for him as he pulled his gaze from them and back to the soon to be rulers of France.

"Do you know who that is?" Morra asked, keeping her voice low.

"Not with any true certainty, but I have an idea of who it might be," Kahadin replied quietly, his gaze firmly on the older man.

All voices hushed as Mary stopped at the altar. An archbishop stood ready to perform the ceremony. Halfway through, Morra had to force down a yawn at the long and boring speech. She couldn't wait until it was done, but she knew there were hours ahead of them, hours that could be life or death.

Once the ceremony was done, the happy couple made their way to the home of the archbishop where the wedding reception took place. Slowly, the courtier filtered out of the cathedral.

"Come on, let's follow them," Morra suggested as the couple paraded outside to cheering commoners. Kahadin stood tall and offered his hand.

The pair were let in without fuss, which they were both thankful for. All the rooms in the archbishop's house were made of thick stone, decorated with intricate carvings and lit by wrought iron sconces that held candles. Larger candles flickered in the glass chandeliers, throwing light and shadows across the tapestries and the rest of the room. Lavishly decorated with wallpaper drenched in golds and reds and royal blues. Tapestries hung on the walls, depicting hunts and royal events. Even the floor was a work of art with a mosaic of precious stones and metals.

"This is beautiful," Morra exclaimed, her eyes taking it all in.

"You wouldn't say that if you had to clean it." Kahadin's voice sounded ominous.

Morra rolled her eyes, barely resisting the urge to shove her posh cousin. "As if you have ever cleaned anything in your life."

He smirked at her before strolling off.

Looking around, Morra caught sight of the man, the one from the balcony. With narrowed eyes, he tracked her every move. Morra continued to stare at him. His eyes met hers, unyielding. A tap on her shoulder broke the staring contest.

"And who might you be?" a soft feminine voice spoke up. Turning, she found the woman dressed in an extravagant white dress with black accents. Her moonlight hair fell to her waist and her lips were in a pursed smile.

With a small curtsy, she replied, "My name is Morra, my lady."

"Why have I never seen you before? I know all of those in this court, but not you." Her French accent softened the scrutiny of her questions.

"My cousin and I have never attended a French court before, but my family is an old prominent name."

Diane examined her with a smile that never reached her eyes. They held curiosity and danger. She wasn't one Morra wanted to piss off. Morra was smart enough to recognize that Madame de Pointe had kept her position through her wits as much as her... relationship with the king. The gleam in her eye told Morra that she was assessing her, trying to figure out if she was a threat or asset.

Friend or foe.

She was neither, and she hoped it would stay that way.

"And who might that family be?" She used a demure tone as her shield, but before Morra had the chance to use hers as a sword, she felt a presence behind her.

"That would be my family, Madam de Pointier." A deep voice rolled over her body. She glanced behind her and saw the familiar stormy eyes. His dark, well-groomed hair complimented his simple but elegant clothing. A doublet of dark brown sat over a white shirt tucked into brown breeches. His boots were polished, and his posture was straight and proud.

"Ah! Duc Seelie," she slipped the young girl a sly glance, "you should have just said. Duc, how do you know this... Morra?"

"She is my niece, my sister's daughter. She wanted me to bring her here as her debut to the French court."

Madam de Pointier giggled like a young girl despite her being in her late forties. "Hunting for a husband, I see." Well painted nail gripped Morra's chin, turning her back and forth, "With a face like this, who wouldn't want to marry her, no?"

"Diane!" Beckoned by the king, the woman released her hold and walked away without a goodbye.

Turning to see her rescuer, she gazed at him up close for the first time. Light skin and dark features framed wild grey eyes, and his voice rumbled from his broad chest. Crows' feet wrinkles sat on the edge of his eyes, telling of both age and joy.

"Thank you for your assistance."

"No need for thanks. We are family." Setting a hand on her back, the older man guided her to a place less crowded. Fewer ears to hear a very private conversation, she assumed.

"I must ask when you are from, who you are here with, and why you are here." He grilled, eyebrows knit together in thought.

"I am here with my cousin; I am sure you saw him during the ceremony. We come from 2012."

"Huh. That is rather far away." He paused, surveying the room before peering at her intensely.

She silently hoped he wouldn't question why they were here again. She didn't need anyone to stop her. But to no avail, he caught on instantly to the moment of hesitance. He didn't ask again, just raised an eyebrow at her impatiently.

"We came here to save someone's life. To do so, I need to speak with Nostradamus."

"The queen's soothsayer?" he mused, leaning back against the rough stone wall casting an imperious shadow.

"Indeed," Morra said softly, in case others were listening. It seemed strange that he referred to Nostradamus like he was the queen's pet versus a family member, she thought. Maybe he didn't know he was part of the family. If he didn't, she wasn't going to inform him.

"He is a recluse, from what I heard, very private. How do you plan to get an audience with him?"

Scanning the room from the balcony, her eyes spot the figure who she needed help from. "By getting a private audience with the queen herself."

Disbelief swam in his face. "You must tread carefully; she is not someone who is easily approached. Especially since the court is foreign to both of you. But Nostradamus is dangerous."

Morra nodded. She knew all too well how cunning this queen could be. She was called the serpent queen for a reason, but Morra knew she was the only chance. Not only of meeting with Nostradamus, but getting the right information from him.

"I would have thought you would have warned me against meeting with queen, not warning against Nostradamus himself," she said, raising her eyebrow at him.

"He is not to be trusted," he cautioned again. The duke wouldn't look at her, keeping his gaze averted. "He bears watching. As family, it is my duty to help you."

She shook her head at him, not wanting him involved. It never ended well for those who got close. She didn't even want Kahadin here; she couldn't come into this man's life and ruin it in her attempt to absolve herself and give breath to Atlas' lungs. If the reaper hung around the corner, she couldn't put him in the path and make him an accomplice.

"That is just it. I don't want you to get hurt." The gravity of her words made her voice crack. It shook her to the core, leaving her hollow.

The duke's eyebrows furrowed as he scanned Morra's face. She knew he probably wasn't used to real emotion, and she knew her face couldn't hide the weight of the ghosts she carried on her back. Shadows danced in her eyes and demons nipped at her heels. Morra knew that he saw it as his scrunched brows softened. "I won't get hurt." Grey eyes that looked just like her own stared at her with such sadness as he murmured, "I better introduce you to the queen then."

Morra let out a heavy breath, thankful but unable to say so. All she could do was look at him, at his dark hair and angular jaw, and try not to give in to the protection he offered.

"Thanks," she said after he led her back into the ballroom. He led her through the throng of people and out into the elegant gardens. Someone had carved the hedges into different animals, some rearing up on their hind legs, mouth open in a silent howl. The opulence was impressive, with a large garden, hedges, and fountains. Ostentatious, but less so than the ugly perfection of Versailles. Turning her eyes to the crowd, she spotted Kahadin's tall frame talking to a younger girl, well dressed, probably noble born. Catching his eye, Morra motioned him to her. She watched as he excused himself from the girl, gazing at him with stars in her eyes. Once the blond sauntered to them, she made introductions.

"Kahadin, this is..." Morra paused, glancing back at the taller man. She had never got his name. The man looked between them, an amused smile stretched across his face, and she saw the flash of recognition. Kahadin knew he was family; his smile matched Balin's.

"What is your first name?" Morra asked, the tip of her ears turning red.

"Berluse."

"He's going to introduce us to the queen," she informed him as they made their way to the queen. A trumpet stopped their movement as the bishop declared the official bedding.

Morra listened, head cocked to the side, with an inquiring glance to the duke who in turn smiled at her naivety. "It is tim e to watch the couple consummate the marriage."

Her nose scrunched up. "We have to..." she trailed off questioningly.

Berluse chuckled quietly, shaking his head, "No, that is the job of the King and Queen of France and those within the church. Unfortunately, that does mean we will not be meeting Queen Catherine tonight."

Morra and Kahadin shared a small glance but before either teen could talk, the duke interjected, "Naturally, it would make sense for the two of you to stay at my chalet. Since the court already is aware of our relations."

"We would not want to trouble you sir," Kahadin told him warily.

"It is no trouble for family," he told them while guiding them out to the carriage that waited to take him home. "There are details we must discuss, though."

Morra felt a lump forming in her throat as they drove up the winding road that led to the Seelie Chalet. Berluse's voice was low and steady as he planned their cover stories; they were here ostensibly for Morra to make a marriage match. Her stomach lurched as the road dipped sharply. The plan was a good one, even if it caused her mind to revolt. She had received many proposals the last time she was here, but that was before. But like Kahadin said, *'It only matters if we can't bring him back'*.

The chateau was nestled in the hills, well-hidden yet conveniently close to the palace. Berluse wasn't worried about being watched, which Morra was thankful for. The carriage rocked back and forth, and her eyes grew heavy. She shifted slightly under the weight of Kahadin, who fell asleep on her shoulder, she didn't want to wake him. Morra knew he hadn't slept as much as she should. Her eyes drifted from her cousin to the man in front of her.

Noticing her gaze, he looked up. Morra hoped the man could help, and as she watched him look between her and Kahadin, she knew he would. It was the look her mom gave her when she thought Morra wasn't looking. Of course, she didn't know what it meant back then, but that look of *whatever it takes* had become familiar.

Early in the morning, the group, now accompanied by Duchess Charlotte of Clermont-en-Beauvaisis, made their way to the palace. After being announced, they were shown to a lavish room off the grand hall. Gilded furniture adorned the room, with it a marble fireplace and dark grey tapestries hung on stone walls. An intricate rug covered the floor.

The duke and duchess perched onto a settee while Morra and Kahadin took chairs opposite them. A servant entered with refreshments and left shortly after. "Have you thought about how long you'll be staying with us?" the duchess asked warmly.

Morra glanced at Kahadin before answering. "We're not entirely sure yet," she admitted.

Charlotte nodded in understanding. "Well, while you're here, we'll do everything in our power to help you. We have connections all over the court, but you must represent us well here. It's the only thing we ask in return."

Tradition was paramount to the French court, and that perception was everything, Morra knew that. She wouldn't jeopardize them.

She could hardly keep still, her knee bouncing nervously as they waited. When the large doors creaked open, it signaled for them to rise to their feet. As they walked into the greeting room, a herald announced, "The King will see you now." The nobles stood and made their way to the throne room. They had to wait a while until they finally glimpsed the king and queen.

Morra's eyes widened when she saw the woman in black and white sitting next to the king's chair. The mistress greeted the nobles, and they bowed as if she held the station of the queen. "Where is the queen?" Morra whispered to Charlotte.

The duchess replied, scathingly, "Running the country while they do this." Morra smirked at Charlottes quite words. There was no love lost between her and the mistress. Morra also smiled at the trust; those words could be treasonous in the wrong hands.

As they approached the thrones, Morra curtsied and paid her respects, while Charlotte and Berluse stood behind her. "Lord Duc Berluse, it is a pleasure to see you again," the king said with a nod.

"Your highness, I would like to introduce my niece, Lady Morra, and my nephew, Sir Kahadin." Berluse gestured.

"It is an honor to meet you, sire," they spoke at the same time, bowing slightly. The lords and ladies in waiting filed into the room and greeted the pair one by one.

They stood off in a corner of the room waiting. "She said she would see us, right?" Morra asked Charlotte, who nodded.

After a moment a servant approached them, bowing respectfully before leading them away from the other nobles. He led them to a small open room that overlooked the gardens. The chandelier sparkled in the light twinkling off of its numerous crystal drops. Warmth encased them as the smell of fresh bread wafted through the air. In front of them sat the indomitable queen.

Catherine de Medici was a formidable person. One Morra knew she shouldn't cross nor belittle, so standing in front of her, she would treat her not as a dainty queen that was no more than a political chess piece. No, Morra knew Catherine embodied a predator. Sharp, perceptive eyes watched as she dipped low in a curtsy. She wasn't an expert at playing this game of chess that they seemed to breathe, but she had to try.

Brown eyes tracked her, and Morra fought the urge to submit. Instead, she stood taller, tipping her chin in defiance; not enough to be disrespectful, but enough to seem strong.

"It is nice to meet you, mam'zelle Morra." Her voice was like velvet, smooth and warm. Morra marveled at the refined way she spoke. "What brings you to our court?"

"I come seeking a favor," Morra told her, jumping straight to the point. What she read and heard of the queen in front of her alluded to a cunning woman who didn't like to be lied to or led.

Catherine looked at the girl in front of her, assessing.

"Marriage?" She pursed her lips. Morra watched as disappointment flashed in her eyes, even though it never crossed her face.

Looking back at Berluse, Morra continued, hoping she didn't mess this up. "No, that is a cover we are using to explain my presence. I am here because I need to talk to Nostradamus." An eyebrow raised on her face and curiosity lit up the queen's eyes.

"What could bring you here? What is so important, child?" She spoke in a soft voice, each word commanding authority and confidence.

Morra paused.

As if seeing her hesitation, the Queen of France ordered everyone out of the room with a flourish of her wrist. Her dark eyes trained on the girl before her. Kahadin's jaw rocked, words on his tongue ready to argue, but with a reassuring glance from Morra he nodded and was guided out by Berluse. Finally, they were alone.

Never shifting her gaze, the queen, in a whispery voice, commanded, "Do not lie to me, child. For I will know, and you will not be successful." It was a warning.

A threat.

For just a moment, Morra could picture Queen Catherine holding a knife to Atlas' throat. She could hear him take his last breath, gurgling as the silver slipped through his neck like a ribbon. She closed her eyes and willed the image away. It wouldn't help her to be emotional. Steeling herself, she locked those images up in her mind.

"I am here because he may be the only person who can help me save the man I love."

"And where is this man?" the queen questioned.

Telling the queen about when she was from felt like a monstrous task. Lying was an option, but if she did, the queen would most likely know and not help. If she told her the truth, though, the queen might think she was mad, and that would not help. Catherine could use anything to her advantage. Either way, it was a risk and gambling wasn't one of her skills.

She swallowed nervously. "Already dead, but with help, I could stop him from dying."

"Ah." Silence hung between the two. The queen drank her cup of tea while Morra waited for more, but it never came.

After a few minutes, Morra broke down.

"That's it? No question, you just believe me?"

"Would you like me to yell witchcraft, and have you burned for heresy?"

"Well, no, but-"

"But you expected me to validate your circumstances?"

"I-" The blank look on the queen's face was infuriating. Morra couldn't think of a single thing to say.

"You are looking for Nostradamus because he is a seer," Catherine finally said.

It was an answer. "He told you? He said something about this?"

"No. Why else would a young girl, who likes to play pretend, find herself in the French court? I should think a seer would be the perfect man to have an answer for you."

Morra nodded, relieved. "Then you will help me?"

"Perhaps, but what would it benefit me?"

"Benefit?" Morra asked, appalled, her voice raising, "I watched the man I love bleed out in my arms. I held him and felt him breathe his last breath and now I have a chance to save him, and you want to know how I can benefit you." Morra's voice shook as she spoke. She had trouble finding the words. When she found them, it was with a practiced edge. "You honestly don't want to help me? The man I love is going to die and you say I have nothing to offer *you*? Have you a heart in that chest of yours?"

Catherine stared, unimpressed, "Do not play me, child. I have been a queen for twenty-seven years. I have witnessed horrors you could not begin to imagine. Do you think I do not know the feeling of love?"

She looked at her then. "I have it for my children, those who died and those who live. I have it for my husband, who has loved another woman for those years. I have it for this country, and I will do anything I can to protect it. So do not for one minute think that I know nothing about losing loved ones. I know it better than you." Speechless, Morra peered at Catherine de Medici, who apparently loved deeply and admitted it. Both admirable and terrifying.

She stood tall in her elegant green gown, "Get out or I will have you drug out of this room."

Morra felt as though someone had punched her in the chest as the weight of what had just been said hit her like a ton of bricks. No help? What else could be done?

She felt her heart drop into her stomach and the room around her became hazy. "I understand," Morra croaked, effectively ending the conversation. But she couldn't walk away, not from this. Something else needed to be said first, because if there was any hope of saving Atlas at all, Morra must tell this woman everything.

All of it.

Even if it meant coming clean about who she was and where she came from... even at the expense of her own life. Morra would tell this woman what she really wanted if it meant saving Atlas' life.

Morra's feet shuffled against the marble floor as she turned, her breathing shallow and ragged. Her heart thundered in her ears like the beat of a war drum, and within her thoughts, a voice was screaming desperately for a way to make this situation right. "I am from the future."

Catherine's eyebrows raised minutely. "Go on."

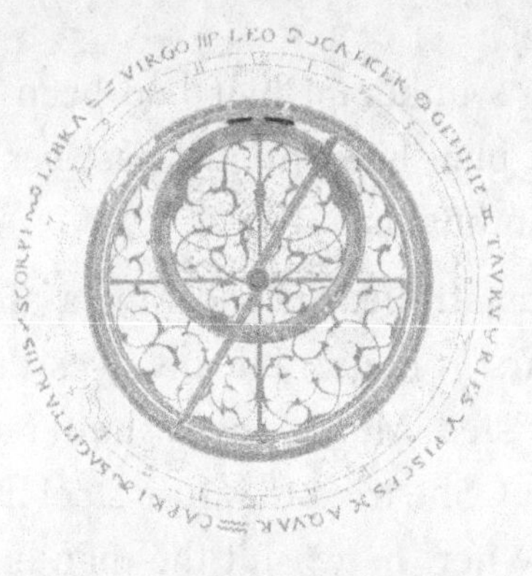

CHAPTER TWENTY

❖

Morra's leg bounced uncontrollably in anticipation, causing the floor to rattle. The nerves sat heavy in her stomach, pinning her to her seat as she waited for Nostradamus. The man himself didn't scare her. No, only the possibility of being turned down again frightened her. She hoped this younger version of the seer would give real answers.

Sat in the grand guest chamber of Queen Catherine, along with her cousin and Berluse, Morra couldn't help but spin in anticipation. Could she save him? The question occupied every inch of her brain, of her heart.

Catherine, adorned in her striking slash of green, stood watching out the tall, arched windows. The queen had changed after their initial meeting. Her new gown looked stunning on her, despite her plain face. Morra had changed as well after being chastised by the queen. Plain purple dyed the lace of the dress and Morra's unkempt hair had been forcefully wound back into a tight plait hanging just past her shoulders by one of Catherines handmaids.

Nostradamus strolled in and Morra almost mistook the man. Thirty years younger, but his eyes didn't change, still haunting and twisted. Morra's eyes shuttered, swallowing the lump in her throat. She tried to infuse steel into her spine. This man didn't know her; he wasn't the man he would be. There was still hope. Grey eyes met the black spheres and for a moment Morra became drenched in irony. They resembled scrying mirrors.

"The queen has informed me you requested my presence." His deep, scratchy voice scraped across her skin like sandpaper.

In the back of the room, Berluse lounged with Kahadin, watching. The two men knew that Morra had to fight this battle on her own.

"Yes, I did," she acknowledged, looking up at him as she stood.

"You wish to know the future? Come to me and I will tell you." As he spoke, Morra noticed the difference the years had made. Being around the man was still like dancing on a gravestone, something about it felt intrinsically wrong. But this time it was undercut by the performance of the soothsayer. "Everyone has the potential to know their own fate," he almost sang, walking around her, sizing her up. The air shifted behind her as the man circled her.

Flinching, she took a step back before jutting her jaw. "I want to prevent the death of someone I love. Tell me my future, tell me how to stop it," she demanded with a hardened voice.

Nostradamus paused and turned back to her. "Are you sure you want to know? Knowing your fate won't change it."

"Would you tell me if I could?"

Nostradamus looked down into the girl's anxious, desperate, stormy eyes gripping his own. "Yes, I will tell you. You are family, after all." A sharp inhale came from behind her, Berluse, she guessed. He knew that seeing powers ran in the family. Those who had a higher amount of fae blood inherited more gifts than just time jumping.

Morra analyzed Nostradamus, searching for something. She didn't find it. Lifting her hand, pausing just before she touched his face. As soon as her palm grazed his stubbly cheek, Nostradamus' eyes went milky white.

"Daughter born under the horned goats setting sun

Orphaned by the future and the past

Seek for the bones of the loved

Until the drip of time caught up

The present time together with the past

Two will rise in distant lands

Two powers that must be kept apart

And she who was proscribed will return to the kingdom

The one who will play the bravest parts

For times good for evil, the sweeter for the bitter

Sacrifices shall return again, and blood shall be spent

Until ancestors and forebears come forth through the depths,

Lamenting to see thus dead."

Nostradamus came back to himself with a chest tightening gasp. Heavy, oppressive air clung to the walls of the room as the silence became palpable. Suffocating. Morra stood in the center of them all. Surrounded by Kahadin's concerned gaze, Berluse's intense focus as he mouthed the prophecy, and the queen's piercing stare that seemed to weigh every word before coming to a rest on Nostradamus with a glimmer of intrigue.

"I don't care about the damn prophecy." Desperation clogged her throat. "What about Atlas? Can I find him in time and bring him back?"

The queen joined the young girl, guiding her into a chair with an unexpected softness. Nostradamus watched her with sadness and shook his head. "There is no saving him. Choices were made, one life was saved and another..."

Morra could have sworn her heart stopped beating. *What's the point of this if you can't save the people you love?*

"The drip of time caught up," Catherine echoed gently, kneeling in front of her, taking the young girl's hands in her own.

She couldn't breathe and the tears threatened to spill out.

Atlas was really dead.

"No," she keened, body collapsing into the queen. The guttural shout shook the windows with its force and echoed down the halls. Miles away people shuttered, the sound didn't reach them, nor did they know her loss, but for just a minute, the world could feel it. Like a roar from a lion rippling the water nearby, the earth absorbed her screams of sorrow and cast it across time.

Outside, the clouds parted, dumping rain on the once sunny day as if mother nature wept on her behalf.

Crazed, she began rambling as tears worked their way down her reddened cheeks. "What if, what if we... I. If I go back, I can stop it... I can fix it. Stop the revolution, kill..." Her words halted as her brain registered her words. Her horrified grey eyes stared blankly ahead. No, she couldn't do that. Atlas wouldn't want that. She glanced at the queen in front of her, completely broken.

Catherine held her steadfast, and Morra was thankful for her tight hold as she cried. When her tears started to slow, being replaced with gentle hiccupping, Catherine leaned back and looked at the damaged young girl in her eyes.

"Take that pain and stand back up and fight. Clutch it, hold it tight and never let anyone forget that the cruelty of this world did not break you. All you can do is make the pain mean something," Catherine whispered the words in her ear.

Pulling back, Morra stared at the Queen of France, knelt in front of her not knowing if she should hug the woman or scream again, but she saw the pain echoed in her face. This was a person who knew what she felt viscerally.

"What now?"

Catherine leaned back and stood gracefully. "What now indeed?" she replied with the soft-spoken grace. "Now you figure out how to move on."

Slinking back into the dark room, she curled up on the nest of blankets and glared at the letters in hand. It was like looking at a Pandora's box with no clue if the contents would soothe her or crush her. Honestly, she didn't know which would be worse.

She looked at the first letter in the stack, dated with scribbly writing, and carefully slid her finger under the seal. Morra read through each letter slowly, each one caused a knife in her heart.

At first the words were marked by happiness and longing but slowly devolved as the time sickness overtook him. The final lines of his last letter nearly broke her. '*I don't know how much time I have. I have prayed you will come back in time for me to tell you this in person, but in case... in case I don't live that long, know that I love you. I have for a long time. I wish I could have loved you longer.*'

Most days, Morra stayed in bed. She found comfort in the darkness and silence of her room. Too exhausted to move, barely able to lift her head from the pillow. Kahadin and Berluse tried their best to nurse her through her grief, but nothing seemed to work. They'd bring food for her, make sure she was comfortable and even read stories, but nothing seemed to help. Even when she did manage to get out of bed, she could wander listlessly around the chateau's grounds by herself.

One afternoon, in mid-May, a knock on the door alerted her. "Not now, Kahadin," she sluggishly yelled. The door opened, causing light to pour into the once pitch black room.

Morra squinted as her eyes adjusted. "I told you I am fine," she grumbled, turning in bed.

"Is that how you talk to the Queen of France?" Catherine scolded, her voice soft, but the hard undercurrent made Morra shoot up. Patting her hair, she tried to tame the wild locks that hadn't been brushed in days. Floating to the windows, the queen pulled the curtains and while Morra wanted to protest, but she knew the queen wouldn't take it well.

"You are going to get up and get presentable."

"Why?" Morra taunted, as anger simmered under her skin. It was childish but she couldn't help herself.

Catherine raised a challenging eyebrow and stared at her. Deflated, Morra stood up, grabbed a dress from the wardrobe ducking behind the privacy screen in the corner of the room.

"Now you are going to come with me, and you are going to help me."

"Help you do what?" she asked, getting dressed. Morra wore a burgundy square-neck dress that had a fitted bodice with long sleeves and a full skirt that flared out from the waist. Delicate pleats framed the neckline, and the thick fabric was made of sturdy and comfortable material.

She couldn't help but feel somewhat better being dressed.

And upright.

Catherine, once Morra looked up, had a soft yet devious smile on her face. "You will see, come along."

Tendrils of emotion rose in Morra, and it took a moment for her to recognize it through the grief. It was excitement.

The carriage ride rattled down the bumpy road. Morra, who despite her doubts, was now interested in whatever Catherine had planned. She shifted uncomfortably as the carriage hit another divot on the uneven road.

Catherine, on the other hand, seemed unfazed by the movement and continued to lean back against the seat in a relaxed position. Her eyes were closed as if she was napping, but Morra could tell that she wasn't sleeping but was deep in thought.

She cleared her throat to break the silence that had settled in the carriage when Catherine spoke up.

"You know I was never meant to be queen," she said, slowly opening her eyes to stare out of one of the small windows in the carriage. "I had to *learn* how to become what I am. And now, while I may not be well-loved, I am respected and feared."

Nodding slowly, she took in Catherine's words. The Queen then turned her gaze towards Morra and fixed her with a resolute look. "That is what you must do," she said seriously, "to become what you need to be in order to survive.

You must learn and move on. Life will and so shall you." She thought about her words as they continued.

Eventually, Morra asked, "So, who is abusing power?" Catherine had told her they were going to strip someone of their *'perceived'* power.

Once again Catherine paused for a long while, Morra began to think that it was a power play. It made people wait for her and the queen only spoke on her terms. Half of her words were riddles, not answers.

Morra started paying attention.

"There are some people in my court who believe they are above the rule of both France and God. We don't let it stand."

"I won't hurt anyone."

Catherine chuckled demurely. "To hurt another, you do not need to be physical. The longest lasting impression will always be with words rather than blows. And if I needed to hurt someone, do you think I would seek out a teenage girl to do my bidding?"

Catherine paused and then looked lazily out of the window again. "We are going to undermine Diane de Poitiers, the King's mistress, who has been using her influence to control the court. We will teach her that there are consequences for abusing power, and that even a mistress's reach has limits."

Morra nodded slowly, trying to understand the full implications of her words. Politics were still so foreign to her.

She wondered what the queen had in mind, there was little point in asking though. The queen would speak when she was ready.

When they arrived at Château de Chenonceau a few minutes later, Morra was still thinking about the discussion. Catherine had answered a question she didn't even know she had cared about; she had given Morra a way to move forward.

Catherine stepped out of the carriage with a grandiose air, Morra instantly fell into step behind her with a more reserved presence. It was a cold, drizzly day, but she hardly noticed as she paid attention to the way people scattered as Catherine walked.

They indeed feared her.

Morra also saw some faces of the people lingering about. The great, powerful, and feared Caterina Maria Romula di Lorenzo de' Medici, Queen of France, was wrong. There were some in France that loved her.

Morra's looked back at her when Catherine started speaking. "I will introduce you to my court as my new ladyin-waiting. It's all for show, but it will keep you close to the inner workings."

Narrowed eyes examined the queen, but Morra didn't protest.

"All you must do is listen. You will learn much from them. I will see to it that you have access to the palace and the court."

"Why are you doing this?"

Catherine smiled and gazed at her with tired eyes. "Beca use you remind me of when I was young."

Morra couldn't help the small smile forming on her face. The Queen of France had had a soft spot for her.

It was an honor.

Morra spent the day with Catherine and some of her courtiers, builders, and designers. She had ordered the removal of Diane's signature crescent moon in Louvre Palace in Paris. Diane had been trying to catch the king's ear about the war with France in *'an attempt to excel hostilities'*.

Catherine wouldn't let it stand and removing her from the Louvre showed the people her influence didn't mean much.

Catherine told Morra that it would help quell the fear people had about Diane convincing the king to go to war. To bring war to French soil.

"What do you think you are doing?"

Both Catherine and Morra looked up. Diane stood there in enraged glory. A large brimmed black hat draped across her face obscuring her expression. Yet still, Morra could see the twist of her lips as she watched the chisel destroy the monument constructed in her visage.

Catherine tilted her head, speaking softly, "Renovating."

"That was constructed by the king. For me." The woman's pale face reddened indignantly.

"Then take it up with Henry." Catherine smiled again, "Unless you believe he will choose myself over you, being I just secured the future of his line. By all means, please tell the king."

Diane tilted her head in defiance, but her eyes, glimmered in fear, bouncing between the two of them. Morra stood four paces behind the Queen; she remembered this game. So, as Diane's beady eyes shifted back and forth, Morra couldn't help the small tilt on her lips. Biting the inside of her cheek, she kept her laughter in.

Diane twirled, storming off in a flurry of black and white, and Morra couldn't help the slight giggle at the older woman's disappearing form. Catherine raised an eyebrow at her in question.

"I think she fears you," Morra stated, amusement curling her lips.

"If you don't terrify people a modicum, then what is the point, my dear?"

Catherine spotted the sculptor, chisel firmly in hand. "You." She began barking orders, causing the wisp of a man to squeak and tremble under the firm orders.

Morra looked on with a macabre fascination. Now a distance away, she could not hear their conversation, but the man shook like a leaf. The woman held a power Morra had never once felt. Not when she was forced to move, not at the group home, not as she watched Atlas die. Not even now.

In that moment, Morra knew she wanted to step into that power. She wanted to be Catherine Medici when she grew up.

When she arrived back at the home of the duke and duchess, exhaustion weighed her down, but for a few moments she had forgotten what happened. Guilt rushed over her as she padded in. She had been out there trappsing around while Atlas was... and not to mention that Berluse and Kahadin were trying to save her dad all while she was-

Arms wrapped around her pulling her thoughts. Kahadin embraced her tightly, she hadn't even heard him come close. For a startled moment she didn't move, and then Morra melted into him. With her face pushed firmly into his shoulder she mumbled, "I'm sorry."

He sighed, his breath tickling her curly hair. "Morra, you are an idiot."

Morra just wrapped her arm around him tighter. "I messed up so many times. I have been a horrible cousin and even worse friend. I killed him and have been such a coward since," she said, face still tucked into his chest. She didn't want to look at him, shame welling inside her.

"Morra, I never blamed you, at all. This is the risk we take when we agree to be a part of this life. I am devastated that Atlas is gone, but that is not your fault." Kahadin pulled back to look at her. "Now, if you are ready, we have something to show you. Atlas had so much in his notes."

He tugged her to a beautiful room filled with ancient artifacts where Berluse slumped over a large red leather tome.

Next to him was the astrolabe.

The brass instrument was built with carefully crafted metalworking and delicate detailing. Oval shaped, the astrolabe was encased in smooth metal housing an open center ring. Intricate gold and silver symbols were etched on the face of the metal, like the stars in the sky.

Morra strolled over, picking it up and flipping it in her hands. It's smooth surface was cool under her fingertips as she graced over the gentle curves and beveled edges. With a reverent gaze she turned the knobs on the side watching as the inside machinery spun.

"Is this complete?" she asked with renewed hope. It was impossible to save Atlas, but maybe she could save her dad.

Just maybe. *Learn. Move on.*

"Not yet. This is just the base of the machine. Berluse and I have been researching and found where some of the pieces are. We can give this to the family when we return." Kahadin vibrated with excitement. Her mouth twisted, not ready to go home.

"Kahadin, I- I am not ready to leave. It's only been a few weeks, I can't."

He scanned her thin frame and hollow cheeks before nodding. "Then we stay, in a month from today we will talk about leaving again," then he paused before turning to their elder, "that is, if you find this acceptable."

He gazed at both children with fondness. "You are always welcome in my home." Morra couldn't contain herself and hugged the older man.

Morra and Kahadin stayed in the chateau and quickly forged an unbreakable bond. Their afternoons were filled with laughter, shared secrets, and grief. When she wasn't with the queen or Kahadin researching with Berluse, they were together. Morra finally confided her old dreams of playing softball and having kids of her own and settling down in Chicago.

"It seems silly," she told him as they wandered by the rive on the grounds at Château de Chenonceau. The sounds of birds chirping in the gardens, of water lapping against the riverbanks and reflecting off the castle walls, the echo of laughter playing around in the courtyard surrounded them as they strolled. The gentle breeze rustling through the trees that line the banks of the River Cher swept up their hair as Morra spoke, "To have had such simple dreams before all of this. Now I can't imagine play ing it professionally."

Kahadin shrugged as they strolled along the bridge. "I think it's good to have some sort of dream, no matter how far-fetched it might seem." A distant gaze washed over his face as he halted at the bridge's apex, observing the courtyard below. "Even if it won't come true."

Morra clutched Kahadin's arm in worry. He stood there motionless, and she tracked his stare. A boy, barely a handful of years older than they were, stood in the courtyard, fervently honing his swordsmanship abilities.

"Oh..." Morra murmured under her breath. She knew, of course she knew, but she had never felt like it was her place to bring it up. Kahadin's jaw was locked tight as a horrible longing shadowed his face. She linked arms with him, standing steady by his side. "When I came out to my mom as bisexual, I was terrified. Not because I thought she wouldn't accept me but because I didn't want to her to see me any different."

He looked at her, eyes widening at her confession. Morra just smiled at him. "She told me she's always known the person I am inside. That nothing could change the way she sees me. And that's all that mattered."

Kahadin's expression softened as he looked down at her. She squeezed his arm gently before continuing, "Nothing could change the way I see you."

"I wish it was the same for the others. It just simply is not done in our family."

Morra nodded sympathetically. "I know, but you don't have to hide who you are from me."

Kahadin's lips curved into a small smile, but it didn't reach his eyes. "It's not just about hiding, Morra. It's about the disgrace it would bring to the family. They have expectations of who I should be, and I fear I can never live up to them." Morra's heart ached for him. She knew the weight of their expectations all too well. "When I become the matriarch of this family, no one will be judged on who they love."

Kahadin smiled with a sheen in his eyes. "That would be nice." The pair stood there in silence for a few moments until Kahadin nudged her. "Ready to go spar?"

"Only if you are ready to get your ass kicked."
"You wish."

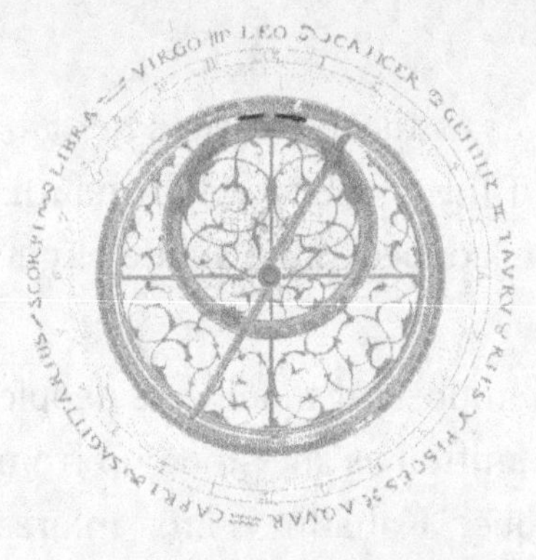

CHAPTER TWENTY-ONE

* * *

"He wants me to leave."

"That blond cousin of yours?"

Morning dawned bright yet cloudy, and Morra took the early hours to enjoy breakfast with Catherine. Relaxing back, she watched her spread jam on a scone before handing it to Morra. She took a moment to contemplate how different this time was than two hundred years in the future.

She smiled at the thought of the French court of the eighteenth century trying to force Catherine Medici into the pomp and ceremony. Morra shook her head "Yeah, Kahadin."

Catherine did not speak, forcing Morra to glance up. Seeing the disapproval on her face, she nodded before flashing a sardonic smile. "Indeed, your majesty, thy own kin's name, the one with the golden visage, hails by the name Kahadin."

1

She laughed as Catherine turned her gaze away, a hint of a smile playing in the corners of her mouth. Morra had won this round, but she conceded the subtle etiquette lessons were helping.

"It is always important to address people by their proper titles," the queen sniffed as she stood up from the table and brushed off her robe. "Kahadin is an... interesting individual. I hope he will find his own path, despite how difficult it might seem." Giving the younger girl a perceptive glance, she continued, "The question remains, are you ready to go?"

Chills worked up her spine. Sometimes Morra worried the woman had telepathy. She seemed to always guess her thoughts. Morra had dismissed the whispers she heard over the past month about the 'gifts' the Black Queen held as nothing more than rumors.

But Catherine had an uncanny ability to sense what people were thinking.

"Know you are welcome here until you are ready. I would happily continue to train you."

Morra nodded gratefully. Her stomach dropped anytime she thought about going home, seeing the faces and the grief. Having to bury Atlas. She just didn't think she could do it yet, but she understood Kahadin needed to go home. Now she just had to tell him.

Strolling through the courtyard and opening the door into Berluse's home, Morra could smell the sweat and leather filling the room. She watched Kahadin and Berluse circle each other, swords glinting in the dim light. Their movements almost choreographed as they lunged, parried, and dodged each other's blade with incredible speed and precision.

Morra could only hope to be as good. Over the last month, both had helped her with her fighting skills, but watching the two, she saw how they pulled their hits with her.

Kahadin twirled his sword in his hands as he turned to Morra, scanning her from head to toe and then peered back to the man holding his fighting stance. Berluse looked between them, Morra with dejected worry plain on her face and the slight heartbreak in Kahadin's eyes. The quiet man sheathed his sword and stepped back.

Lightly touching her hand on Kahadin's shoulder, she glanced at the older man. "Berluse, I need to borrow him for a little bit." She didn't want to leave him, but she knew he couldn't stay.

Pain and rejection filled Kahadin's eyes despite the stoic set of his face.

"Kahadin, I'm sorry," she said softly. "But I can't go home yet, I can't be there right now. I can't bear to lower him into the earth, not before I find a way to mend the void in my heart." Her trembling hand rose to her own cheeks, which were stained by tears. "I will do something incredibly stupid, like try to make it not happen."

"I promise," Morra explained with determination in her voice, "when I am ready, I will come home."

Steel eyes watched Morra; her face painted with uncertainty. She hoped he would listen, he had to let her go. For her own safety and sanity. With a heavy heart, he stepped forward and pulled her into a tight embrace. "I understand," he muttered softly into her hair. "If you ever need me, you know where I will be. I'll be waiting for you."

"You will see me soon." A small smile graced her face, tears still making their way down. She didn't promise when, couldn't. Not when her heart was still bleeding.

Kahadin left to pack and go, but Morra couldn't stay to say goodbye. The queen had informed her they were going on a trip, so she, too, had to pack.

The sun glinted off the calm waters of the river as the queen's carriage rumbled under them. Morra stared out the window, watching the trees pass by with a sigh.

Birds sang as they progressed, and horses trotted as men shouted. A small spark of excitement in her chest ignited in Morra. It had been too long since she had left the kingdom, though she wasn't sure what this journey was for or where they were headed.

"Where *are* we going?" she asked Catherine when she noticed her silence.

"Marcoing."

Morra wanted to roll her eyes, as if she knew where that was. Sometimes she thought Catherine forgot she wasn't from here; but then again, Catherine Medici forgets nothing.

Sighing, Morra turned away from the window to watch the stoic woman instead. She sat tall in her carriage, her hands steepled in front of her chin, eyes closed in contemplation as if trying to memorize every detail before her. *What could be so important at Marcoing?* Curiosity bubbled in Morra's gut like a pot on a stove, begging to boil over.

"How long is the travel?" The questions wanted to tumble out. She had to gnash her teeth to stop the overflow. She felt this was some test, and she didn't want to fail it.

Catherine distractedly waved a hand. "We should be there in the morning."

They traveled for two days. The trip took longer because of a rainstorm, but finally they reached their destination. Stepping out of the carriage, her every movement dripping with grace and poise, Catherine surveyed their surroundings before turning to Morra, who had yet to budge from her seat.

"Come," she commanded with a nod of her head towards the entrance of the castle.

Morra swallowed tightly. The majestic walls towered above them, the white stones reflecting in the sunlight like diamonds. Somehow it exuded subdued and understated grandeur, yet there was something foreboding, something that made her feel uncomfortable.

Catherine didn't seem to notice as she walked through the grand entrance, her stride becoming more purposeful as they walked further in.

"We are here for a meeting," the queen informed her as they swept into a large room. "We shall see what kind of agreement we can make between us and the Spaniards. We need to end these wars."

Tension in Morra's chest loosened knowing the plan. Her step lighter as she silently followed behind Catherine as a footman led into another room them. Around a large wooden table sat men dressed in various fine clothes. The pair waited just inside the door, Catherine tilted her head, examining as an announcer shouted each name in rank. The men stood as their name was called.

Francisco de Ávila, Morra Seelie: Héritière Duchesses of Clermont-en-Beauvaisis,

Morra's eyes widened at her own name.

Fernando Álvarez de Toledo: 3rd Duke of Alba. A man larger than the rest stood and relaxed back on his heels like he owned the world.

The announcer continued:

Michel de L'Hôpital: Chancellor of France, Antoine

Perrenot de Granvelle: Cardinal, 1st Archbishop of Mechelen, Ruy Gómez de Silva: 1st Prince of Éboli, Antoine de Bourbon, roi de Navarre.

The man finished with the queen's name, out of breath, before stepping out of the room.

She stood there stunned; she never expected to be included. She thought she was here for the queen not to take part in peace talks.

Not as an equal. Not as the heir to Berluse's estate.

Catherine stood, waiting until all eyes were upon her before introducing herself and giving her thanks for the audience with them. The men rose to their feet at once, bowing deeply in respect before taking their seats again. "For the sake of time, let us do away with formalities," Catherine began. "We are here to stop the wars and find terms we can agree on.

It is not our wish to enter a conflict, but rather to find a peaceful solution."

Granvelle, a man with a long face and dour set of his lips, sneered, "Stop wars? Tell that to your Duke of Guise!"

Morra disliked the man immediately. He glared at the queen, offended by her presence. By a woman's presence. She fought the urge to roll her eyes; the lecture wouldn't be worth it.

Morra sat quietly in her seat, racking her brain as she tried to make sense of their words. Isolde's words about French history echoed in her head as she struggled to keep up with the conversation around her.

Finally, the Duke of Alba stood imposingly, "The duke is following orders of your king. How are we to believe that peace is wanted?" His deep voice rumbled like a distant avalanche, his words carefully articulated, his accent heavy and guttural.

The comment was met with bitter responses from Bourbon and L'Hôpital, who both took unkindly to the duke. Arguments broke out between them until no one could be heard over the noise.

"Enough!" Morra shouted, unable to stand the noise and the pettiness. Immediate regret washed over her as the room went silent. The men turned their ire to the girl brought along and Catherine stared at her with a single eyebrow slightly raised and gestured for her to continue.

This was her time to step up and be the person Catherine saw or tuck tail and go home, and that wasn't an option. She would rather face a million angry men than Atlas' dead body.

Swallowing her nerves, Morra launched into her questions. "Alvarez, you are the King of Spain's closest council, yes? And you can speak for him during these negotiations?" she clarified

The Iron Duke shifted in his chair, his bulk filling the room. He was a tall and robust man with chiseled features and dark hair with a long, well-groomed beard. Morra understood why he was called 'The Iron Duke'; he was physically impressive, an imposing figure whose face was the map of his conquests. The man nodded, his eyes alight like bonfires.

Morra met Alvarez's eyes; her grey gaze unflinching. "The war you speak of will be lost for Spain." Alvarez bristled visibly, and Morra held up her hand, pausing his response. "I do not mean that as an insult, but as an inevitable," she continued calmly. "The only way to win this war is to come to terms with each other and find a peaceful solution.

"Jean Carrebe is leading your army. Commanding three thousand men, but the Duke of Guise has four times that. Even if you hold off French forces for some time, you will lose half your men and we will only lose a few hundred."

She tried to soften her words, but the facts were facts. "In the end, Carrebe will surrender unconditionally, and he and the Spanish soldiers will leave home with nothing. I do not say that as a victor because people are dying and there are no victors in death, but it will not cease until we hold peace talks." She paused, looking at them with more confidence.

"So, may we hold them without prejudice of what is currently happening?"

The Iron Duke stared hard at Morra, his dark eyes burning with frustration, before finally he spoke, "You speak words of wisdom beyond your years, girl." He nodded slowly before turning his attention back to the others in the room.

Catherine, with a gentle but firm voice, decreed, "We understand your concern, but we must all come together if we are to make progress here today." She paused for a moment before continuing: "Now please, let us focus on finding solutions rather than pointing fingers."

Talks went on for hours, and after the eighth bottle of wine, a break was called. The group agreed to reconvene in the morning. Before she could head off to her room, Catherine pulled her to the side. "I am impressed, more than I thought I would be."

Morra looked up at the queen's face, gratitude in her eyes. "Thank you, your majesty." It truly was an honor to serve her.

"Good," Catherine exclaimed. "You seem to have a decent handle on the situation. Maybe you can continue with the negotiations?"

Morra could hardly believe she was being given the chance to speak on behalf of the French. "Yes, your majesty."

Despite the eloquent speech, peace talks quickly devolved into petty squabbling. The shouting reverberated through the room, causing a migraine to start to form behind her eyes. The queen must have felt the same based on her pinched look.

Morra sat quietly. Wine had been poured into goblets, and she slowly sipped hers. The red wine tasted like blood in her mouth, but she wanted to fit in. She needed to be seen as equal

Her eyes shifted to Michel de L'Hôpital, who spoke aggressively about the situation between France and Spain. He wanted the Spaniards gone for good. L'Hôpital's war-torn arm hit the table with a thud as he gestured for effect, and she could not help but wince.

After another round of shouting, Morra leaned forward, her hands wrapped around her goblet, giving her some courage. "Us being here has nothing to do with the rights of the French or the Spanish government. This is about the people of France, and their lives. What will you do when the people are dead? They are not just bodies of flesh, but they are people with lives, hopes and dreams." Her voice shook with anger as she spoke. "What will your family do, L'Hôpital? What will you do, Alvarez? This is more than just blood and bodies. People make our countries run, not you." *Despite what your over inflated egos say,* she thought to herself.

She paused, rubbing a hand down her face, Morra made her decision. Leaning toward Catherine, she quietly whispered in English, "Your majesty. I was thinking perhaps..." she trailed off, unsure of how to continue.

"Yes?"

"Perhaps a compromise is needed," she said, taking another sip of wine to steel her nerves. "Spain wants to keep the land it has taken from the French. France would like to have it back. We cannot do this if both sides have their hearts set in the same direction."

"So, you are suggesting...?" Her eyes sparkled. It made Morra nervous.

"That we give them what I already know will be given, but not a single thing more."

The French queen stared at her hard for a moment, then gestured for her to take her idea to the group.

"I suggest a preliminary compromise. I do not speak for the king, but I can give my opinion, and if we are in agreement, we take the offer to both our rulers."

The assembly stared at her, a young girl who talked to the battle-worn men like children. Some had hate in their eyes, others respect. She didn't know what to do with either emotion, Morra just knew this moment could change everything.

"King Henry of France will recognize King Phillips of Spain as the sovereign leader of Milan and Naples while denouncing his own claim to these territories. France will recognize Spaniard control over the Kingdoms of Sicily, Naples, and Sardinia." Morra continued to list French concessions, much to the complaint of the other French men, but the queen sat on and watched. Listened.

The men on the Spaniard side watched content until Morra listed the demands of France. She spoke, hoping memory did not fail her.

"France will retain the Three Bishoprics of Toul, Metz, and Verdun. We will retain five fortresses in northern Italy: Turin, Cherasco, Pinerolo, Chivasso, and Villanova d'Asti. Spain will give back Saint Quentin, Ham, Le Catelet, and all other places in northern France."

Morra glanced at Catherine for permission to continue. With a nod, Morra took a steady breath before finishing.

"Lastly, the Duke of Savoy will marry King Henry's sister." With a pause of hesitance, she finished. "And Elizabeth of Valois, the king and queen's eldest daughter, shall wed your King Philip." Chaos broke out.

The assembly erupted at Morra's suggestion. Many of the French generals argued that the terms were too lenient on the Spanish, and some of the Spanish generals thought it was too generous. Catherine silenced both sides with a glower, her eyes full of determination. "This is a compromise that both sides can approve," she said firmly. "Concessions must be made."

Morra watched with admiration as Catherine commanded the room. She could only imagine how difficult it must have been for her to trade her daughter for peace. After a few moments of silence, Catherine addressed Alvarez again and asked him to bring back their respective kings' approval of the compromise so they could sign a treaty and end the war.

"I have one amendment to this." The Iron Duke started across the oak table. He sat back, eyes dark as his clothing glinted off the light of the setting sun. They had been there all day and many of the men's eyes were now red rimmed from wine. His fingers drummed at the table as his rings sparkled.

"I want the hand of your heir duchesses."

Morra's eyes widened; he wanted to marry *her*. The war hung on the balance of this proposal. Her grief still consumed her, and she didn't belong here in this time. She couldn't marry him. Wouldn't. Her gaze flickered to Catherine.

Catherine acted quickly informing him, "Sir, I must inform you the heir duchess is in mourning for her beloved fiancé. His passing is still fresh, and it would be improper to ask this of her now."

Morra's reactions marked her words; eyes welling up as images of Atlas dying in her arms swam through her vision. With a tight smile, she stood, her chair screeching against the stone clattering to the ground as she fled the room. Morra's hand covered her quivering lips as she choked back sobs.

She stumbled through the mostly empty hall in an attempt to get to her rooms. Falling into a door frame, a strangled wounded sound tumbled from her parted lips. She dug her fingernails into the wood as she fought against the tears. The weight of the skirts pulled at her, and her corset dug into her ribs. The tight fabric squeezed her torso like a sarcophagus, trapping her in what surely felt like death.

As she blindly followed the curve of the stone walls, she grasped the fabric, needing to not be there. It was as if the ghost of Atlas was here, surrounding her. She could feel him close. The phantom sound of his dying breath rang in her ears until she felt like she would burst. Sweat pricked at her skin even as her teeth began to chatter.

Finally, her legs collapsed. The cold stonework dug into her back as she hugged knees, burying her head in the tight fabric. Footsteps echoed in the hall but Morra couldn't hear them over the phantom voice whispering, '...*know you were worth all the pain.*'

A rough, calloused hand hovered above her head before smoothing her hair in a soothing motion. Startled, she glanced up to see Fernando Alvarez. Light of the setting sun glowed behind him and for a moment she thought him to be a specter as he shone with an almost unearthly glimmer. His outfit caused rays of light to bounce off his shoulders, surrounding him in a halo.

"Duchess?" he asked in a rough voice. It scraped her like sandpaper, yet somehow the pain was grounding.

Morra looked up briefly before focusing back on her hands as she tried to shield her tender wounds. "I... I... I just need a minute."

Moments passed, Morra thought he had left until a warm shoulder touched her own. The Iron Duke sat on the dusty cobblestone floor beside her. "I apologize that my request brought you grief. I did not know you were in mourning." He sighed heavily, fiddling with a ring on his hand. The gesture surprised her; he seemed to be the type of man who didn't waste time on such sentimental nonsense. "I know your pain. My wife passed away about eight years ago and the pain lasted a better part of those years."

"I am very sorry, sir. I wouldn't wish this pain on my greatest enemy."

He nodded, understanding. His demeanor shifted back to the hardened warrior with his moment of vulnerability over. "I wanted to tell you personally that I will not require a marriage to serve this proposal to my king. It's a fair one, despite what my companions may think." The Iron Duke stood, knees betraying him with their noisy cracking, and he offered his hand to the younger girl who took it. "I insist on escorting you to your rooms. This is no place for a girl to wander unprotected."

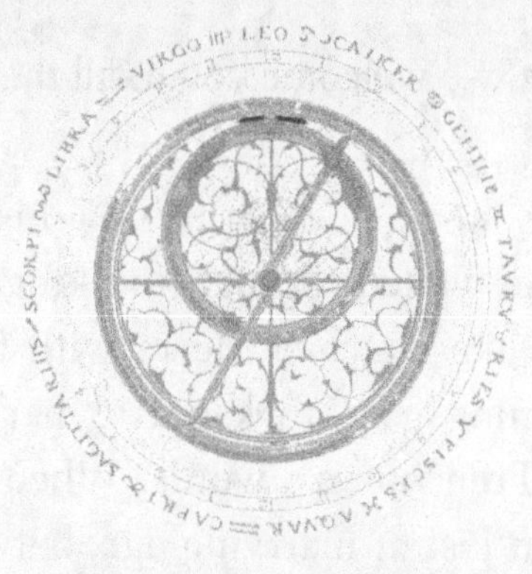

CHAPTER TWENTY-TWO

It had been almost a year since Morra sat and successfully negotiated with the Spaniards, and now they were back. Time had changed the young girl.

This time, she knew what to expect and was ready for their demands. She had grown into a woman and seen the world. Catherine had trained her well. She was ready to face the Iron Duke with the same determination that she had in the past. Now, as an adviser to the king and queen, Morra spoke with authority.

"Thank you for joining us today. We hope your travels were pleasant and that the accommodations are suitable. While we hoped your sovereign would be here, but we understand his position and thank you for coming in his stead," she said with a cordial lit. Wine was passed around as she continued her speech. "In fourteen days' time, our two realms shall be bound in matrimony as one. Until this happy union is complete, we welcome you to all the pleasures France has to provide."

King Henry stood, Catherine by his side, and Morra stepped back. She waited through the king's speech, all the while the Iron Duke watched Morra with fire in his brown eyes. The darkening gaze flickered to her lips, completely oblivious to the Frenchman's words. When he had seen her last, she had been just of marrying age, but now Morra wore the grace of a woman. She walked and spoke with the poise of a queen.

After the king finished his portion of the speech, everyone stood and the Duke Alvarez looked on, much like the cat who ate the canary, spoke, "Heir Duchess, I will not demand nor even ask but know, if you were to ever decide, my offer still stands."

Morra threw her head back, unable to conceal the chuckle pressing from her lips. The burgundy dress that dripped from her body swayed with its force and the duke gazed on in awe. Her grey eyes shone silver, like the moon reflecting off the waters of the Seine. Morra had changed much in his time away. Her dark hair, almost black, hung in ringlets down her back, complimenting her warm tawny skin that glistened in the candlelight.

Her wide smile gleamed with a look that could only be described as a she-devil. Morra walked like the sun; people orbited around her warmth. The duke, too, got caught in her gravity.

Alvarez, with an unwavering focus, locked on to Morra. Gaze never faltering. His eyes had a special intensity to them, burning a hole through the air. No sound came from him, no words or movements, just the dense silence of two people starving. Even the silence held a certain energy, practically screaming his desire for her.

She dragged her eyes down his large muscular frame. The Iron Duke hadn't changed much. He was still imposing but now it was... attractive.

"I will keep it in mind, sir. Good day." A soft chuckle tumbled from her red lips as she turned and sauntered off, feeling the passion radiating from the duke. The man tracked her every movement until she was out of sight.

Morra had an appointment she couldn't, and wouldn't miss. Refuting men that lavished her with attention had become a pass time, but with the duke it was something sweeter, sadder. The cuts in her heart had healed, the scabs still caught on rough times and quiet moments. Only occasionally did they sluggishly bleed. All in all, it seemed the old adage of time healing all wounds was true. The pain lingered in her, far away but not completely gone.

She had grown, not just in age, but in many other ways. Becoming a diplomat, a negotiator, a strategist, and most of all, a survivor. Seeing the duke reminded her of that; she had come a long way from the girl who ran from a proposition.

The sun shone down on her as she walked out of the palace and, and a warmth imbued inside her. Poise and grace exuded from each strike of her heel, hitting the stone pathway.

As she arrived at her uncle's home, her shoulders softened at the peace. Her time had been spent mostly in the castle at the king and queen's behest, but in her down times, the stonewalls covered in ivy became her home. It, in many ways, resembled the manor. A pang shot through her, thinking about that house and the people she left behind. The broken pile of her own self had now been tempered in pain, time, and wisdom, like steel in a forge. She knew she was ready to go home, but that could wait until the wedding. She wanted to watch it through.

Opening the doors to what had been her home the last year, she sighed in relief. It seemed so very strange that she had been here longer than she had been with her other family. In that time, she had formed an incredible bond with Berluse and Charlotte despite staying busy as a prominent member of the French courtier.

Morra found Berluse and Charlotte hunched over a piece of metal, examining it with careful touches. They shared whispers, something about math or arithmetic. She paid it no mind as warmth spread through her chest at seeing the loving pair.

Berluse had spent every free afternoon teaching her, training her, expounding on her time at Camelot Manor.

She had learned Galahad's manner of teaching was... frowned upon by the standards of the family. Suddenly she remembered a conversation they had after Kahadin left.

Morra furrowed her brow in confusion. "I don't understand," she said.

Berluse let out a sigh and rubbed his temples in frustration. "What I mean is, why did your grandfather entrust a child with the important task of being your timekeeper?" he asked. Morra's eyes widened as she realized what he was getting at.

Berluse nodded grimly. "The timekeeper is not just responsible for documenting time, but also for knowing the past and future. Their whole job is to keep devastating information from the head of the house. Your grandfather knew this and used that knowledge to his advantage."

Morra had shifted back and forth, not quite sure what to think about that. Galahad had taken her in, protected her, and given her a family.

Morra still didn't know what to think. Here in the past, the Seelie's lived like everyone else and only intervened when the Enemies of the Past got involved.

The only thing she did know with certainty was that Galahad often kept secrets. Good or bad, she wasn't sure. Berluse hadn't hidden who they were. He never hid anything from her, and it was refreshing. When Morra had told him of the circumstances of her arrival at the manor, he became angry at her *'mistreatment'*. From then on, he helped anyway he could.

Berluse even went as far as gathering pieces for the astrolabe. Morra smiled fondly as she remembered her time spent with Berluse and Charlotte.

She watched for a few more moments before clearing her throat softly to announce her presence. Berluse peered up from his work with a start and jumped up from his chair to embrace Morra in a tight hug.

"Ah! My dear niece! How lovely to see you after all this time!"

A twinge of guilt sparked through her. It had been weeks since she had been here, the wedding preparations had kept her busy.

Charlotte also stood up and gave Morra a warm hug. "We have something for you." She walked back to the worktable, picking up the round bit of metal.

"Is it finished?" Awed, she took the cool brass, flipping it over. They had been working on it for months, searching high and low for the pieces. Atlas had done most of the heavy research, but Berluse had collected most of the pieces.

"Almost. Just a few lost pieces." Pride infused his tone, and Morra thanked him profusely.

Looking up, she gazed at the people who helped her heal when she was broken. "I think after the wedding I am going to go home. You both have been the best to me. I can't tell you how much you helped me."

"What? Are you sure? You know you can stay as long as you want," Berluse said with genuine concern.

"I love you both, but I think I need to go home. I have been away for a long time, and I miss my famly and my friends," she said with a smile.

"Morra, you know you will always be a part of our family," Charlotte added, hugging her. Jasmine perfume infused the air and Morra knew she would miss it, miss her.

"I know. Thank you. I would like to leave after the wedding, but I wanted you to know first."

After some time Charlotte left, leaving just Morra and Berluse; they both sat looking at the astrolabe when Berluse informed her, "I found the location of another piece."

"You want me to go with you?" she asked, eyebrows

raising in surprise. He hadn't asked her to go with him for the other pieces, but looking at him, she noticed a sheepish expression on his face. The tip of his ears were painted cherry red. "Why?" She leaned in with a splitting grin on her face. Morra had a feeling she was going to love his answer.

"Well, I might have pissed off the man who has it. I may have slept with his wife..."

"Who?" The grin, somehow, became wider. A mumbled response was all she got as he rubbed the back of his neck.

"Did you just say Genghis Khan?" she clarified. Her eyes went wide with delight. "So, you're telling me you pissed off the greatest conqueror in history by sleeping with his favorite concubine when you were young? Does Charlotte know?"

Sighing, he wiped a hand down his face. "Yes, she knows, and I was young. And stupid."

"How did you live? From what I know, he doesn't seem like the forgiving type."

Berluse shuddered as he leaned back in his chair. "He isn't."

Morra leaned against the desk and thought it over. It wasn't the best time; Catherine had her running around trying to perfect the wedding, but could she really refuse?

"Why me?"

With a deadpan look, one that told her she was being an idiot, he explained. "The Khan has only one weakness." He paused, expecting her to understand. She just stared back blankly. "Women. You are young, pretty, and intelligent. He has conquered most of Asia and so to him, with your skin and hair and makeup. Well, you will be an exotic thing for him and he will be curious enough to let us in. Hopefully."

Morra hesitated at the plan laid out before her. "You want me to seduce the Khan?" she asked, unable to believe what she was hearing.

He shrugged. "Seduce is such a strong word. Think of it as distracting him long enough to get an audience. Your tongue is sharp enough to convince him. We just need to get inside the palace."

She knew it would be a terrible idea, but it seemed to be the only way for her to retrieve the treasured piece that could save her father. With no other plan in sight, she sighed.

"What will I even wear?"

Berluse smiled at her with a glint in his eye.

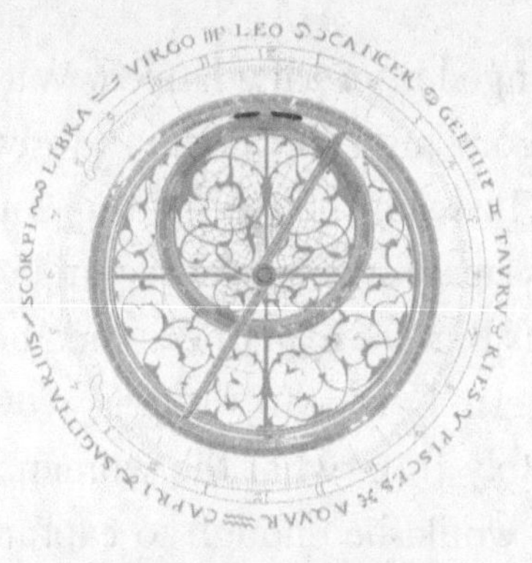

CHAPTER TWENTY-THREE

When they arrived in the beginning of the thirteenth century, Morra's eyes flitted around. The world looked untouched by civilization, even though she knew it was brimming with people. These people lived with the land instead of against it and it showed.

Morra stood on the outskirts of the encampment, gazing over the valley at the bustling population of warriors, merchants and commoners that had gathered here. They landed in what Berluse called the Palace of the Great Khan.

The smell of rich grains, fresh fruit, and sweet nectar drifted on the wind. As did the aroma of blood and the harsh clanging of sparring swords. Spices, candles, and incense mixed with the heady smell of desert. The entire city was ravishingly beautiful in its profligated excess. Butterflies erupted from within and sweat prickled on her palms.

She had changed after they landed. With the sun beating down on them from high in the sky, Morra wished she had shorts or a skirt. Instead, she wore a thin long silver-blue silk slip gown. It was heavily embroidered and cut low enough to be *'interesting'*, as Berluse explained when he handed it to her. There were eastern European designs woven in while still differing completely from what the women around her wore. Berluse hoped it would be enough to capture the curiosity of the man who already had hundreds of women.

Morra took a deep breath before walking further into the city. Everywhere around her, people were selling their wares, trading goods. They stopped as she walked past. Her heart beat faster as she approached the guards surrounding the Khan's building. Berluse walked beside her, tugging his head piece in an attempt to disguise his face.

The building itself was exquisite, white and gold, with steeples of marble. Morra couldn't believe the craftsmanship of it. A hand touched her back, Berluse pushing her along.

With her head held high, she looked at the guard, who stopped her.

Under his thick eyebrows, he looked her up and down before wordlessly moving aside. She smirked. *If that was any indication,* she thought, *this would be easy.*

Inside was an unexpected sight; it was cozy with colorful fabrics draped over walls and comfortable pillows scattered around on carpets. Men and women of all types sat around, but in the middle of the palace sat the Khan himself, dressed in fine silks and jewels with an air of regal power surrounding him. He glanced up expectantly when the strangers entered, brows furrowed in anger by the intrusion, but his expression softened almost immediately.

Slowly, she glided towards the raised dais. Bowing her head respectfully before taking a few steps forward,

"Greetings, your highness..."

She once had such a small view of the world; her worries were wrapped up in softball and friends and being the new kid. But now, at eighteen, she held an audience with the greatest warlord in history.

"Not many would come before me without an invitation, so who are you?" His deep voice reverberated off the walls. It reminded Morra of standing near speakers at a concert, a frequency that rattled her bones. From under her eyelashes, she examined the man in front of her. His tall and stocky body was littered with scars, battle-hardened. She could tell even through his silks his wide body housed muscles like no other she had seen. The khan could give the Iron Duke a run for his money.

Morra found it odd. This is what she expected a king to look like. In two centuries, those who ruled the lands in Europe would all look soft, pliable. But the man whose gaze trailed after her with fiery amusement was the epitome of a warrior.

Berluse stepped forward to answer the man's question. "Great Khan, we came for the chance to meet with you."

Suspicious eyes gazed at him. Morra saw the doubt. The Khan was a smart man; he could read a lie.

She stepped forward, delicately placing a hand on Berluse before walking even closer to the Khan. The moonlight dress swayed, showing the slit in the leg. Only her heels, tapping against the stone floor, could be heard as everyone held their breath in anticipation. She stopped in front of the steps leading to where he sat.

"It was my idea to come. I heard tales of your brutality, and warmongering." Clocking the anger rising on the face of the man in front of her, she contained a smirk and Morra heard Berluse whisper her name in warning. "But I have also heard of your religious tolerance, your tolerance of culture."

She walked up the steps until she stood right in front of the hulking man. "And your.... high-minded treatment of women." The smirk finally broke through and she knew as intense intrigue clouded his face, he was hooked.

Berluse's plan was *actually* working.

With a nod from the Khan, one of his servants brought out a chair for Morra. "Please, sit."

Berluse backed away, finding a seat as far as possible with out completely abandoning his niece.

"So, what is your name?" the Khan asked.

"Morra."

"And do you always come to the Palace of the Khan uninvited, Morra?"

Her eyes flicked to his. "Only if I wish to," she responded. "I am just a woman, a traveler, a seeker of knowledge."

The Khan slowly tilted his head, lazing back on his throne. His posture screamed disinterest; his face spoke a different story. "You wish to learn my trade?"

"I do. Among other things."

"What would you do with such knowledge?"

She smirked at him. It was an act. Inside, she quelled the tiny voice of doubt. This was the same game she played time and time again, and she was excellent at it. Catherine would teach nothing less than perfection.

It was sundown when the Khan brought Morra out of his palace. She had spent the day listening to stories and watching him interact with his people, impressed with his abilities. Morra smiled as she watched, thanking everything out there that Catherine was unable to time jump. If she had the ability to be around people like the Khan... she shuddered at the thought.

Berluse hung back at the palace discussing *'trade'* while she and the Khan had walked to a secluded spot. He led her to a garden. The dogwood trees were flowering, and the air was full of light perfume. The birds were silenced by the Khan as they walked. Morra had never heard anything so quiet. As they strolled about, they circled a pond that looked to be made of sparkling gold. The reflection of the water from the setting sun bounced off the man's face, looking as if it, too, was crafted of gold.

"You, Morra, are an interesting creature. One like I have never met." It was a far cry from the sultry remarks she exchanged with Duke Alvarez in France. There, every word held fiery passion and candor.

He leaned in close, and his immense hand cradled her face, tilting it. Here, the flirtations she flung were nothing more than games of political prowess.

"I want you."

She smiled politely at his words. "I apologize, Great Khan, I am not yours to have." Morra detangled herself from his light touch and flitted a few steps back. It was a risky thing to declare, but she hoped he would accept it. "I do have something that could be yours, though."

Dark intrigue sparkled in his eyes, her dismissal forgotten.

"What is that?"

"Knowledge of the future, but it comes with a price."

He slid her a skeptical look, silently debating if it was a ruse, but intrigue weighed heavily on his features. The future was something that had eluded him, and she knew the thought would tempt him.

"What do you want in exchange for this knowledge?"

"I was informed you hold a piece that I need. It may seem like nothing, but a compass made of solid gold," she said boldly. Berluse had told her on their way that the pieces he had found were integrated, hiding their true nature into things still of value. A solid gold compass from a time like this wasn't likely to be destroyed.

The Khan hummed in contemplation, "I may know of the piece. It was given to me by a friend many years ago. I have never had any use for it, but if you want it so much, it makes me curious about its value."

Morra took a deep breath. This was the moment she had been waiting for. "The value is more... sentimental of nature."

"I will not trade for nothing," he informed her.

"I understand," Morra conceded calmly, "but I assure you that my knowledge will be well worth it."

The Khan thought it over for a moment, and then nodded. He was an impulsive man, but she could tell he was not one to act without strategy. One of the greatest warriors alive did not accomplish what he had without thinking.

Raising an eyebrow, he studied her with an intense gaze, his lips twisted in thought. Morra knew he was used to magicians and charlatans passing through trying to fool him with false promises; she also knew none of them looked like her, talked like her.

"Very well," he said after a few seconds of deliberation. "But first, please stay as a guest. Enjoy yourself and rest." He turned away, "Oh, and remind your uncle to stay away from my wives. He should give you his thanks. Without you, he would be dead."

She had been in the palace for two weeks now, two weeks of feasts and parties and entertainment. Berluse tried to lie low after the warning while Morra charmed the men and women in Khan's court. But as the full moon closed on them, Morra knew she had to leave soon. France awaited her, and then home.

Genghis sat down to eat with her. He plied her with the best of what he had to offer. Morra deduced this was another attempt at courting her, despite her steadfast refusal.

"Will you not just stay? I could give you a lavish life," he asked, his tone alluding to begging.

Morra shook her head, chuckling as she placed a sweet berry to her plump lips, humming slightly, "I told you, great khan," she spoke with a smile, "I like my men to only be with me. And you are..." She fumbled for the Mongolian term, only being passable in the foreign language. "You could never be with one woman."

He sighed at the rejection. Morra had to give it to the man; he was tenacious. "I have to leave soon, but before I do, I need that compass."

He stood up then and walked over to the gilded throne. He reached behind and pulled out a simple compass made of solid gold. "You can have it." He handed it over to her. The light glinting off the sparkling metal. "But I want to renegotiate our terms."

"Go on," Morra said simply.

"Instead of telling me of the future, I want you to come back. At least once."

A rush of fondness flooded her. It was hard to believe that he, the man responsible for the death of ten percent of the population, could be like putty in her hands.

"Okay, that seems like a reasonable offer."

He nodded. "This is all you've talked about. Tell me what it is."

"It is a compass."

He stared at her, knowing she was lying or not telling the whole truth.

"It's not a compass," she recanted. "My family hid something in that compass a very long time ago, and I need it back. It is one of the last pieces. That is why I must take my leave now."

The Khan pierced her with a stunned look as she stood to leave. "You are a bold one, to ask me to let you go, knowing how much I wish to keep you here."

Morra smirked and leaned in. "I am brazen, but I do not lie. I will take your compass and be on my way."

Again, he heaved a sigh, unaccustomed to being refused. Morra's honeyed words and demure smile protected her secrets. She knew he knew this; and that he admired it. She could tell him something that could change the world, but he respected her too much to ask.

Instead, he let her leave without protest. "I will see you when you return to my court," he called after her, tracing the curves of her form as she walked away.

With a grin, she left. She had the piece, and she had all she needed to do was time jump. She had a wedding to attend.

She knocked on the ornate door, waiting for an answer. It was late, but she knew Catherine would be awake. The woman barely slept, it seemed.

A call from inside echoed out and the servant at the door reached for the knob before stopping at Morra's sharp look. She had been here too long and now no longer suffered the pomp and precedent this place oozed, although it wasn't nearly as bad as the future.

The doorman quickly slides back into place, allowing Morra her own entry. Alfie should know better by now.

Just inside, she slipped off her heels, bare feet padding through the entryway. "I come bearing gifts," Morra yelled, setting down the goblets. They clink gently clinking against the decanter of wine. As she unwraps her bundle of food carefully wrapped in cheesecloth, Catherine emerges from the back room.

"What's this?" Catherine asked as Morra sat down in a chair next to her. They were used to this routine. Many long nights had been spent in these chairs, the same one they sat at during their first meeting.

Morra poured them wine, handing a goblet to the queen. "It's called Aaruul. From my travels." Morra showed off the chunk of dried cheese. She had liked it and the Khan had insisted she take some with her.

"Where did you go?" Catherine took a sip of the wine and a bite of the cheese before nodding appreciatively.

Morra paused, gauging whether she should tell her. She shouldn't tell her, but Morra knew the look in the queen's eyes and she sighed over the red wine. Did it matter now? After everything she had done, this seemed like a minor infraction.

"Mongolia... Genghis Khan." Her voice almost echoing her quiet whisper. They were alone, but she wasn't dumb enough to think the walls didn't have ears. Servants were everywhere and knew everything.

"How was he?"

"Like all men. You did truly teach me well."

"Ah, so he is like your Iron Duke, hmm?"

A blush flooded her cheeks as she took a healthy swig of her wine. "How was the meeting?"

Catherine cast her a sly look. "That was not covert enough."

"I did not mean it to be. Was Diane there?"

This quickly spurred the queen in the right direction. Catherine sighed heavily. "No, but she may as well have been. I love that man, I truly do, but when his mouth opens, her words come out."

Morra smiled around her cup. Catherine and Diane's rivalry was almost magnificent to watch. The queen had been right all that time ago. Watching truly did teach her many things.

"I still won't hurt her," she jibes, recalling that conversation long ago. Catherine must too because she chuckled.

"I still wouldn't ask you. You were never that proficient in poison."

Morra conceded with a nod. Cosimo had to create antidotes for her on multiple occasions after her training went... poorly.

"You know there is an upside to Henry's mistress parading aboutthe castle." Catherine stared at her hard doubt written all over her face. "I am serious. Mistresses provide a buffer; in the sameway you hear her voice, so do others."

"How could a weakness like that be used in my favor?"

Morra couldn't tell if she was being sarcastic or not, so she just forged ahead. "When a decision goes wrong... it's Diane's fault. When there is a drought and the commoners are starving, well, then it is the king's mistress who is using valuable resources. The crown is not responsible." She had seen what happened when people didn't have someone to blame, royals lose their heads.

Catherine must have seen the faraway look on her face because she nodded. The two sat in silence. The moon rose and their wine deplenished until Morra felt relaxed and tingly. She had missed this while she was away.

"So," the queen said, "what is going on with you and the duke?"

Morra looked at her, and then at the wine. She should have known. With a shake of her head, she replied, "I am not sure, but whatever it is, it's nothing."

"How so?"

She sighed. "When I leave and I will have to leave, I get back to my time and he will have been dead for hundreds of years. It doesn't do well to love someone from a different time." That lesson was one she wasn't willing to repeat. She wouldn't sacrifice her present and future for a love that could never truly exist.

Catherine sat with her silently for only a moment before sipping on the last of her wine. "Who ever said anything about love?"

One week later, Morra stood tall and proud in her unique gown, fitted at the waist and billowing out at the skirt. The dress was a deep blue, with intricate silver detailing that shimmered when she moved. Pinned in a loose bun, her dark hair cascaded down her shoulders. She wore a delicate silver necklace that sparkled in the light and drew attention to her graceful neckline. She stood next to Catherine as she watched Elisabeth and Iron Duke, as the king's stand-in, get married.

Fernando Álvarez de Toledo's gaze raked down Morra's body before he met her eyes. They burned with passion. She smirked at him. Morra would never admit the flutters dancing in her chest, especially to him. But as she watched the man kneel next to Elizabeth, she couldn't help feeling incredibly powerful.

The pope's voice faded, leaving her feeling as if they were the only ones in the church. She lifted an eyebrow at him, an impish grin still on her face.

The Iron Duke gazed under his brows, looking like a man who would happily kneel at her feet. The look on his face was a mixture of ecstasy and agony. A wholly inappropriate expression while at the feet of a church delegate. Shivers worked down her spine at the thought. It was a heady feeling having a man of such power and strength look at her like he was starving.

Begging.

Claps and cheers broke her out of her trance.

Morra and the duke caught each other's eyes over the next three days. She enjoyed his company, and they spoke often. She sat next to him during the jousting competition. Their hands brushed lightly against each other as he handed her a goblet of wine. Sparks trailed from his fingers to hers, causing her breath to hitch.

The tournament started right after the wedding ceremony.

Now, days after the wedding, the jousting still continued. Each contender for the tournament wore a new suit of armor from the previous day. They all glistened in the sun, looking like heroes of old. The lances cracked sharply against shields, and the crowds roared. The din of horses whinnying as their riders sought an advantage lapped behind their conversation.

"You look exquisite today, Lady Morra." The Iron Duke's voice rumbled as his eyes dragged heavily down her frame. They were, once again, sitting together on the raised dais with the royals.

"Thank you, sir," she replied with a coy smile, feeling his gaze linger on her curves. "But I think it's the dress that looks exquisite, not me."

"Ah, but it's not just the dress," he said, leaning in close enough to whisper in her ear. "It's the way you wear it. The way you move and carry yourself. You have a grace and elegance that is unmatched."

Warmth flooded her at his words. She knew she was playing with fire, but she couldn't help herself. Her own eyes deliberately lingered on his sharp, chiseled jaw, trailing down his intricate leather tunic before snapping back to his. He lifted his wine to his lips and Morra wanted to speak, but her words were cut off.

Fanfare played loudly as the king of France, riding a black stallion, came onto the field. He lined up across from a knight. The wind whipped around Morra, blocking her view as memory suddenly took hold, but it was too late.

Everything went wrong.

A lance gave a sickening crack, and a scream echoed across the field. The king of France lay motionless on the ground. Morra's gaze whipped to Catherine as the crowd waited with bated breath for their king to stand.

"Get the physician." Morra yelled, standing from her seat. Blood spurted from his face as wood stuck between his visors. "Help your king."

Suddenly everyone sprang into action. Diane screamed hysterically as Catherine moved faster than she ever had before running down the stairs.

Morra and Alvarez ran right behind her. Fernando held the king down as he tried to sit. Blood poured from his helm, coating the man's hands. Catherine screamed orders to her servants as she desperately tried to rouse her husband, tears running down her face as she whispered pleas.

Over her crying form, Morra and the duke shared a look. They knew this pain. Helplessness curled around Morra as she wrapped an arm around her mentor, whispering words of comfort in her ear. Catherine gave her a pleading, watery look, staunchly refusing to believe, but Morra slowly nodded once. The queen closed her eyes before steeling herself, knowing it wasn't the time for tears.

Diane finally made it to her king's side, frantically she gripped his helmet and quickly Morra slapped her hand. Not having the patience for the mistress's outrage, Morra glared at her scathingly. "Do you want to kill him?" Tears fell down Diane's face, yet Morra couldn't find sympathy for her.

At last, after what seemed like an eternity, a doctor arrived. The knights gathered around, helping lift the king. Morra stepped back, letting them while watching Catherine fret. Fingers wrapped around her wrist, the duke squeezed gently, his face sympathetic. "Follow your queen. I will check in later." He turned around, ushering people away, and finally the king was secured. They carried him to Château des Tournelles. The queen followed with Morra in step.

Catherine whirled around to face Morra before they stepped into her husband's chamber. Her voice broke as she pleaded, "I must know the truth!"

The fire in her eyes faded slightly as Morra spoke the grim words, "The lance pierced his eye. Wood fragments split and logged into his brain. He has only ten days remaining before death takes him."

With a quivering lip, the older woman stepped across the threshold. Time was running out.

Morra watched as her friend's shoulders collapsed inward, her breath wheezing out of her in a jagged exhale. She stayed close, a silent witness to her friend's fear, attempting to provide some sort of comfort.

King Henry's dying form laid on the bed as the surgeon fretted over him. Pallid and drawn, the king's hands lay limp at his sides. The silver of his armor contrasted against the deep red of the blood-soaked bandages wrapped around his face.

Catherine walked to her husband's side, standing strong even in the face of grief. As she took his hand into hers, he opened his eyes, just as wails from down the hall caused everyone to look up.

Catherine held Morra's gaze, her command clear.

Moving swiftly out of the chamber, she blocked Diane's entrance. She had transformed in her mourning; her black dress hung loosely on her small frame, a single white rose clasped in her hand. Damp patches on her cheeks spoke of recent tears.

"Let me see my Henry," she begged, voice trembling. Stepping forward, Morra rested a comforting hand on her shoulder. "He needs me," Diane choked out before Morra quietly guided her away.

"I'm sorry Diane, but the king's last wish was for Catherine to stay by his side during his passing."

Diane shook her head in disbelief, tears streaming down her face. A twinge of guilt pinched her insides as the lie rolled off her tongue; she knew that Henry would've wanted Diane there too. But she understood that Catherine shared Henry during his life; his death was for her only. The guilt grew as she imagined not being with Atlas in his last moments, but her friend came first.

Diane scoffed, pushing past her, attempting to move past the guards. With a flourish of Morra's wrist and a tired sigh, the guards blocked her way. "Diane, I do not want to make a scene. The king's word is still law. Leave or I will act appropriately."

The guard's gaze shifted uneasily between Morra and Diane before finally relenting and barring the weeping mistress from the room. They wouldn't go against their King's words.

Catherine banished Diane from the castle. Days passed, and the doctors went from hopeful to resigned and on the tenth day, Morra visited the king and queen in the room.

A faint whisper came from King Henry's lips, the last words he would ever speak before departing this world. A final plea for peace and understanding hung in the air around him like a ghostly reminder of his mortality. His prayers drifted as he fell asleep once more.

Morra had brought medicine with her when she jumped. Simple things like ibuprofen and melatonin. She had crushed them with poppy making a drink to ease his pain. Catherine was thankful.

Morra pulled up a chair next to them and sat in silence for a few moments before taking Catherine's hand in hers.

"He was special, wasn't he?" The question seemed unnecessary as it was obvious, he meant the world to her.

The king's eyes were firmly shut, the medicine easing him into sleep.

Catherine nodded and gave a watery smile. "Yes, he was my everything. I remember when we were young, and I first came to this country. He was so kind and gentle, even after...." She laughed while brushing the back of the king's hand. "We had horrendous fights, truly horrendous. Still, he never stopped being kind, and I never stopped loving him."

King Henry's breaths became short and strained. His heart beating slowly in his chest, a faint thudding sound that grew weaker with each passing moment. Finally, after what seemed like an eternity, King Henry inhaled one last breath before going limp in Catherine's arms. She brushed his hair back from his face and tenderly gazed at him for the last time. The king was never an imposing man, but he was a steady presence. They were friends and partners, and Catherine was enormously proud to have had him in her life. It was no wonder that so many people loved him.

Morra left Catherine to her grief. She slowly left the chamber and closed the door behind her.

"Thomas?" The guard outside the door turned to attention. "Alert the guards, ring the bell. The king is dead." Not long after bells rang across the country. The royal court fell into mourning as everyone prepared for the funeral procession and burial of their fallen leader. Morra made the arrangements, said goodbyes to the foreign dignitaries, and stood by the queen. The duke stayed by her side as a silent support, and she leaned on him at night over a glass of wine.

The days and weeks after Henry's death were chaotic. Between coronation preparations, scheming lords, Diane, and Mary, Morra was busy running around. Catherine mourned, and Morra tried her best to help so much of the concerns were fielded to her. She had become a pseudo-ruler in the absence of one.

The kingdom called for a regent, and Catherine wasn't the first choice. Rumors of her meddling spread along with whispers of her poisoning the king. Morra ended them swiftly; it caused people to look to her for stability. Many nobles called for her to be regent until the coronation of the Dauphin Francis, but she turned it down. That was a job for Catherine, but Morra knew if the queen didn't step up, she would be stepped over.

"Catherine?" she asked, knocking on her chambers. The widowed queen perched in a chair at her desk, looking outside over the gardens forlornly, not registering her presence.

Morra knelt next to her, approaching her like a wounded animal. "Catherine. I know you are grieving, but France needs you, Francis needs you. They are deciding on the Regent today and if you do not go, someone else who isn't family will be ruling France. The Bourbons or the Guises will control your country. Control Francis."

Her words caught the queen's attention. Finally, she looked at her and Morra could tell she was getting through. "You once told me to stand back up and fight. You said to clutch my pain and show the world it didn't break me." Morra continued, gesturing to the door and the palace that lay beyond. "Do you really want them to think you are nothing more than a woman broken hearted, or do you want to show them who Caterina Maria Romula di Lorenzo de Medici truly is?"

Later that day, the Queen of France walked into the meeting of the king's council. Morra stood silently by her side. Adorned in a black gown with an embroidered sigil. A broken lance with green and silver words that read *'lacrymae hinc, hinc dolor'.*

From this come my tears and my pain. Morra thought the words were fitting and watching her mentor and great friend, she knew Catherine would be perfectly fine.

It was time for Catherine to flourish and for Morra to go home. She needed to stand tall and face her own demons.

She was ready.

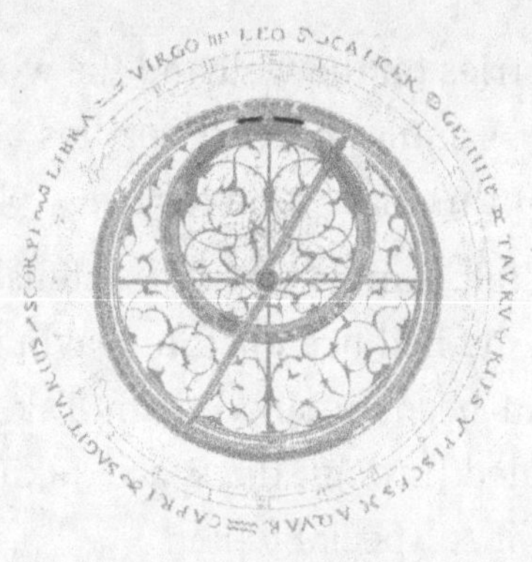

CHAPTER TWENTY-FOUR

Carolina's air differed from that of France; the noises, the animals, and the people. English felt foreign to her tongue. She hadn't spoken it in months. Almost a year, actually.

Her flight had been a long thirteen hours, with a stop in New York City. She was glad to be back, even though she already missed her home in France. It seemed she was destined to always miss a home left behind.

Dark curly hair bobbed as she walked through the doors of her old home. Everything was untouched and for a moment Morra forgot that she had spent sixteen months in another time. She almost felt like that young girl.

Almost.

Drawing in a deep breath, Morra stepped into the hallway of her old home. Everything was just as she remembered it, down to the tapestries on the wall and the wooden floorboards beneath her feet. A smile touched her lips as she recalled all the memories that this place held for her.

The Manor felt almost like an extension of herself; a reminder of who she had been before leaving Camelot Manor and what she had become since then. Taking another deep breath, Morra glided through the space, taking in all the little details that made it so special to her.

A flurry of arms wrapped around her as Kahadin and Ladianna bombarded her. Morra called her favorite cousins before getting on the plane in France, wanting them to know she was headed home.

"We are so glad you are back," Ladi gushed, letting her go finally. Kahadin and Ladianna both looked just as Morra remembered them; their skin pale as snow and their eyes still glowing with the warmth of a summer's day but the color of a moon silvered night. Their bodies were slim but muscular, unchanging.

In the time that passed, Morra had blossomed. Her hair had grown longer yet still curled in untamable waves. She had grown an inch and her once youthful face was now sharper and more femininely defined. Even her walk had more grace, as did her speech. The girl in front of them had grown into an adult.

Kahadin gave her a meaningful look. "It's been a long time for you, hasn't it?" he asked.

Morra smiled and nodded, knowing full well how much time had passed since she left. It felt like an eternity, yet it had only been sixteen months since she left for France.

Morra hugged her cousins tightly again, relief washing over her. She hadn't realized just how much she had missed them until now. "It's so good to see you two," Morra said, smiling as she stepped back from the embrace.

"We missed you too!" Kahadin wrapped an arm around her shoulders, leaning into her side, "Grandfather wants to see you," he whispered with an edge to his tone. Galahad was angry; she expected it.

"I will see him once I have showered and changed." She was not some child to be ordered around. She was an adult, even though she was technically seventeen. Morra shook her head at her own thoughts; she understood why everyone stopped counting.

But now, after being in the presence of a queen who taught her not to take orders, it was hard not to bristle at them. It made her think of what Berluse would say right now, and she smiled.

Feet traveling a familiar path to her room, Morra reveled in the familiarity. Though she hadn't lived here long, it had been the first time she felt like she truly had a home, one that wouldn't change. One she knew she could always come back to. She missed it thoroughly.

And water, she missed plumbing intensely. Hot water cascaded down her back, loosening her tight muscles and cleansing her travel-worn skin.

After a quick shower and slipping into a clean blouse and trousers, she made her way downstairs, the weight of her delay heavy with every step. When she stepped into the office, the head of the house, Galahad, glanced up from his paperwork with an expression that held both relief and irritation.

The impending lecture didn't come; instead, Galahad stalked up to her, face pinched, and without a word he wrapped her in his large arms. A surprised gasp escaped her rosy lips as he lifted her off her feet.

"Hello Grandfather!"

He held her close for a moment before setting her back down and leaning in to examine her. Looking back into his face, she found that even though his white hair had thinned, and his wrinkles had deepened, nothing else had changed. Not even the dark circles which still hung heavily around his eyes.

She felt the sting of guilt on her tongue as she said, "I'm sorry I had to leave, but I just could not force myself to stay."

"Kahadin told us of how you blamed yourself. While we are not happy you left, we are grateful you are back. Everyone wants to see you but..." Silence filled the room for a moment as his knitted brow softened. "I wanted to see you first and tell you we buried Atlas in the graveyard behind the horse field. We didn't know when you would be back."

"I understand. I will go say my goodbyes tomorrow," she said with kind eyes, somewhat relieved she didn't have to watch him be buried. Her heart panged, dully. The time had lifted the weight of her grief, but now that she was back in these walls, some had come back. The guilt would never leave. She accepted that long ago. There were certain things in life that would forever haunt, but you just had to deal with it.

Before she could think, people burst into the room surrounding her.

Sofia got to her first, pulling her into a hug, and Morra couldn't help her smile. After cheek kisses, Balin pulled her into a bone-crushing hug and again Morra relaxed.

"Look at you," he said, pushing back so he could take her in. A melancholy smile tilted his lips. "You have grown so much." Balin pulled her in again. "Your father would be proud."

Standing next to her son, Sofia nodded. "We are so glad you are home." Tears welled in Morra's eyes as she realized how much she missed her family. It was such a relief to be surrounded by loved ones once again.

After a moment, Balin released her from his grip, giving her a small smile before turning his attention to the others in the room. "Alright, alright," he said with a laugh. "Give her some space, people. She's just gotten back after all."

Morra took a deep breath, feeling a sense of calm wash over her. She had been away for so long, and the world had changed so much. But in this room, with these people, nothing seemed to have changed at all. It was a comforting thought. Even the glare from Madoine was a weird comfort.

Galahad clapped his hand on her shoulder. "Let's go eat. I am sure you are starving."

As they settled into their seats, Galahad filled her plate with food, piling it high with roasted meat, vegetables, and bread. Morra looked around and her heart panged at the empty seat in the filled room.

"So, tell us about your travels," Sofia said, a smile on her face.

Morra looked up, grateful for the distraction. She caught up with them and told them stories about her time away, and after a loud and happy dinner, she crawled into the cool sheets of her bed. Morra had desperately missed them, and it seemed her return brought some light to their still fresh grief. Hopefully, her news about the astrolabe would help bluster their moods even more.

The next morning, she took the astrolabe and Atlas' letters and tucked them in the pockets of her wool pants along with her hands, attempting to stay warm from the cold winter air. The heaters didn't work as well as the fires in the castle. She missed it. Despite the cold, she decided she needed to say goodbye to someone.

Putting on her coat and boots, she made her way outside through the training grounds and back behind the horse field, the alpacas sounding off in the distance. Fresh dirt mounded up, alerting her to his resting place even before she read the tombstone.

Trudging through the mud, the pungent scent of wet earth engulfed her. She stopped in front of the headstone and gently touched the cold marble. A rush of sadness washed over her as she read the name carved into the stone. Memories flashed in her mind as she recalled their last conversation from what seemed to be a lifetime ago. She had gone away to France seeking answers, but instead found healing. Though she felt at peace about what she had found, guilt for having healed still lingered.

Morra sat on the ground next to him and started talking.

"Hi. I miss you." She chuckled bitterly. This didn't feel like enough. It would never be. How do you apologize for missing a funeral?

"I hoped to go to France and find a way to save you. When I couldn't, I never thought my heart would heal, but it seems it did. The missing you hasn't left. I do not believe that it will. Just know that I loved you. And I always will. Thank you for everything you gave me."

Nostalgia bloomed in her, causing a single tear to roll down her cheek. Tucked away in another pocket, she pulled out their letters. "I thought it only seemed fair for me to keep yours if you kept mine. I never got to tell you thank you for helping find a way to save my dad. I know you loved him, the letters said so. I will tell Arthur what you did for him. For me. I will always love you, Atlas." Taking a deep breath, she brought her hand to her lips and kissed it before touching it against the cold marble headstone of her beloved one last time.

It felt like a real goodbye, an end of a chapter. But now, as she walked back into the house, she knew it was time to try to save another. She just hoped this time she succeeded.

She walked into Galahad's office, thankful for the fireplace. The aging man looked up as she crossed the threshold. Before a lecture could begin, she held up the chunk of metal. "I have something for you."

His eyes lit up.

"How is that even..." Galahad trailed off as he stared at the almost put together device. Handing it over, he examined it.

"I had some help from the family. A man named Berluse in France helped me tremendously." Morra watched as Galahad tensed imperceivably.

He walked to an old painting on the wall. Fiddling behind it, his old fingers caught what he was looking for. With a click, it lifted up, revealing a safe.

Inside, he pulled out a cloth bag gently dumping the contents on the desk. Morra walked over and immediately saw the missing pieces to her Astrolabe. "How did you find these and how long were you there?"

Morra gave a distracted shrug as she attempted to get the pieces together. "We found these pieces from the research Atlas did. And I am not sure on the exact time, but I am eighteen now."

Galahad's gaze shadowed with worry. He wasn't pleased she had been gone for so long. The tight pursed lips and furrowed brow told her so. It made her curious, but before she could ask, he began rummaging through his desk. A sheet of paper was thrusted at her, distinct handwriting covering it.

Moving to the fire to rid herself of the chill, she took a moment, gazing into the flame. Galahad opened his mouth to warn her but paused. Time was a funny thing; it changed and dulled reactions that could once consume. The heat of the flames no longer invoked terror, and seeing his handwriting no longer made her cry.

"It truly has been some time for you," Galahad remarked. A half shrug was the only reply as she scanned the papers. A paragraph caught her eye, and she reread it:

'Time vortexes do not work as time jumping does, it produces a stasis that can only be survived for a limited time. Due to unknown vortex data, we can only guess sixteen and a

half to seventeen years being the viable time frame for a body to withstand the force of time lashing. Time lashing is the process when not in a solid timeline. It slowly burns the fae blood out of the body.'

She kept reading, as her aunt and uncle joined her grandfather in the study, talking in low voices.

"Grandpa, have you seen this?" No response came, so she repeated herself more loudly. "Did you read it?"

"Hmm?"

Frustrated, she shook her head. She watched the man sitting at his desk surrounded by his children and recalled Berluse's words. Curiosity flared in her; who was the time keeper now? But then, as she reread the passage, something else caught her attention. Those questions could wait. None of that mattered with the information she had in her hands.

At last, he looked up as she slammed it down on the table.

"When did my father disappear?"

"Over sixteen years ago. Why?"

She read the passage out loud and Galahad's face paled dramatically, and then he cussed. "We need to do this soon or he could be lost." Her grandfather began to panic. Isolde placed a hand on her father's shoulder, squeezing briefly.

Her lip curled into a sneer. "You are really going to let her retrieve Arthur after she killed Atlas."

Morra paused, glaring at the older woman, her jaw ticking. She had enough of this. In a flash, her murderous expression fell away into a shadow of demure.

"Dear aunt, please know that if you are going to continue to act as a child, I will, in fact, treat you as such." With sure, steady steps, Morra prowled towards her. Both men froze in place by the harsh shift of personality. "Do remember that I am the heir to this family? If you continue, the consequences will be... detrimental to your future." Isolde's mouth pinch as heat bloomed across her face.

"Let me put this together, grandfather, and then you and I will go. Only you and I," she said with a hard look to Isolde. She wouldn't let her come; Morra was going to do this and do it right.

It took hours to slot in the other pieces, but when they slid together, nothing happened. Morra didn't know if something should, it just seemed to be a hunk of metal.

Picking up Atlas' notes, she read through it again. He had done thorough research. In it, he explained that only someone who has seen the person stuck can accurately pull the trapped person out of the time vortex with great risk of falling in. She skipped through that part, searching for...

When she found it, she knew exactly what to do.

'To pull someone out of the vortex, a device of immense power is needed. One has been rumored. Looking much like a medieval astrolabe, these pieces were forged in the fires in Avalon by an ancient goddess known as Mythala or 'the Empress of Time'. To activate it words of the ancient order must be spoken. This is to ensure only the family of the Fae may harness it.'

Morra ran to where she first met the boy, who hastily scribbled all the answers they needed. She threw open the heavy door, running to the statue. Morra didn't know why, but she knew that this was Mythala. She had thought it was Morgana, but now she knew.

Holding the ancient device, she scanned the inscription etched in stone and before her eyes, old words flowed into her mind and she, on instinct, echoed them.

An ainm Mythala, siubhail sinn am amann,

Airson an t-am gun tealladh,

Gus an t-am far am fuirich i a-rithist.

As Morra spoke the archaic words, her eyes fell shut. A humming filled the room. It started off low and grew in intensity until it filled her ears like a distant storm, making the whole room pulse, wrought with living energy. A faint blue light began to flow out of it and surround the device. The light flickered and grew brighter until it was like a beacon, radiating a bright blue glow in all directions.

The surface of the device now lit up with a pulsing light that seemed to call out to something beyond. Vibrations moved through her body as she spoke each word. Until finally, with a loud pop, the blue light turned to a soft glow that surrounded the mechanics of the device. She waited with a held breath.

The gears began moving, and she beamed, holding it up to Galahad, who looked disturbed.

Quickly recovering, he wasted no time commanding, "Let's go."

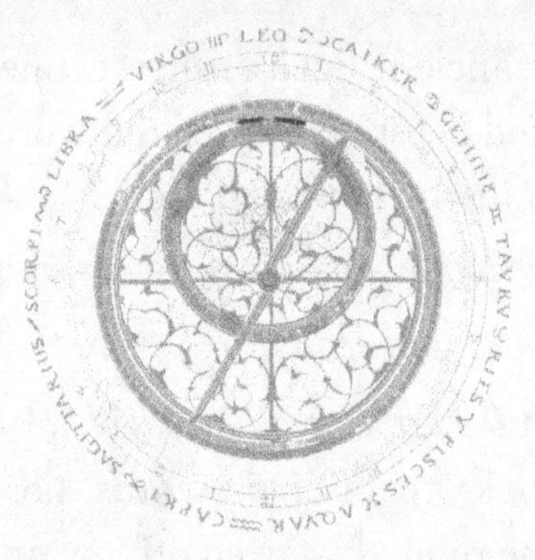

CHAPTER TWENTY-FIVE

The wheels of the private plane screeched across the pavement below and Morra couldn't help the lurch of air that forced its way past her throat. They landed in the town she only lived in for a month before.

Before her mom died.

Her throat tightened and her eyes stung as she walked off the plane into the bristling cold. The frigid temperature didn't help. When the plane took off, Morra asked her grandfather to get a hotel in town so she could walk around. She wanted to see the place she left behind.

Morra hoped to feel nothing.

She hoped to be over it; she hoped she could walk around this town and not be bothered. Hoped it wouldn't hurt.

Nothing she hoped for came true.

The rush of frosty air on her face stung her skin like needles. Picking up her feet quickly, she clasped her body into a coat and started to walk away from the small terminal. It was oddly quiet. The lack of sound reminded her of a ghost town. Everything seemed to move in slow motion, and she stopped thinking about her mission.

She only had the rest of the day to explore. Tomorrow they would jump. Galahad wanted to do it that day, but Morra needed time, just a few moments to breath, to remember.

As she walked down the street, her heels clicked. It made her pause, when she first came to this town, furious at her mom as she wore high tops. Black, ratted. A rueful smile graced her face as she thought about it. She would have laughed if som eone told her that in over two years she would prefer heels.

The grin dropped.

She wouldn't have believed any of the things that would happen. Tomorrow they would jump to before she met Galahad.

Ignoring the torrent of emotions, her feet pulled her down streets, remembering them all too well. Trauma either wiped memory from the mind or burned the memory in until it couldn't be forgotten.

She passed houses, the shops, and the places she used to visit before she left. It was all too familiar and once she passed the cafe; she swallowed the lump in her throat as she peeled her eyes from the pavement. In front of her was her mother's shop, charred and blackened, the bubble letters beneath barely visible behind where the fire graced it; she hadn't seen it before she had been taken away. No one touched it, this blight on the town. The windows had been boarded. Her eyes caught on the yellow caution tape.

She had been wrong. Workers with hard hats moved in and out of the building. Somehow that stung worse than if they had left it a horrible memorial. Suddenly, Morra remembered she never found out where, or if, her mother had been buried. She fought the waves of anger and despair as she gazed at the sign that seemed to crumble in the wind and her jaw rocked back and forth. Seeing it hurt and reminded her of how desperately she missed her mom. She fought the emotions for a few moments, but it was futile.

The emotion and memories washed over her like a flood, yet no tears came, only anger and resolve. Morra came to say goodbye, but instead, it was her way of bidding farewell to the life that was stolen by her mother's death. Grief was a beast she had become used to taming. The seasons had changed, and Morra with it.

Not wanting to sleep yet unable to stay still; she decided to wander around town aimlessly until sunrise. She followed the same path that led to their old house, though this time the only thing familiar was the grass and trees. A pristine white car sat in the driveway as kids ran through the house joyously behind each window. A bitter smile crawled on her face as she walked away.

Hours later, Morra watched the sun rise over the crest of the hill. Leaning against the hard cheap stone, Morra dug her now numb fingers into the cold ground. The dirt here wasn't fresh, yet the grass had not completely grown over it either. A bitter chuckle escaped her. It seemed to be a metaphor for her life; always in between.

When Morra's cell phone rang, she jumped, startled.

"Hello?" Her eyes were still unfocused, but she knew who it was.

"Morra?"

"Yes?"

"It's time. Where are you?" her grandfather asked, his voice unable to contain his warring emotions.

She snapped out of her trance and her voice hardened. "Meet me on Main, I will be in the coffee shop next... next to my mother's shop."

The line clicked dead.

She met her grandfather sometime later. Morra sat in the comfortable chair, sipping her steaming latte. Galahad sat across the table from her, not saying much, just waiting for her. Pushing the black coffee toward him, she took her time. Deadlines be damned.

This place, well, she deserved the caffeine. Part of her had hoped the man behind the counter would recognize her. He didn't.

They sat in silence for a while until Galahad finally spoke.

"Are you sure you want to do this?" She nodded.

"Okay."

They got up and walked to her mother's shop. The black and charred visage of the past would be the jump point. It had to be forced, of course. Bitter rage simmered inside her. Even the universe didn't think her death was substantial, no they had to force it because Adelaine burning to death didn't make enough of an impact.

Her eyes drifted over to her mother's ruined shop. It hung above her like a dark cloud.

She took a deep breath, trying to collect herself.

Her eyes were drawn back to the shop as she clung to the astrolabe. Galahad was quite overwhelmed with his own feelings; she knew he didn't have time to deal with hers as well. This was the last chance for him to save his son. Tension pulsed between the pair as they tried to prepare themselves for what they had to face.

Morra swallowed down her doubt and took a deep breath. Tears prickled at the back of her eyes, but she refused to let them fall. Her father depended on them.

Galahad placed a hand gently on her arm, his gaze heavy with emotion and understanding. "Let's do this," he said quietly.

Morra nodded and opened her palm to reveal the astrolabe that was entrusted to her. She felt its weight in her hand, like a conduit of power. A physical representation of hope.

She closed her eyes and imagined that day. The leaves had been falling, the faint sound of music and the memory of her mother dancing with frosting laced hair.

With an unsteady breath, Morra brought the astrolabe between them. The cold metal was grounding yet hollow. Her lips ghosted the bronze as Galahad laid a heavy hand on her shoulder, the other wrapping around her hand. With whispered energy swirled around them and, with a burst of light, they were gone.

When she opened her eyes, a noise tore through her throat as she stared at a now intact bakery. Her mouth cracked open in a quivering gasp, too scared to say the words out loud. Lips trembling, she breathed out the word, barely able to form it through the tears that lined her cheeks.

"Mom?"

Standing in the bakery was her beautiful red-haired mother. The astrolabe, still warm with blue light, became Morra's only anchor to reality. She would give anything to walk in and wrap her arms around the woman. Without permission, her feet began to move.

Galahad's hand gripped her upper arm, stopping her in her tracks. "You can't."

Her eyes were wide, wild with the need to run to her mom. Morra tried to pull herself free, but Galahad gripped harder, pulling her between buildings. "But she is right there. I - I have to try."

Her breath came in rough pants, and her vision came in waves of white. She couldn't breathe. The only thing she could feel, as her hands went numb, was the hot tears tracking down her face.

Galahad pulled her into a crushing hug, and, with a sad sigh, he pulled back and gave the girl a choice. He folded her hand around the astrolabe, "Dear, you can choose your mom, or you can choose him," he told her, voice cracking as he nodded to the image of his son who appeared.

She had until he walked away to decide.

He continued, "Throw her into the barrier where she can live for a number of years and hope the machine works enough to get her back one day or save your dad. We don't know what this will do to the Astrolabe, but I am giving you a choice and I will respect your decision." She didn't want to do this.

She didn't want to make this choice. How could she choose? It felt like free falling. Save her mom? Save her dad? Choose differently and go save Atlas? Time slowed as she looked into Galahad's aging grey eyes. A scream built in the back of her throat.

The world was cruel and in that moment; she hated everything and everyone. If she believed in any Gods, she would hate them, too.

But she had to choose.

Their family depended on it. Even if she didn't like it, she had to do it. It was the only way.

Learn. Move on.

Her mind went to Catherine and how she dealt in the wake of her husband's injury and death. She tried to remember the training and be infallible under pressure. *From this come my tears and pain.*

With that, she made her choice. She would honor her promise she made to her mom all that time ago and save the man she loved. Morra would save her mother's wind. She would save her grandfather's son. He had brought her into his house and world and let her have a family and home. He deserved to have his son back. It wasn't a time to be selfish.

The anger could wait.

Grey eyes bore into her with surprise as she yelled,

"ARTHUR!" And then she ran. Time was running out. She turned the corner to see his back, so she yelled again until he heard her. She reached out for her father's hand, astrolabe clutched in a death grip with the other.

"Morra," Galahad shouted, tension radiating from him.

The air crackled, and the daylight darkened. Like a beacon the astrolabe pulsed in her hand. Galahad looked at her intensely. "Hurry."

As if on cue, a group of people suddenly appeared around them. Clad in leather, they moved in sync. Weapons were drawn and Morra watched as Galahad unsheathed a sword, she hadn't seen him put on.

"Enemies of the Past! Get your father."

She didn't need to be told twice. With one last glance at the group of strangers, Morra's fingers trembled as she held the astrolabe in one hand and reached out with the other to take her father's hand. Her heart pounded in her chest, and she tried not to focus on the fear that threatened to overwhelm her. "Arthur!" She reached out as his wild eyes stared at the outstretched hand.

Nails gripped her arm, pulling her from the rippling barrier that held her father. She turned quickly, relying on muscle memory as she twisted, throwing her attacker off balance. Without hesitating, she stomped down, catching his shoulder with the heel of her combat boot and she was intensely grateful she changed out of her stilettos. A vicious grin faced her as she swung again.

Her attacker twisted his head quickly, and spit a thin stream of blood, and spit a thin stream of blood.

The crunch of boots on gravel caused her to look up. Galahad attacked his assailants with his sword. Fighting skillfully against impossible odds, Galahad managed to hold them off.

A low growl escaped his lips, and she imagined his face to be filled with fury and revenge, but she couldn't see. Blood dripped into her eye, stinging sharply.

Distantly, she couldn't recall being hit. Wiping the red liquid, Morra's arms and legs moved quickly as she took down each of her attackers. A leg collided with her side, knocking the air from her as a fist drove into her face. A burst of copper filled her mouth.

More people were coming at her. As the enemies closed in around her their weapons coming too close for comfort, she felt the touch of death around her and she refused to let it take more people. A cold blade slid through the flesh of her arm that

held the device. Her fingers twitched, almost losing grip on the metal as blood rolled down it.

Surrounded, with only one option, she turned. Hands grazed her as Morra threw herself into the vortex with her father. A scream tore from her throat, her skin felt like fire. As she fell to the ground, she looked at her skin. No burns but it still felt on fire.

The man who had cut her stood in above her eyes whipping around wildly. "Come out, sweetheart." The man's voice was muffled as if he was behind a thick pane of glass. "You can't hide forever." His face was hidden behind a mask, but she could see his mouth twist into a sardonic smile. She desperately wanted to wipe that smirk off his face.

She stood, watching the man search for her. In here she was nearly invisible. A noise behind her caused her to whip around.

"Who are you?" Arthur asked, fear and awe swirling around his face.

The last time he saw her she was nothing more than a child and now she was anything but. With a grin, blood trickled down her lip where she was hit. "I am your daughter, and I am here to save you."

He looked at her, opening his mouth to pour out questions she didn't let him. Instead, she threw herself into him, hugging him as tightly as she could. "There is a time to talk, but not now. Can you fight? We need to make it to your father."

She felt his nod as she pushed him slightly back and with an unhinged smile she put the ancient astrolabe, still glowing, in his hands. "Do not drop this or we are fucked."

Morra could see the weakness in her father; he shook as he stood there. The time vortex hadn't been good for him. She knew he wouldn't have lasted much longer. His body was collapsing into itself. She hoped he survived. Grabbing onto him tightly, she pushed, throwing them through.

Searing pain encased her, and she let out a scream as she burned from the inside out. Concrete met her as her head slammed into the solid ground under her. Color burst behind her eyes.

She had to get up.

Morra made it out alive, but she wasn't sure about her father's health. She needed to fight. She couldn't lose now; she wouldn't, not after everything.

She didn't have the strength to fight all of them off. The Enemies of The Past had turned their attention from her grandfather to her.

A knife slid over her cheek as she took a step back. She didn't even have time to process the pain before the next blow hit. She kept fighting, but her injuries began to weaken her. A boot connected to the side of her knee and her face hit concrete.

She peered into the window and saw her mother with a smile dancing around as Morra was pulled across the ground, blood splattering everywhere.

The icy steel of the blade pressed harshly against her exposed neck, sending shivers down her spine. In a split second, her assailant was hurled away from her as her father's surprisingly strong grip reached down and grabbed her arm, pulling her up to fight alongside him. They both fought in perfect harmony against the relentless onslaught until they reached Galahad's side.

He was on his knees, single-handedly fending off a group of enemies that were swarming him like a pack of wild animals. Morra watched as his sword arm grew weak and saw the terror in his eyes.

She had to help him, and she had to save her father, no matter what. She could see the fight ahead of them, and without a second thought, Morra charged forward. Galahad was fighting for his son and granddaughter. He always had, and he always would. Now it was time for Morra to do the same.

She had to get him out alive.

She clung desperately to her father, straining every muscle in her body as she yanked the astrolabe from his grip. With one hand firmly grasping Galahad's shoulder and her heart in her throat, she quickly began to chant ancient words.

Peering at their enemies through throbbing temples, she saw the glint of a gun being pulled. Just before the metal in her hands shimmered blue with magical energy, a loud bang caused Morra's world to spin. A searing pain raced through her skull as her ears rang like a banshee's howl.

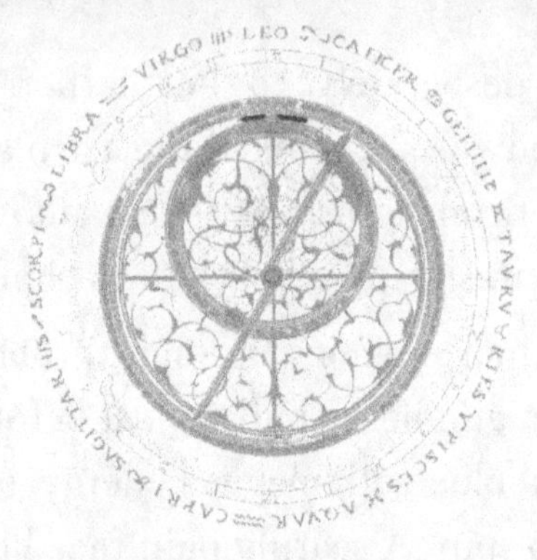

CHAPTER TWENTY-SIX

B loody and bruised, the three people crashed back into time, landing on the pavement. Morra, ignoring her own broken body, looked at the men beside her; her father's skin turned grey and sallow, his body trembled uncontrollably. Morra had hoped removing him from the time vortex would help his damaged body.

It only made it worse.

Then she looked over at her grandfather, his body lay on the pavement, unmoving.

Blood oozed from his abdomen, and his breath slowed, coming in shaky pants.

"Fuck." She rushed to him, putting pressure on the gunshot wound. He needed a hospital. With one hand still pressing on the gushing wound, causing the man to moan unconsciously, she reached for her phone. Blood coated the screen, slipping it clattered on the ground. Shaky fingers grasped it, hitting the buttons.

"Morra?" Balin's distant voice crackled over the speaker and her throat seized. Tears of relief welled in her eyes, and it took her a moment to reply as she surveyed the carnage around. With a shaky voice, she replied, "We did it, but I need help. They hurt grandpa. We need the pilot, a hospital. Something, please hurry." She dropped the phone as blood continued to ooze out in between her fingers.

If he keeps bleeding like this, he won't make it.

It would be her fault. She should have let the others come, but no, she wanted to prove herself and for what?

She pushed harder on the wound before scolding the unconscious man. "You don't get to die. I told you; you weren't allowed to die for me. You better not die, do you hear me?"

"Dad?" a croaky voice echoed. Arthur crawled to where Morra sat on her grandfather's chest, pushing with all her might despite her injured arm and swelling face. He bent down and whispered into the older man's ear.

"I am trying," she said tearfully, hoping he understood when his whispered words stopped. It was easier to watch someone die when she knew it was going to happen. Staying strong for Catherine wasn't hard, she knew Henrys fate. But this... real life had more stakes.

Father and daughter looked at each other and Arthur nodded. "I know."

Suddenly, the squeal of tires kicked smoke as an SUV came to a quick stop. Her muscles tensed as she crouched over

Galahads body. With no weapon, all she had was hope that it was someone rescuing them, not more assailants.

Arthur thought the same as he tensed his body, maneuvering himself in front of his daughter and his father. Ready for another fight.

If they came, the three of them would die. She would die in the same place as her mother.

Instead, their pilot stepped out. Dressed in his usual suit, he rushed to their side. Surprise flashed across his face as he saw her dad.

"Morelli?" Arthur asked as the man ushered him into the back of the car.

"No time." The man responded before he turned to her.

"He is dying," she shouted. Morelli ran to the back of the car and grabbed a bag. He pushed her hands out of the way with strength she didn't know he possessed and inserted something into the wound. The bleeding started to slow even though the thick, sticky liquid covered them. The pilot quickly started an IV pushing medication as she sat and stared, her back against the once again destroyed bakery.

Ash fell into her hair and a smell of burning and screaming flashed through her mind until a face popped into her vision, saving her from her spiral.

"Come on, let's get you home." Morelli lifted her easily, sliding her into the front. In the back seat, Morra saw her dad and grandpa, both pale but alive.

They were alive. She did it. Darkness took her.

When she woke up in a warm bed lined with silk sheets, she groaned. Pain wracked her as she felt her head split open in agony. Choking down another moan, Morra forced her eyes open, trying to examine her surroundings. Through her clouded vision, she recognized the bed posts. Morra was back in the Manor.

The bed dipped, she turned her head and nausea burned the back of her throat as she did. A gentle smile crossed her facing, causing her to wince as it tugged on her split lip.

Laying there on the bed was a sleeping Kahadin. He seemed so young like this. They said the world moves on, but this time it didn't. It stayed exactly the same. She changed, no longer was she a little girl lost in the world.

Shifting, she gasped as pain shot through her arm. Instantly, Kahadin snapped awake and was by her side, bleary-eyed.

"Hey," she whispered, head pounding at the slight noise.

"You're wake?" Kahadin sighed in relief, suddenly looking even younger.

Morra shook her head and regretted it immediately; *I have to stop waking up like this.* "How long was I out?" Sitting up, she grunted in pain. Kahadin helped prop her up. Looking down, Morra saw the bandage on her arm stained with blood before she returned her gaze to her cousin.

"About two days on and off," he confessed. "The doctor said you hit your head super hard. You have a severe concussion."

She nodded. That would explain the migraine.

Before she could ask, Kahadin volunteered, "Grandfather is doing okay. He had surgery and now is resting. Morra, you saved his life, he would have died. Uncle Arthur as well."

"I knew the Enemies were bad but... Kahadin, I thought we were going to die."

"I am so sorry Morra." Kahadin's voice was filled with regret and exhaustion. He reached over to grab her hand squeezing it gently.

"How did they find us? Or travel there. Even we had to force it and use ancient sources."

"I don't know. I am sure grandfather will know more about it."

Nodding and sending searing pain through her bandaged head she slapped on taunting smile. "I must have hit my head harder than anyone knew, if I just heard you say, *'super hard'*. Are you sure you aren't concussed?" He rolled his eyes at her.

She was grateful, knowing Galahad was okay. The memory of blood spilling through her fingers was sure to haunt her for some time. Just another in a line of terrible memories her brain desperately tried to forget.

She wanted wine, the red kind that she and the queen would drink on days when Diane had made life extra difficult. It was the kind that made you forget, for a moment.

"Morra?" Kahadin looked concerned, but she waved him off.

"Can we go downstairs?" she asked him.

Kahadin said reluctantly, "You should rest."

She shook her head, ignoring the pain. "No, I want to see my father."

Kahadin stared at her for a moment before giving her his arm. With his help they walked into the dining room, the loud conversation stopped as everyone stared. Sitting around the large circular table crafted from old wood, polished smooth from a century of use, sat the whole family, except Galahad. Joy and relief evident on their faces.

The bright light escaping the window and shining off the chandelier made her eyes hurt, but she decided it was worth it. A feast was laid out before them.

Morra's dad sat in Galahad's typical seat, but when he spotted his daughter, he stood. On shaky legs, the man who held pain in his eyes and adventure on his face wrapped his bulky arms around her, squeezing tight.

The pain intensified, yet she said nothing. It was the first time her father ever held her. All her long-awaited birthdays, every wish she'd ever made, they'd all come true in this moment. His arms were powerful, and as he held her close, safety settled over her that she hadn't even known she was missing. When she left with Galahad to save him, she thought she did it for him, the family, and her mom.

For years, she convinced herself that she didn't need a father in her life anymore. After eighteen years of living without one, she believed that her wishful thinking was a thing of the past. When he embraced her in his arms, she knew she was wrong.

When Arthur spoke, his deep timber voice reverberated through her bones, "My beautiful daughter, thank you for saving me."

Tears burned her healing wound as she nodded. She hadn't even realized she was crying until she felt the sting. Arthur pulled back, reaching a big, calloused hand and wiped the wet trails from her trembling form. Everyone in the room had stood and as soon as one hug ended, another began. Balin lifted her in his tight hug, whispering with a wobbly voice, "You brought my brother back. I am so proud of you and so thankful."

The rest of the family hovered like birds around an injured nestling, each regarding Morra with a mix of pride and admiration. Each embraced her, giving her praise and thanks. Isolde even walked to her sullenly, and whispered, "I may have been wrong about you." It surprised Morra that she didn't turn to smoke after uttering those words. It wasn't a thank you, but it meant more.

Despite her joy, Morra's legs shook, fragile and weak from being unconscious for two days. Eventually noticing her swaying, her dad led her to her seat and filled her plate. She struggled to chew; the movement causing the bruise on her jaw to smart. Unable to eat another bite, she pushed away her plate.

Her dad and uncle shared a grave look, the kind that made her stomach twist into knots. Arthur's voice became low and serious as he declared, "There is something I need to tell you."

Morra's heart stopped, her body rigid as she tried to brace herself. Words Morra never expected to hear fell from her father's lips.

"Your mom is alive."

AUTHOR'S NOTE

As I finish writing this novel, I find myself reflecting on the incredible journey I have embarked on. Writing this story has been a labor of love and imagination, and I am filled with gratitude for the opportunity to share it with you, dear reader.

This is the first of many works that I plan to write but none will be as important as this debut novel. It was after a deeply painful and tumultuous chapter of my life that I truly began my writing journey. A year ago, I left a relationship filled with domestic abuse. In the darkness that followed, I questioned my future and struggled to piece together the parts of myself that had been torn apart. But within those shattered fragments, I found the strength to dream again. And so, my debut novel emerged as a beacon of light, guiding me towards a path of healing and discovery.

The central theme of my book is "finding home" – a journey many of us undertake, seeking a place where we belong and a love that embraces us unconditionally, whether that be in family, friendship or in romantic entanglements.

As you read this book, I invite you to join me on this heartfelt quest for home, knowing that it carries a piece of my soul within its pages. It is my greatest hope that my story resonates with you, offering comfort, inspiration, and the realization that, even in the darkest times, there is a glimmer of hope waiting around the corner.

To anyone who may find themselves in an unsafe relationship, I implore you to seek help and support. Remember that you are not alone, and your life is irreplaceable. There is a way to find your way back to yourself and to the concept of "home" that brings you peace.

Thank you, from the depths of my heart, for being a part of this journey with me. Your presence as a reader brings my words to life, and it is an honor to share this story with you.

With love and gratitude,

A. Marie

National Domestic Violence Hotline:
https://www.thehotline.org/
Call 800-799-7233 or text START to 88788

ABOUT THE AUTHOR

A. Marie was born and raised in a small town nestled in the scenic landscapes of Oregon. At twenty-six years old she now proudly presents her debut novel, a labor of love and determination that carries a profound personal significance.

CONNECT WITH ME

Thank you for reading Winds of Time! I'm thrilled that you've joined me on this literary journey, and I'd love to stay connected with you. Here's how you can reach out and stay updated on what's coming next:

The Sequel is on the Horizon!

I'm excited to announce that the second book in the Sacred Time Trilogy is already in the works! If you enjoyed the adventures of Morra in this book, you won't want to miss what's coming next. Expect more action, intrigue, and unexpected twists as the story unfolds in *Bloods of Time.*

Get Early Access on Patreon

Are you eager to dive into the next chapter of the trilogy before anyone else? You're in luck! I'm offering early access to chapters, exclusive sneak peeks, and behind-the-scenes content on my Patreon page. By becoming a patron, you'll not only get a head start on the story but also get a chance to influence its development and interact with fellow fans.

Click on the link or scan QR code below to find all the links to my social media

Let's Stay in Touch

I'd love to hear from you! Whether you have questions, feedback, or just want to chat about the world of Winds of Time, you can reach me through the following channels:

https://linktr.ee/author_a_marie